BLUE
HAIL MARY PREPA...

42

C.A. RENE

Cover by: Black Widow Designs Co

Editing By: Kim BookJunkie

Paperback ISBN: 978-1-990675-01-0

Hardcover ISBN: 978-1-990675-32-4

PLAYLIST

Blue 42 Theme Song - For the Glory - All Good Things

Strong Enough to Live - Late Night Saviour

Born For this - The Score

Big Gangsta - Kevin Gates

What You Know About Love - Pop Smoke

Life is Good - Future ft. Drake

Highest in the Room - Travis Scott

God's Plan - Drake

Godzilla - Eminem ft. Juice WRLD

Astronaut in the Ocean - Masked Wolf

Humble - Kendrick Lamar

Mask Off - Future

All the Stars - Kendrick Lamar & SZA

Emotionally Scarred - Lil Baby

Apeshit - The Carters

Heartless - The Weeknd

I Don't Fuck with You - Big Sean ft. E-40

Too close - Next

DEDICATION

For the Buffalo Bills

Thank you for giving me a love for football and awakening this story in me.

"The harder you **WORK**, the harder it is to **SURRENDER**."

- Marv Levy, Buffalo Bills

PROLOGUE

I can say with utmost confidence that every decision made—even the smallest—leads you down a path well traveled or through the dense foliage forcing you to forge your own. Every single word uttered from your mouth and action your body makes has you spinning in the darkened space, pushing you in another direction. Therefore, oftentimes we feel lost, confused, or disoriented and ask ourselves *how did I get here?*

Over the past year, I have muttered this very line to myself numerous times, and the answer is always the same: I got myself here. My choices and my actions continued forcing me down a path I had to forge on my own, the injuries I obtained along the way were because of me, and in the end as I stood on my very own path, I knew how I got there.

Now that I'm at the end, looking into the darkened abyss, where will I go next? And who will be there when the darkness slips away and reveals my life vividly? There's only one way to find out … you must take that first step into the black void and hope you find your way to the end in one piece.

In one piece.

Dixon

The Memorial Stadium field shines a vivid green in the early morning sun, and the smell of freshly mowed grass is intoxicating. Tonight is my final game with the Clemson Tigers, and everything I've worked so hard for is coming to fruition. My family needs me to succeed, and I need to be the father figure my brother is so desperately searching for. The pressure would crush the typical college kid, but nothing about me is typical.

I jog down the hill and head toward the locker room knowing Coach will be pissed if I'm late. He's going to have us running plays for hours, perfecting every single toss, analyzing every catch. It's why we're number one in the Atlantic Coast Conference and playing our final playoff game against the Alabama Crimson Tide. We've had an undefeated season so far, and I want to leave here a champion. I won't accept anything less.

"North!" Coach snaps from his office. "In here."

I step inside and see his forehead wrinkled in concentration.

"Sup, Coach?"

He looks at me above his reading glasses, his brown eyes narrowing and his thin mouth pursed. "Why are you late?"

It's five fucking minutes, and I can guarantee no one else is even here. I can't say that though because I respect the man. He's the reason why I'm here, the reason why I am who I am, and the father figure I had so desperately been seeking.

"Sorry, sir," I nod my head. "I stopped to look over the field."

His eyes soften a bit, and he gives me a brusque nod in return. "How's the knee?"

I took a hit a few weeks ago and landed hard on my left knee, luckily no damage except for bruising.

"Good," I flex my leg. "Strong."

"Okay, son." He waves me away. "Go on and get ready for warmups."

"Yes, sir." I head into the locker room.

Clemson University is located in South Carolina where the weather is mild and the team pride here is amazing. We're number one each year for a reason. I know it's due to our hard work, but it's also in our determination to never let our fans down, which they repay us in unconditional love. The rush their screams give us, that adrenaline coursing through our bodies when they chant our names, and the exhilaration when that pigskin kisses our fingertips, sending them into a frenzy. I live for those moments. It's sad that I'm in my fourth and final year, but I'm excited for the future.

The silence of the locker room greets me, telling me I don't have much time left to myself. Our lockers are lined in perfect rows of bronzed metal, and each one has a silver plaque, our names etched into the surface. I stand in front of mine and rest my forehead against the door.

North.

One day, I will have my name on an NFL jersey, on an NFL locker, and engraved into a championship ring. I won't settle for anything less.

I have been scouted since my senior year of high school. I decided I would never let this opportunity pass me by, and I would succeed for the people who need me most: Ma and my little brother, Danny.

St. Francis Academy gave me my first taste of football, and thankfully, Clemson noticed, offering me the chance of a lifetime. I needed that chance because Westport, Baltimore is one of the roughest places to grow up in; crime is high, and gangs run it.

I would've been swept up in a gang if it wasn't for Ma working three jobs to get my ass into St. Francis and then continuing when I needed equipment. I will forever be indebted to her, and as soon as I can, I am getting her and Danny out of Westport.

Danny.

My little brother who shows no interest in sports, doesn't like academics, and thinks 'bitches' are a pastime. He's quickly becoming a victim to the streets of Baltimore, yet I can't do a single thing about it right now. Ma tries to make things sound great at home, but I know they're not, and I know Danny is on his last leg at school. It's his final year, and the principal is threatening to kick his ass out for skipping class and fighting.

Like I said, the pressure's on, and I need to get them the hell out of Maryland.

"North." A hand claps me on the shoulder, and I turn to see our quarterback, Andrew Mills.

"Hey, man," I spin and grab his hand in mine, pulling him in for a hug.

Andrew is our team's star. He's dedicated, and he's pulling points scouts are salivating for. He keeps his brown hair short, and his green eyes are always analyzing. It's part of who he is and what makes him a great QB. He's a bit shorter than me, and his body is leaner, but he's quick. His skin is also unnaturally pale looking, so when we have long days in the sun, he turns into a lobster.

"You looked down for a bit there," he remarks when we break apart. "Everything okay? How's the knee?"

"Nah, everything is fine." I bounce on my leg. "Leg is strong, just pregame nerves."

"That Buffalo scout will be back tonight," his smile widens. "He has his eye on someone."

"I just want that draft pick." I grin back at him, and we bump fists.

Guys begin to trickle in, and my silent pleas against my locker are ended. Now all I've got is my talent and drive.

There's a buzz in here this morning. We're hyped, and we're ready to play this last game like our lives depend on it. We all share the same energy, and it's swirling thick over our heads, potent in our blood.

"C'mon, ladies!" Coach calls into the locker room. "Let's get these drills down, and then I want to run a few plays with the Taxi Squad. We are winning this one tonight, girls!"

The guys all collectively roar around me, and I stand still, letting my eyes shut as I breathe in this moment. After tonight, it's going to be gone.

The steam from the hot showers drift around me as I stand in front of the mirror and stare into my dark brown eyes. I can still see the hunger, and I can still feel the desperation in my muscles. My warm brown skin is coated in dried mud, and my uniform looks the same. This year I really filled out and now fit the look required for my position, wide receiver. I'm quick, and I worked hard on my runs, dropping my yard times consistently. I splash water on my face and watch as the drops run over the angular slopes of my cheeks, dripping off my chiseled jaw.

I pull my gloves off my hands and stare at my long fingers. They're nimble, and Coach says the best hands he's worked with yet. They're like magnets, drawing that ball swiftly into their clutches then nestling it safely as I run my ass to the end zone. These hands are fucking magic. I run my fingers along my short, black hair, watching as the steam rises from the showers in the reflection.

"North, are you nervous?" Mills asks when he gets out of the shower.

"Not nervous," I shake my head, searching for a way to express what I'm feeling, "I'm … psyched to finally start my life."

"Everyone knows the scout is coming for you." His hand claps down on my shoulder. "I'm here for another year, but I'm ready to show you off tonight."

I nod and beam at him. Andrew and I have been working together for three years now. We play like one unit, think on the same level, and react as one. When that ball flies from his hands, I am always in the right spot to bring it home, and we do cause quite the sensation in the stands. Some even call us married.

He grips my shoulder before sauntering off into the locker room, and I am once again looking at my reflection. I've only got this one chance.

It's the fourth with ten seconds left in the game. We've got ten yards inside the Alabama line, and we're all tired. We're tied at a touchdown apiece, and the tension has brought the stadium down to a nervous hush. My head pulses inside of my helmet in time with my erratic heartbeats, and my muscles are shaking with fatigue.

I see the look in their cornerback's eyes as he watches me warily, and he's fucking dog tired too. But this is it, a make it or break it play, and I won't settle for mediocre. I give him a nod of respect because he's working hard, and he gives one back. There's no hate between our teams regardless of what people see on the field. We just want the same things, and only the best can get it.

The play is called, and instead of running forward, I hop back and dart around the cornerback. I zone out what's happening behind me and look up to see the ball sailing toward me. Then my fingers are digging into the leather. My vision tunnels, and the end zone is a pulsing beacon of light, everything else dims. The energy snakes up my legs, and I'm bolting forward, darting around Alabama's defensemen. I hear them behind me, but it's too late. I hit that end zone, and elation spreads all over me. We fucking did it.

The crowd goes insane as I fall to my knees and cradle the ball to my chest, my blood pumping through my veins. I lean back and throw my face up to the sky, roaring my victory. I hear my teammates screaming as they rush toward me, throwing their helmets, the force of their footfalls vibrating the earth under my legs.

I'm hoisted up in the air as the crowd begins to chant my name. *North! North!* The bright stadium lights burn into my retinas, and white dots color my vision. I pull my helmet off and hold it above my head.

"Dixon North!" I scream.

CHAPTER TWO

The collar of my dress shirt rubs against my neck, and I can feel the sweat collecting at the base. It's loud in here with the excited chatter and the atmosphere pulses with frenzied energy. My mother and I are sitting inside the Selection Box in Grant Park, Chicago. It took us eleven hours to drive here, and I barely spoke full sentences the whole way. I'm nervous, and it shows in the bouncing of my knee.

"Dixon." Ma reaches out and pats the offending knee. "Try to breathe and relax."

Relax? This is just determining the rest of my life, no big fucking deal. Not just my life either, but hers and Danny's also. I wanted Danny to come with us, to show him where he could go in life with hard work and determination, but he's been slowly withdrawing from me. Our relationship is becoming more and more strained as I spend more time away from home, and it's difficult watching my little brother slip between my fingers.

The large screen up on the stage lights up, and the words 'First Round' shine brightly. My heart crashes into my ribs as I once again am reminded of how pivotal this moment is. I feel like I'm walking a tightrope and I could fall at any moment. My name skates across the screen with a picture of me in my Clemson uniform. The growing crowd begins to cheer, and I can't hide the smile that widens across my face.

"That's my boy," Ma mumbles, holding her clasped hands to her chest. She prays a lot and always did while I was growing up. Her belief in God is what she accredits for where I am today.

I don't believe in any of that. I can only accredit myself for my achievements, and Ma can continue to pray to whomever she wants as long as I can get her out of that neighborhood. She was telling me about a drive-by the week before and how one of our front windows is now boarded up. Yeah, that's right, our house was hit with a stray bullet. Luckily, my mother was in her room, and Danny was out somewhere. She found the bullet lodged into the sheetrock of our kitchen wall, at about the same height her head would've been had she been cooking.

That's the shit that scares me but also drives me to be the absolute best I can be because failure really isn't an option.

"So this Buffalo Bulls team is really going to sign you?" Her brown eyes—exactly the same shade as mine—shine with unshed tears.

"Bills, Mom," I chuckle. "And I really hope so." I reach up and tug on one of her greying, tight curls.

The Buffalo Bills were dead last in the league last year, and they get first pick tonight. I know I'm here because of their scouts, and I have been assured they want me on the team. They believe I can bring them back up to the top, and I want to do that for them if given the chance.

My knee begins to bounce again as more faces pop up on the screen, and my heart rate accelerates when I see a few other wide receivers. I've investigated their stats out of curiosity, and it only made me more nervous. As good as their stats are, mine are better, and I still feel like I have room to grow.

"There are a lot of people gathering out there." She points to the park and the large, glowing Ferris wheel.

"This is it, Mom." I squint my eyes to hold back the moisture. "This is as big as it gets."

"You've already made me so proud, Dixon." She pats my bouncing knee again. "This is just the icing on the cake."

"Thank you, Ma," I nod. "This is just the beginning."

"This is what you've always worked for, what do you mean the beginning?" Her eyes crinkle on the sides as she squints at me, her face looking older than what she actually is.

"I want you and Danny out of Baltimore."

"We're fine for now, son." Her wrinkled hand pats me again. "We're doing just fine."

They're not, and it bothers me that she wants me to believe that.

"You guys deserve it."

The screen goes black, and a hush falls over the crowd. This is it. I've watched the draft picks every year for the past ten years, and I know this is where they begin. Voices begin talking over the sound system, and the announcers you hear every Sunday are here, talking about the lineup for today. I wish I could say I hear everything they're saying, but I don't … it's a rumble of voices and laughter from the crowd.

My head begins to pound, and my vision loses focus as the screen once again lights up with a commercial. I can't even take it in because my stomach is twisting with knots.

"You look like you might pass out, boy," Ma tsks. "Get yourself together and quick."

She's right, I know she's right, but my body isn't listening to reason.

Suddenly, the crowd cries out as the Buffalo Bills logo zooms in on the screen, first pick of the first round. Then there's a compilation video of me that I signed off on for them to use, but what I didn't see the first time are the actual game plays they put in there. They have a clip of the final game against Alabama when my team rushed me in the end zone.

My head is thrown back, and I can see my mouth moving as I scream out my name. The sweat pouring down my cheeks, the black makeup over my cheekbones smudged, and the tears leaking out of my eyes. I will never forget that moment, the high and the accompanying relief. I put my everything into that game.

As the video moves on to the other player's compilations, I turn my head and look around the area. I see a few of the draftees sitting at the tables, but I know some are also sitting at home watching. We had the option to do either one, but I knew I needed to be here.

"Today is exciting!" one of the announcers declares to the crowd. "Did you see that lineup?"

The crowd screams, and the sounds amplify the anxiety coursing through my chest. It feels like time has completely slowed down, and the moment I'm waiting for is taking forever to get here. I want my name called, I want the bidding to start, and then I want a fucking steak dinner.

A hand lands on my shoulder, and I turn to see an usher. "Time to head to the Green Room."

I swallow thickly. The Green Room is where the picks who show up to the draft selection wait. Once their names are called, it's a waiting game until a call comes through. Then you either head to the stage or you don't.

"Good luck, baby." Ma pulls me in for a hug.

I nod and stand from my seat, following the usher to a set of stairs to the left of the large draft selection stage. I take the stairs one at a time, letting the weight of my foot hit the metal, the sound reminding me to stay grounded. This is a memory I want to store and remember for the rest of my life. I won't let nerves take it from me.

The top of the stairs opens to a large room with couches and a couple fridges. The room isn't green at all, nothing in here is green, save for the Packers emblem stuck to the wall, and it gets lost in the sea of team emblems.

There are two other guys in the room, and one I recognize from the list I read. He's another wide receiver, and he's really good. He's a popular choice, and his stats are phenomenal. He stands when I enter the room, and he's fucking tall and fucking wide. His grin spreads across his face. His blue eyes twinkle with mirth, and his blond, shaggy hair flops over his forehead.

"Man," he claps his hands, "I heard you were going to be here today." He holds out his hand. "I'm Greg."

His grin is contagious, and suddenly, I feel my own inching across my face. "I know who you are." I clasp his hand in a firm shake. "I read up on you."

The speaker over our heads crackles, then the crowd below starts its loud booing. The announcer's voice floats through the room as he announces the NFL Commissioner to the stage. The booing intensifies, and the three of us in the room begin to laugh. Every year it's like this. The Commissioner walks out on stage, and the crowd boos him. I looked it up the first year I heard it and laughed at what I read. He is the most hated person in the whole organization.

I watch the large TV screen hanging on the wall as he walks to the podium, waving to the crowd and keeping a large, forced smile plastered to his face amid the boos. He's in a perfectly tailored suit, the grey linen rippling in the breeze as his hair flies up revealing his bald spot. The guys behind me titter, and I smirk as he tries to pat it back into place.

"Welcome to the first round of draft picks," he announces into the mic as the speakers overhead crackle with his voice.

The booing continues, and the three of us break out into laughter again. I needed this. The nerves have slowly dissipated, and it feels good to be in a room with guys who are probably feeling similarly.

"Our first pick tonight is," he looks down to his card, asshole. "Buffalo Bills. Who will be their choice?"

I watch as a large timer starts on the screen behind him. Fifteen minutes until my fate is decided. The screen flips to the table of announcers you would normally see on a sports broadcast as they talk about my stats from the three years of playing with the Clemson Tigers.

"Good luck, Dixon," the second guy in the room stands up and holds out his hand. "Stanley. I heard Buffalo has had their eye on you."

I take his hand and give him a nod of acknowledgment. I'm back in my head again. Those nerves are inching back up again, hard to ignore.

"That phone is going to ring, and that's when your new life will begin," Stanley says with a smile. "Let's have a beer in the meantime."

He heads over to the small bar fridge and passes each of us a can. I take the smooth, cold metal in my hand and pop the tab, the fizz of the carbonation loud in the otherwise silent room. The timer keeps dialing down, and with each second, my blood pressure rises.

There's a random guy in a suit off to the side. He's sitting in front of the phone, and his eyes are dead center on the countdown. We're at the ten-minute marker now, and I want to fling my can across the room and scream. Are they purposely making me fret?

"It's probably about money," Greg mutters. "What salary to give you."

Right, my multimillion-dollar deal that will change the course of my family's life and propel us into a whole different culture. A rich man's culture. Something that makes me feel both elated and terrified. I've seen what that much money can do to a person who has no idea how to handle it, and I'm thankful I have my mother. She'll never let me lose focus on who I am.

The sudden shrill of the phone startles me, and my beer sloshes out and over my hand. The room is quiet as the phone screams for the suited guy to answer it. It feels like forever as his hand reaches out, and his fingers curl around the receiver, slowly lifting it to his ear. I look at the screen and see seven minutes blinking in a still sequence.

"Looks like The Bills have come to a decision," the announcer says into the mic, the speakers overhead pushing sound into the room.

I watch as the guy on the phone furiously moves his hand over paper as he writes down whatever is being said. He nods then dips his head to continue writing. I know it's a lot because I read everything there was to read about NFL salaries, and I'm waiting, albeit impatiently, for what the details are, the fine print.

He drops the phone back to the cradle and looks at me with a grin. "Dixon North, you must be one special rookie," he chuckles. "Come on over, and read their offer. You let me know if it's good or if you want a renegotiation."

I walk to him on unsteady feet. With each footfall, my heart tries to jam itself up into my throat, and my brain is screaming at me that this moment is profound. This pivotal moment is going to be that one point everyone has when they think of how they got to where they are in life. This is mine.

I stand at the table, and the guy is still chuckling as he hands me the paper. I blink a few times and will my eyes to focus.

$12,638,000.00 per year on a four-year contract. $2,100,00.00 signing bonus. I quickly read through the other stipulations, but all I can think of is this is it. I don't need a renegotiation, I'm a fucking Bill.

"Looks good," my voice cracks, and I quickly clear it. "Yeah, I'm in."

The other two in the room clap and holler as the guy looks at me then picks up the phone. It takes a minute before my face zooms onto the screen with the Buffalo Bills logo underneath.

"They're asking for you on the stage," the guy says as he extends his hand. "Congratulations, Dixon."

This profound moment set the course for the rest of my life.

CHAPTER THREE

"Rookie!" Buffalo's coach, Trevor Meyers, screams at me. "What the fuck was that?"

I slow my run to a jog and skid to a stop, looking back at him over my shoulder. His face is red and ruddy, and his bald head looks like it's burning in the mild Buffalo sun.

"That looked like a newborn horse, just out its mama's womb," Our tight end Sebastian Avando sneers. "All wobble legged and clumsy."

He hates me, and he's somehow convinced some of the other players to join in on the taunting as well. I don't know why.

"I thought we bought ourselves a wide receiver, and one that can outrun my others. So why the fuck haven't you done that yet?" Coach screams as I slam my fists to my waist and tip my head back on a groan.

He's right. I've been slow, and I can't seem to shake whatever hold my mind has over my body. I've been at the Bills' camp for two weeks now, and we start our season in three. I need to get my fucking head in the game.

I slowly start to walk back to the sidelines just as Sebastian and the defensive end, Ostin Jameson, stride past me. Sebastian is near to my height with broad shoulders. His swagger is always exaggerated, and the way he walks is confident, telling people he's not one to be fucked with. His eyes are amber pools and hold enough hatred to crush a weaker person. I'm not that weaker person.

Sebastian slaps his hand against my helmet, and Ostin begins to laugh. Ostin Jameson is larger than life, and he's Sebastian's sidekick. He's loud and aggressive both on and off the field. I grind my teeth just to hold myself together and convince myself that fighting him will do nothing, but it's extremely hard. He deserves a good knock to the fucking jaw.

I grab a bottle of Gatorade and stand on the sidelines, watching as Avando and Jameson line up across from each other. Sebastian Avando isn't required to run faster than the wide receiver because his job is to do whatever is needed to get that ball into the end zone. Tackle, run, catch … it doesn't matter, and he needs to be able to do it all on the fly. Avando has been crushing my times though, and he's been flaunting it.

I don't know what I did, but it took two days for him to decide he hated me and that he wanted to make my life fucking hell. He has this hold over the others, and I can't decide if they admire him or fear him. He has the tough exterior of someone who grew up with the belief that you kill or be killed.

His body is nearly covered in tattoos. I grew up in one of those kill or be killed neighborhoods, so I know what gang signs look like… Avando has them inked all over him. In the locker room we see everything, and he has no shame in walking the room ass out naked.

Coach blows the whistle, and Avando side skips Jameson, his legs swift. He gets out of Jameson's way easily and runs down the field, his knees pumping fast.

"Look, kid." Coach comes up beside me, and I grit my teeth. I hate that he calls me 'kid.'

"I know," I nod and scrub my hand down my face. "I'll stay and do laps again tonight. I'll get that time up."

"I think what you really need is rest." His hand slaps my back. "We already know the times you can do, maybe you just need a reset."

I haven't rested in weeks because I'm trying to prove that I'm worth what they spent on me. He has a fucking point, I'm drained.

"Okay," I agree.

"Get on out of here, and get yourself some sleep. We'll start again tomorrow morning."

"Yes, sir." I turn to head toward the locker room.

The team shouts behind me, and I can imagine it's because Avando once again crushed his time. I don't have the heart to look back, and my body feels like lead as I drag it into the locker room. Coach is right… I need the rest, and I need to ice my knee. These past two weeks have been brutal on my old injury.

I strip down and toss the equipment and clothing into the laundry bin. I wrap the towel around my waist and head for the showers. I thought Clemson had amazing showers, but they don't hold a flame to what the Bills have. Four shower heads per stall and all uniquely made for different massage pulses. My legs are all that's really bothering me, and these won't work for shit on them. I need a hot bath.

"Who wants to bet the fucker is back here crying somewhere?" Sebastian's voice filters in over the spray of the water. "I marked him a pussy the first day he showed up. All big eyed and scared looking."

I know he's talking about me, and if my career wasn't on the line, I would rip him apart, limb by limb. I hear a few other snickers, and I would bet anything it's Jameson and Ortiz, his two pet dogs.

Ortiz Fernando is a tight end for the Bills, and he's also a large, opposing figure on the field. His dark tanned skin is riddled with tattoos—like his friends—and he curses in Spanish every other word.

His slight accent tells me he's Mexican, and his dark features confirm it. With black curly hair and near black eyes, he's literally the epitome of tall and dark.

The three of them are tight as hell, and they tend to intimidate the others, all except our quarterback, Zeal Flaherty, who doesn't take much shit from anyone.

I shut off the shower and decide to bathe when I get home. It's just not worth it to start some shit here with Avando today.

"Here pussy, pussy," he taunts, and I growl as I pull on my track pants.

They round the corner just as I tie the waist band and cross my arms over my bare chest. I'm not a small guy, and I know I look just as rough with my tattoos as well. I may have stayed off the streets and away from drugs, but I still look the part of where I was raised.

"If you gotta call for pussy to find it," I let a taunting grin of my own stretch along my mouth, "then you got a fucking problem."

"What did you say?" Sebastian's light brown eyes flash with sudden rage.

He's as tall as I am, hitting about 6′3″, and he's leaner than me but no less built. His deep tawny skin speaks of his African American and Puerto Rican background. Yeah, I Googled the asshole the first day I met him.

I don't bother to engage further and keep the grin on my face, infuriating him more. He strides forward, and his hand grabs my throat as he slams me against the tiled wall of a shower stall. I keep myself still, but I let my eyes dance with amusement at his actions, playing a dangerous game with his ego.

"Do you know who you're fucking with, rookie bitch?" His lips are pulled taut against his teeth. His spit flies against my cheeks, but I don't let the grin drop. "Do you want to die?"

"Avando," I hear Jameson call out in warning. "Let's go,

man."

Little bitch is all talk, and I would assume Ortiz is as well, both riding on the ass of Avando who obviously isn't all talk. But I'm not afraid of him.

"Looks like y'all are having a good time in here," I hear Zeal Flaherty say as he enters the showers. "Avando, I think you need to take a walk."

Sebastian releases his hold on my throat and slowly backs up, his body vibrating with anger. With Zeal being our quarterback, a lot of responsibility falls on his shoulders, and one of those is keeping us in line and working as a team. Right now, this is as far from teamwork as it gets, and I feel bad for Zeal, but I won't back down for Sebastian. He will just have to learn to work with me because I'm not going anywhere.

"This isn't over," he grits out under his breath, and I give him a brusque nod. I know it's not.

He turns on his heel and walks back to the locker area, leaving me alone with our quarterback. Zeal is what I would consider a good southern boy. He has light brown hair that falls in waves over his head and always has that messy, just out of bed look. His blue eyes are light and naïve, always searching for the good in people. He's tall, reaching six feet, and he's lean but muscular. He shows respect to his teammates, and he's a natural leader.

"Avando is an amazing player. His legs eat up the distance on the field, and he finds the perfect spots to get into that will guarantee touchdowns." He rubs his hand along the nape of his neck. "When he feels threatened or confronted, he lashes out with anger."

"I haven't done anything to attract his anger," I tell him honestly.

"Nothing you did to him personally, no. But when we found out your stats and what you were about to bring to the team, he felt threatened."

"There's not much I can do about that," I shrug.

"No, there isn't, but I really don't need y'all fighting all the time." He lets out an exasperated breath.

"I don't know exactly when you walked in," I walk by him, "but I wasn't fighting him at all."

I hear his groan as I walk out of the shower area and back into the locker room. Sebastian is standing at his locker, glaring at me as I open my own.

There's no way I'm taking the fall for this man's insecurities, and I won't be blamed for his temper tantrums. Zeal needs to confront him and leave me out of it. He has to get over whatever animosity he's clinging to with me because I'm not going anywhere. I worked too hard and too long to be pushed out by a hot-headed, insecure man.

After grabbing everything I need from my locker, I shut it and pull on my jacket.

"You're a pussy, North," Avando calls out, and I bite my tongue. "You're about to be crushed on the fucking field."

I don't bother to give him the attention he is so obviously craving and bend to pick up my bag. The locker room has fallen quiet, and I know everyone is waiting with bated breath for my reaction.

"See you guys tomorrow," I call out over my shoulder and head out the door.

As soon as it shuts behind me, the noise picks back up, and I hear a few riotous laughs. That's fine. This is one situation where I know I'll get the final laugh.

I head to my rented car and throw my bag in the back. I know I can win them all over, even Sebastian Avando.

CHAPTER FOUR

Sebastian

This rookie needs his head checked, and I will gladly be the one to do it. Since the first day he got here, striding onto the field like his shit didn't stink and his nose so far in the air, I've fucking hated him. Rookies aren't supposed to act privileged, and they sure as fuck don't start mid ladder.

Back home in Rochester, guys like that get capped, and then we send pieces of them back home to their families, reminding everyone of their places. I think I need to teach this bitch his place.

"Avando." Zeal's voice grates on my last nerve and I give him a cursory glance over my shoulder. "Lay off the rookie."

"Pardon?" I turn around to fully face him. His lean body is tense with frustration, his blue eyes hard.

"I don't want tension on the team." His face hardens, and I clench my teeth, holding my fists firmly at my sides. "I want the Super Bowl this year."

"And what? You think the pussy rookie is going to get it for us?"

A few snickers circle the room, and I snort when Zeal's eyes flash with irritation.

"He's an asset, and if we work as a team, we can all get there." He drags a hand through his light brown hair.

"You heard him," Jameson sneers, a sheen of sweat shining along his porcelain skin. "If we all get on our knees in a line and suck the rookie's dick, we'll win the Super Bowl."

Ostin Jameson is a big motherfucker, and almost everyone on the team stays out of his way. He's as tall as me, but where I'm cut and stacked, he's at least two times my size in width, most of it fat. Not that that's a bad thing, we need the power that comes with his big body.

"Maybe Coach needs to hear about this shit," Zeal threatens, and once again my teeth crack as I grind them.

"Go for it," I grit through my teeth. "I think it's time our second string QB had some field time."

Coach Meyers is firmly against bitching of any kind. If he hears it, he drops whoever is bringing it to his table, and he expects his QB to keep us all in check.

"Maybe Flaherty needs a vacation," Ortiz announces. "Maybe a little bit of homegrown loving from his mommy back in Alabama."

Ortiz Fernando rubs his dick through his shorts, and the locker room breaks out into laughter. He's not fucking wrong, maybe Flaherty needs to take his ass home. I have ways to ensure that happens.

"Try to behave," Zeal mutters, his face red from embarrassment.

"Yes, Daddy," Jameson snorts, and the room is once again in an uproar.

Zeal and I stare into each other's eyes, and I smirk when he's the first to drop his gaze, little pussy. He turns and heads for the showers as I look around the room.

"I think we need to welcome the rookie properly." I see a few nervous swallows and some sideways glances. They know what the hell I mean.

"Yeah… If any of you don't want to help, then turn your ass cheek," Ortiz grins maliciously.

"That's not how the saying—" Jameson begins.

"Shut up," Ortiz cuts him off with a shove to the shoulder.

They're fucking dumb as shit, but they're loyal, and if I say to jump, these fuckers ask how high.

I drop the white powder onto the glass tabletop before cutting out the thin lines with my limitless Amex Black. I drag my right nostril along the clear cold surface then my left, back down to where I started, both nostrils filled with the brain numbing elixir.

"We have a piss test in three days," Jameson mumbles as he sniffs his line.

"Well, make sure we get our piss." I look at him with my brow raised.

"I think Coach is onto us," Ortiz states, his pupils the size of pinpricks.

"As long as our piss is clean and we get the fucking ball into the end zone, Coach will leave us the fuck alone," I growl. "If you're afraid then get the fuck out of here."

Ortiz nods, his face void of emotion and his eyes glazed. He and I didn't get off to a good start in the beginning either. Not only did the fucker have my position, but he had a shitty attitude too. Being a rookie at the time, I let it slide until I couldn't ignore it any longer and slammed him into place.

Ortiz Fernando grew up in Corpus Christi, Texas to a poor but religious Mexican household. He and I are the same age at twenty-four, and he's the oldest of four brothers and two sisters. His parents have been married for thirty years. All the good shit you see with those sitcom families … full of love and prayers to Jesus, his family is a carbon copy. That is until he started rolling with me. I hardened him and made him a fucking man.

I pick up the gun that's sitting beside the discarded bag of blow and rub the barrel against my temple. My .22 is always close by because no matter how safe you feel, you're never actually safe.

Ortiz has his dark brown eyes on the gun as he shrinks back into the couch. He knows I don't tolerate fear well. Doesn't mean I don't like to see it in the eyes of the person I'm staring down, and I think that's what has my insides so twisted. Rookie has no fear. It's driving me to want to do things to entice that fear out of him, creating fear is my addiction.

Buffalo has been my in-season home for three years now, and I hope I'm never traded. Yeah, we struggle to win games, but at least I'm close to home, and I can go back to see my boys whenever I want. Off-season, I live outside of Rochester with my family, and I prefer it that way. They don't come to Buffalo to live with me, so I just rent this house while I'm here. That's how most of the guys do it, and the in-season begins to feel a bit like vacation, or a break from the nagging of family.

"I need to get going." Jameson stands and holds his fist out to me. "I'll see you two tomorrow."

I give it a quick bump with my own and nod to him. "Yeah, bro."

Ortiz runs his hand through his black hair and stands as well. "It's an early day tomorrow."

I nod again and watch them leave, letting themselves out my front door then hearing Jameson's car start up. They live in the same gated community, so they carpool like housewives going to book clubs or some shit.

I lay back on the couch and stare up at the ceiling, watching my ceiling fan rotate in circles. It reminds me of the one-room apartment me and Mom lived in back in Rochester and how the summer nights were brutal, our ceiling fan doing absolutely nothing to ease the discomfort. I remember how my stomach would growl from not eating for a whole day, anticipating the next day's school funded breakfast. How most nights I was left alone in that apartment while Mom was off turning her next trick and grabbing what drugs she could with the money.

My father could've been any drug dealer or random guy who picked her up for a few hours. I guess she learned her lesson after me, and abortions became her form of birth control. Until they weren't needed... I'm guessing she made herself infertile. Not that she was upset by it. No, that meant more sex without the worry and more money to spend on drugs.

My first year of college, I came home from class and found her dead in a puddle of her own puke. Looked like she'd overdosed and drowned in her own vomit. I wish I could say I felt sad or traumatized, but that would be a fucking lie. I was *relieved* she was finally gone, and I could pursue this football career without having to give her a cent. Because that's exactly what she was banking on before her death: her son to look after her when she never looked after him.

I was running the streets from eight years old and selling drugs by ten. It was only a small hop from that to joining the local gang and holding down our turf. From twelve onward, I had finally found the family I had always been craving, and they made sure I was good. When Mom got us evicted for the fifth time, I went and lived with one of the guys. When Mom didn't feed me, my boys always had a hot meal ready for me. That's why I will always do everything I can for them. I wouldn't be where I am today if they hadn't taken me in.

They taught me that I am my own person, that I need to

watch my back and always be prepared for something to pop off. I grew a tough exterior before them, but with them, that shit became impenetrable, and no one gets inside. No one. That's why Rookie is pissing me off. He's getting to me, and I fucking hate that. He acts like he's entitled, and I'd bet my left nut that the fucker grew up feeling loved and safe. Most pussies did.

I'm ready to find out exactly what the little bitch is made of.

CHAPTER FIVE

Dixon

Buffalo is quiet compared to Baltimore. No sirens and no gunshots waking you up all hours of the night. I miss my mom, and even though he's been pissing me off, I miss Danny too. I'm lonely here, and I had hoped I would've befriended some teammates by now. Instead, I'm here sounding like a bitch inside my own head.

I roll off my bed and head to the kitchen. I rented a smaller townhome because I don't plan on buying until I can get Ma and Danny out of Maryland. Danny is giving Ma a hard time about it, saying he doesn't want to leave behind his friends and the girl he's seeing. As soon as I have time, I'm heading home and convincing him to leave.

In the meantime, I bought Ma a house, and even though it's a quaint, two-bedroom bungalow, it's still an upgrade from the one-bedroom apartment we were all living in at one point. She's happy to be out of the hood, but we both know Danny is still very much in it, no matter how much we try to ignore it. I know the lure of the streets all too well, the promises of loyalty and the rush of adrenaline. How holding that metal piece in your hands makes you feel invincible and the fear when you watch someone bleed because of it. I know all of it, but I fought the allure, I scraped myself out of the gutter.

Danny is not so strong, he won't be able to fight it, and as the months tick by, he gets closer to an initiation. If that happens, there's no getting him out, and all of this will have been for nothing. If I can't save my brother from himself and if I can't give him what he's searching for, I may as well go down with him.

I've rested for twelve hours straight, soaked in hot baths, and even had a deep tissue massage, but now I feel agitated. I want to move, I want to run. My muscles feel the best they've felt in a long time, and I feel the pull to the field, a place to run out the energy I feel coiling inside of me. I bounce on the balls of my feet and breathe deep. Just a few more hours and I can show Coach just what the Bills acquired with me.

Just a few more hours.

"Today will be the first string against the second string," Coach calls out. "Line up!"

This is my chance to show I'm not second-string material, I belong on that first string.

My legs are buzzing with the need to pound my feet into the field. I jog toward the second-string group where our QB, Allan Samuels, gives me a wide smile.

"How're you feeling, Rookie?"

"I feel like my legs are gearing up to set this fucking field ablaze."

"Yes!" he growls, and a few hoots go up from the others. "Let's hand these first stringers their asses."

Again, hoots and hollers go up, and I revel in the sound of the camaraderie. This is what I've been needing since I arrived here… A purpose to run my ass off and a team worthy of winning. I want to win with this team.

Samuels gives us our play, then he points his finger at me. "Rookie, run that shit home for us."

I give a quick nod before we break the huddle, fanning out across the field. Jameson lines himself up across from me, and I watch as his lips form a grin around his mouthguard, then he winks at me. He won't catch me, and the thought has me grinning right back at him. I look down their line, and my gaze catches on a hostile pair of golden eyes, the hatred in them clear. Avando will never accept me, and the thought has me feeling a bit defeated. Then I hear my Clemson Coach's voice in my head, *"You can't please them all, son."*

I can't please them all, and I will have to live with that, but I won't let him take this from me. I'd much rather leave him in my fucking dust. Samuels calls out our play, and as soon as that whistle is blown, I'm dancing my way around Jameson. He dives to catch my legs, but I skip to the side and watch as his body hits the grass, then I sail over him. My toes dig into the field as I run, quickly looking back to see the ball soaring for me. My hands reach up, and just like fucking magic, it lands in their grasp.

I don't break my speed, I don't falter, and I keep that end zone firmly in my sights. I hear them at my back, the screams of triumph and of frustration, but I keep going. The burn running up my legs is like an extra jolt of energy, and I take off faster, the last twenty yards swimming in my periphery. I sail over that line and dig my heels in to stop, the divots of grass unearthed behind me.

I drop the ball and throw my head back, screaming into the early morning sky. Finally, I'm back to myself. I turn around to see both strings standing there watching me, looking shocked, and one face in particular looking angry as hell.

"Rookie!" Coach calls out. "Is that you, Rookie?" His smile is huge across his face as he scrubs a hand over his bald head.

I can't answer him because my lungs are fighting to suck in as much air as possible, but my lips peel back around my wide smile

"Do that a few more times today, and I'll have you on the first string when the season starts," he calls out, and my heart soars. A rookie on the first string his starting year... It doesn't get any better than that.

I jog back to the second string and pass by a glaring Avando. "You'll suck my dick before getting the first string, pussy."

"Sounds like you'd like that," I counter and continue by. I won't let him destroy my career.

The hot water hits my chest as the steam gathers around my head. I'm still riding the high of running that ball into the end zone five more times. Coach was right... My body needed a reset, and now I feel like I'm on fire. He's promised me a first-string start for the first two games, and if I continue to prove myself, he'll keep giving me the following games. I take the bodywash and ooze it out onto my sponge, rubbing it into the skin of my chest and stomach. The smell is musky and earthy, really masculine.

"Rookie did real well today, boys," I hear Avando's loud voice behind me.

I turn to see him, and standing at his flanks are Jameson and Ortiz, no surprise. They're all naked, save for the white towels around their waists, and all three stand there ominously with their arms crossed over their chests. They wouldn't try anything, right?

"He sure did," Ortiz nods, but it's Jameson who looks the most pissed off. I get it, he's the one I ran circles around all day.

"We should celebrate," Avando claps his hands together.

What?

I go to open my mouth to ask what he means when both Jameson and Ortiz rush inside the stall, flip me around, and push my face into the tile. I try to fight, I'm exceptionally strong, but there are two of them, and they're huge.

"Did you think your little remark on the field would go unanswered? Huh, pussy?" Avando sneers from behind me. "Do you know what I do to pussies?"

I'm struggling against Jameson and Ortiz's hold, and my body is on fire with anger. I can't help but let fear mingle with the anger. I grew up in the hood where we're taught to never turn our back on anyone. What is he going to do? Stab me? He'd never get away with it. Give me a beating? He better hope it's enough to keep me down or else I will easily turn on him.

Sudden shock tears through me and halts my struggles at the feel of his fingers brushing down my right ass cheek. It's so light that I can't be sure I'm truly feeling it right, and my body tenses.

Do you know what I do to pussies?

No.

No fucking way.

"Don't fucking touch me," I snarl into the tile wall, my cheek pressed firmly into it making speech awkward.

His cold chuckle sends ice down my spine despite the hot steam around us, and my stomach drops as bile rushes upward, stinging my throat. His fingers grab my ass in their clutches and squeeze tight, the nails cutting into my skin. The other hand grabs on, and then he's spreading them apart.

"Looks like a nice wet pussy to me," he whistles.

Then I feel the head of his dick slip between my spread cheeks, and I scream, kicking out with my legs. Ortiz and Jameson clamp my legs against the wall, and then Sebastian is stuffing a wet, white towel into my mouth. I struggle, but it's no fucking use. I'm about to be raped. I've heard about this happening in jail, and yes, I've heard about some university scandals involving rape, but I never thought it happened in the NFL. How many others has he done this to?

"She's pretty," he coos as he goes back to stroking his cock along my asshole, never penetrating, just gliding over it.

My screams are muffled around the towel, and when I feel him start to push inside, shame, sudden and hot, flies through me. How did I let this happen? I should've fucking known better than to let my guard down. Tears break past my lash line as he continues pushing inside of me, and the pain is like a hot poker, searing me with each inch.

"She's tight, boys," he grunts behind me. "I think we've got ourselves a virgin."

Why did I have to stay in the shower for so long? Why didn't I get out of here quickly? I knew he was pissed, and I knew I had egged him on today. How did I become so fucking naïve? He withdraws then pushes back in, the pain making me scream once again into the wet towel.

I hear a locker door slam in the distance, and Sebastian hastily pulls out as Jameson slams his fist into my stomach. The force of the hit has me doubling over and gagging hard around the wet towel. Vomit hits the fabric in my mouth and rushes back down my throat. Breathing becomes impossible as the acid liquid spews from my nostrils since the towel still blocks my mouth.

"Remember your place, Rookie," I hear Avando sneer. "Or that little pussy will be mine again."

They hurry out of the shower, and I pull the towel out, inhaling a lungful of air. Everything hurts, so I take my time getting to my feet. The room spins, and I stumble into the wall, my hand slipping on the tile. I lose purchase and slip to my ass on the floor, grunting through the pain radiating back there. I refuse to scream, and I refuse to walk out of here weaker than I walked in.

If Avando thought he could break me this way, he was sorely

mistaken. I won't give him the satisfaction. I stand again and lean against the cool tile, taking deep breaths and spitting out the bile that's collected in my mouth. I stumble back under the water and let the cooling liquid roll over my back and down my ass. I will never be caught with my back turned again.

There's no way I can go to Coach about this, and even if I wanted to, the thought of telling anyone has my stomach rolling again. No, I will deal with this the only way I know how, and fuck … How fucking sweet my revenge will be.

CHAPTER SIX

Dixon

Getting out of bed is extremely difficult this morning. I spent half of the night stressing about having to wake up and then the other half convincing myself that I could handle anything. Could I actually handle this, though? As much as I've been through in my life, this is a first, and I don't know how I'm supposed to be feeling.

I was raped.

Rape. A word I'd never really associate with men being on the receiving end. I know men can be raped, obviously, but not like that. I don't know ... I feel detached from myself, like my emotions about the whole ordeal are locked up tight, and I am thinking about it like it didn't really happen to me. I know why I'm doing that ... I'm so fucking ashamed.

It's an hour before I have to get back to the field, so I must force myself out of bed. My stomach is aching where Jameson punched me, and I have other aches in places I have never ached before. The feeling that surges up inside of me is crippling, but I push myself to keep moving and step into the shower. Once the spray hits me, my body stands rigid, and I can't seem to calm my heartbeat. The water mixed with the feeling of the tile beneath my feet has me tottering on the edge of losing it. It feels like I'm right back there.

My fist hits the tile on the wall, and I let loose a scream that's been trapped in my throat since I pulled myself out of that shower stall yesterday. I let it roar from my chest until all the air is expelled from my lungs, and my voice is hoarse. I didn't work this hard to be brought down by a group of bullies. We are grown, and I won't let them think they got the best of me.

I smash the tile one more time and breathe through the myriad of emotions I'm feeling. They're twisting inside of me like a kaleidoscope, and unfortunately for Avando, anger seems to be the most prevalent. I smear the body wash over my chest and angrily scrub it into my skin, scraping my nails across the surface. I feel my skin become irritated and slightly inflamed, a mirror to how my insides feel. I rinse myself off and slam down the faucet, effectively shutting off the water.

After I have myself dressed and my protein shake in hand, the contents shaking from the onset of nerves, I head out to my car. I can face them and be a constant reminder of what they failed to accomplish. I won't be chased out.

The drive there is about ten minutes tops, and I blow out my breath as I park my vehicle. This morning, a longer drive would have been preferable. I'm not ready to just waltz in there, and my stomach picks that time to roll. Nausea hits me hard as I press my forehead to the steering wheel.

Get it together.

I grasp the door handle roughly and quickly pull myself out. I don't want to sit here wallowing. I keep my head down and watch my shoes hit the pavement, one after the other in a slow jog. Each impact jars my stomach, forcing me to harden up my insides. Nothing happened that I can't handle.

Opening the door, I take my final nervous breath and drop my shoulders back. Nothing happened here yesterday. The thought stays firmly in my head as I pass the weight room and head into the locker room.

"Hey, North." Zeal holds his fist out to me from his seat on the bench. "That was amazing yesterday. Welcome to first string."

"Thanks man." I bump his fist with mine.

"You really are fast." He comes up beside me and leans in close, his hand hitting my shoulder. "They'll get over it," he says quieter.

Zeal wasn't there when I was attacked, but his closeness is chipping at my carefully constructed wall of defense, and that can't happen.

"No worries." I slide out from under his hand and close my locker. "I got it covered."

"I know," he nods with another smile. "Today we hit the gym for a few hours and then the field."

"Cool," I swallow thickly.

The thought of being in that closed space with the three guys who attacked me threatens that defense once again. I close my eyes as I hear Zeal head off to the gym then breathe slowly. No, they won't take this from me.

My mom's face appears behind my closed eyes, the awed look on her face when I bought her new place and the excitement when she had a proper kitchen to cook in. Then Danny's face appears, hard in anger, toughened by the very streets I'm working to get him out of, and his eyes saddened with what he's had to do to stay there.

They won't take this from *them.*

My stride doesn't falter as I make my way to the gym, determination for my family once again blocking out everything else as I swing open the door roughly, letting it bounce off the wall.

The sound reverberates around the room, and I feel eyes on me as I stalk over to the leg press machine. If I can't take my frustrations out on Avando's face, then I may as well put it to use in here. I feel his eyes on me, and I can tell it's him because it always feels the same. Like something dark and inky slipping its cold, dark fingers along my spine. Thankfully, him and his rape posse don't say a fucking word because I'm ready to rip out of my damn skin. I wouldn't be able to control myself if I heard his voice right now.

Two hours later and with my muscles aching, I head back into the locker room and change into my uniform. I know he's here in the room because I can feel that same feeling, only this time I've expended my energy, and I don't give a fuck. I can feel my anger continue to rise as I get dressed, slamming my locker closed. I grab my helmet from the rack and storm out to the field. I pity anyone who tries to tackle me today … I can't guarantee their faces won't be pressed to the fucking grass.

I run toward the gathering second string as Coach blows a quick breath into the whistle, "North, you're playing with first string today. May as well get used to them."

North, not Rookie. It's a start, and I can't deny the pride that squeezes my chest. It's where I want to be playing, regardless of who I'm playing with. Zeal holds out his hand with a wide smile, and I firmly grasp it in my own.

"Welcome to first string, North." His eyes are shining with excitement.

"Thanks, man."

Just as I'm pulling on my helmet, Avando, Jameson, and Ortiz run onto the field. Avando raises his brow when he sees me in the huddle.

"You lost, Rookie?"

"Coach put North with us today," Zeal claps me on the back, "and probably for every day afterward. Get used to it."

I can see the words getting to him, *get used to it,* and he probably wants to bend me over right here in front of everyone, just to put me back in my place.

As Zeal begins to tell us our play, I can feel Avando's eyes boring into the side of my face, that inky darkness trying to consume me. I push it from my mind, concentrating on Zeal and preparing revenge in the form of outshining the three pricks beside me. That's what Avando is most worried about with me being here, that I will steal his spotlight, and I'm going to do just that. Then laugh in his fucking face afterward.

Coach blows the whistle, and we line up, Jameson brushing my shoulder as he passes me. I run by Avando to my spot, hearing him snarl, "pussy bitch," as I go. Zeal calls out the play, then I feel the heightened energy as everyone moves into place. The ball is hiked as Zeal steps back into the pocket, then I'm running past the defensive line. Zeal bides his time as he waits for me to get open, and as soon as he sees his chance, he's throwing me the ball.

My fingers glide along the stippled leather surface, then I tuck it to my side, running by and watching as a few guys try to catch up with me. My anger, my stress, and my shame are seeping through my feet as I run, slowly leaving my body.

Out of the corner of my eye, I see our defensive tackle, Dex Carver, getting too close, so I take my chance, running out of bounds to avoid taking the tackle. The last thing I need is to risk fumbling the ball the moment I hit first string. Heading back to the line of scrimmage, I can still feel the hatred radiating off Avando, but at this point my adrenaline is kicking in, and it's only fueling me to play harder.

At the snap, I take off like my feet are on fire, pushing myself to the limit, wanting to show everyone just what I'm capable of. I can feel someone gaining on me, so I look back to see our defensive end, Alonso Lopez, just as he's diving at me from behind, attempting to trip me up. I hurdle out of his reach just in time and keep on going.

As if our minds are in sync, I turn right as Zeal is throwing the ball my way. I dodge another tackle and watch as the ball spirals perfectly toward me. My heart is thundering in my chest from the exertion and adrenaline, but there's no way I'm missing this. Jumping up and reaching with both hands, I catch the ball with the tips of my fingers. Not wasting a second, I quickly tuck it tight to my body and take off toward the end zone.

My feet pound the earth in a quick staccato, and as that end line rushes forward, I scream into the air. This is why I'm here, and no one is going to take the love I have for this sport away.

Once we're back in the locker room, my body is begging for a hot shower, and I refuse to acknowledge the anxiety that's threatening to resurface. I need to face my trauma, and I need to be prepared.

I grab my towel and head into the showers, shedding my clothes into the hamper along the way. Once the cool tiles touch my feet, nausea begins to swirl low in my gut, but I tamper it down and head to the same stall as yesterday. I won't let my fear rule my decisions.

I hang up the towel and turn on the hot water, waiting for the steam. I step in, keeping my back to the wall, then I dip my head under the water, letting my eyes close. The hot water sluices down my back, soothing the tired muscles, and I groan at the feeling.

I open my eyes and see the three of them, my vision blackening with anger. I rush forward, naked, uncaring, and grab Jameson. I use his and the others' surprise, to slam his head into the tiled wall, satisfaction coursing through me as he sinks to the floor.

"What the…"

The sound of Avando's voice sends my anger soaring, and I turn on him, slamming my fist to his mouth, grinning when Ortiz raises his hands in surrender and begins to back away.

I stand over Avando while he's on his knees and spit at his feet. "I may not act like it, but I'm from the streets, you little bitch. You got the drop on me yesterday because I had my back turned, but don't think I'm soft because of it. I can guarantee it will never happen again."

As Sebastian gets to his feet, I watch as his tongue snakes out, running along the blood gathering on his bottom lip. My chest is moving rapidly up and down, my eyes never leaving his golden ones. I can see the rage simmering in the amber orbs and I wait for his retaliation. Jameson's groan from beside me breaks our stare down as Sebastian's eyes flick to him then back to me.

"You think you're street?" Avando sneers.

"You think you're straight?" I retort, and his eyes flare again. "Were you coming back for seconds?" I let my lips curve upward slowly, taunting him.

He takes a few steps back as Jameson stands to his feet, giving me a once over. It's in his and Ortiz's eyes that I'm beginning to see respect.

"Watch yourself," Avando warns, and I laugh.

"No, you watch yourself," I throw back as they leave the shower.

I know how to watch myself, and with these guys, I must be on my guard constantly.

CHAPTER SEVEN

The rookie has a fucking death wish.

He actually asked if I was straight. Does he want to fucking die?

"Bro, where did he come from?" Jameson has an ice pack to his swollen temple.

"Clemson," I growl as I throw a bag of coke to the table.

"Nah," Jameson shakes his head and winces. "Where did he grow up?"

I should know this, it's something we're all told about the rookies before they get to camp, but I missed North's bio. He's tougher than I gave him credit for, but that doesn't mean shit, and it makes me want to prove it to him that much more.

"I know that look," Ortiz grumbles beside me. "This shit will get you kicked out of the league."

"Ain't nothing going to get us kicked out of the league. You think that pussy bitch will say anything?" I look from Ortiz to Jameson. "He has a family he needs to feed too, I'd bet my life on it."

"He handed us our asses today," Jameson whines, the noise grating on my last fucking nerve.

"You want to suck his dick now?" I sneer at him. "Is that it?"

"Bro—" his face screws up in confusion, but I cut him off.

"Don't call me 'bro' if you're ready to suck the rookie's dick." I grab my own dick through my pants. "Because believe me, you're either sucking dick or getting your dick sucked, you choose."

"Sebastian," Ortiz cuts in, "we're on your side, but fuck, this shit has gone too far."

Bunch of pussies wouldn't last a day in Rochester, and it makes my insides boil when I think of the rookie making them piss themselves.

"I don't need you anyway," I grumble as I pour the powder on the glass top. "I'll take it from here. You guys make sure you suck on those balls too."

They're smart to keep their mouths shut as I run my nose along the white oblivion because I'm ready to fucking snap, and I have no problem adding to the nasty bump on Jameson's head.

Ortiz starts cutting the weed and rolling a blunt into the Backwoods Tray as I sit back and watch him. I can't involve them in messing with North any longer. The rookie thinks he's too good for us and needs to be knocked the fuck down, but these two aren't ready for that. They're small-time gangsters, used to being told what to do and never overstepping orders.

The dirty shit needs to be done by me, that way I control everything, and no mistakes are made. I can still see the fear in Jameson's eyes as he holds the ice pack to his head. I would bet my life this bitch has never had a gun pulled on him, has never been thrown to the ground with the barrel of a pistol cold against the back of his head while some rival gang member searches his pockets for that night's drop-off.

Yeah, I've had plenty of guns held to my head, knives slashing my skin, and even a few bullets shot at me. But I'm here, and you better believe I'm not going any fucking where.

Rookie is probably basking in the win he had today. I hate that he took us by surprise, and I hate that he thinks he's won. I'll let him have it though because when I finally tear him apart, I'll laugh at the defeat on his face… And right after he thought he'd won.

He's renting a townhouse in a nice, little, private, gated community. Like a good little rich boy now. Too bad the guard at the gate recognized me, and when I said I was coming to meet a teammate, he was all too happy to let me in. Now I'm sitting in my car, watching his house like a fucking stalker.

This shit takes time … watching someone and how they move, finding out what or who their main priority is. When you figure that out, you find the person's weakness, and if I want Dixon North to actually go away, I need that weakness.

I hate that this bitch thought he could just come on the team and land at the top, no work, and no struggle. That's just not how this shit works. Every one of us fought and bled to be where we are, and he needs to do the same. Respect is earned, and I worked hard for this team's respect. That's why everyone listens to me when I talk.

It wasn't hard to find out the simple things, like where Dixon North comes from, where he went to high school, and what college he attended. When you're picked first in the draft, that becomes public knowledge, and everyone is salivating for every last detail they can get.

He was born and raised in Westport, Baltimore, Daddy dead, Mommy working three jobs, and a little brother who likes to get in trouble. Westport isn't a good place to grow up in, a lot of gang violence resulting from turf wars, and soaring dropout rates for high schoolers.

His front door opens, and I watch as he steps out onto his porch, his eyes on the sun rising in the sky. He's wearing an orange tank top, and the color makes his rich skin pop, glistening in the early morning light. He's stacked, his muscles defined and flexing as he stretches. He puts earbuds into his ears, then he's jumping off the porch and jogging down the street.

I get out of my car, pop my hoodie over my head, and jog to the side of his house. He has a corner unit, which means access to the back that the others don't have. I keep tight to the brick wall and slowly follow it to the open concept backyard with no fencing to separate it from the neighbors. There's nothing back here, no patio furniture … not even a barbecue, telling me this place is temporary.

He doesn't plan on staying here, or he's waiting for someone to come live here with him. A girlfriend? A wife? Or maybe his mom and brother. If he's smart, he'll keep his family far away from his work. Those two never mesh, and family has a way of dragging along drama.

I get to his rear, sliding glass door and try to see inside the house. I soon realize I'm staring into his kitchen and the brand-new looking stainless steel appliances. Does he do anything more than sleep here? The place looks spotless, like maybe he has one of those cleaning OCDs and can't stand anything out of its place.

How long does he jog for? Would he have armed the alarm even though he lives in a gated community? Is this door locked?

I tug a bit on the handle and snicker when it slides open, no alarm alerting anyone to my presence. He really is a dumb little bitch. He said he's from the streets but has no problem leaving his house unsecured? To this day, I still need my windows and doors locked before I sleep or leave the house. On top of that, a gun sits loaded inside the table by my bed. No one will get the drop on me; I'm always fucking ready.

My boots squeak on his shiny clean floors as I step through the kitchen, running my finger along his immaculately cleaned counters. The complete opposite of what my house looks like, but in all realness, I am not keeping that place for my family, and this is exactly what this looks like … a family home. Does the rookie want his mommy to come here and take care of him?

I stand in the middle of his family room and look around. There are no pictures, nothing that personalizes the place, and nothing to help with what I'm looking for. It looks like this place is barely lived in, and if I didn't hate him so much, I'd feel sorry for the little bitch. The stairs are to my left, and I bound up them, taking two at a time. We're all due at the field in two hours, and I don't know how long I have in here. There are three doors up on the small landing, and I open one to find a closet, empty save for two towels. Again, it's quite sad. The next door is a large bathroom. Every surface shines—even the fucking toilet seat—and then I open the third.

The bedroom is exceedingly plain, and the guy is still living out of his suitcase even though it's been over a month. I kneel beside the suitcase and push aside the clothing. There's absolutely nothing. No pictures, no books, and nothing telling me this guy has a personality. It's like everything about him and this place is temporary. What the hell is his plan?

I pull open his small closet and find a few sweaters hanging along with a suit. I shut the door, and then my gaze lands on his wallet sitting on his side table. Fucking yes. I sit on the perfectly made bed and flip it open, seeing a Baltimore driver's license. I pull out my phone and take a quick picture before shuffling through a credit card, old school IDs, and a Baltimore bus pass. Weird. Until my eyes zero in on the name: Daniel North.

Not Dixon.

I turn the card in my hand and find a picture, the film over the top scuffed with age. It's looks like a younger, thinner version of Dixon, but this kid looking back at me is tough, and he's fuckin angry.

It almost looks like I'm staring at myself. I see that look in his eye, and I know it all too well. Before I can think twice about it, I slide the card into my hoodie pocket and set the wallet back on the table. Finally, something useful.

I slip back out of the house the same way I got in and jog back to my car. Not fifteen minutes later, Rookie comes back into view and jogs up his driveway, giving a quick look over his shoulder.

You feel my stare, little bitch?

CHAPTER EIGHT

Dixon

"Come on, North." Alonso Lopez claps me on the back, his black hair dripping water. "It's our last day of training camp. We always hit up the club!"

"We really do." Zeal wraps his towel around his waist.

"We all get so fucking drunk, then we have a few days to recover," Dex chimes in as he walks buck naked to the shower stall. The man is a fucking tank, and now I understand why the announcers call him The Carver. The guy could plow a path out on the field.

They're all trying to convince me to hit up the local club tonight to celebrate the end of training camp. I don't drink often, and the thought of partying with these guys puts me on edge. Will Avando, Jameson, and Ortiz be there? Because them coupled with alcoholic drinks sounds like a recipe for trouble.

"What club?" I can feel myself caving and make myself promise not to drink.

"Sky Lounge." Zeal gives me a wide grin. "North's in boys."

"Yes!" Dex yells from inside the shower. "Let's get him fucking wasted."

"No," I shake my head, "only a few drinks."

"Yeah, yeah," Zeal chuckles.

The neon blue, fluorescent lights cast a glow around the room and the small, dimmed lights hanging over the bar do nothing for clarity. It's your typical club, dark and thumping with bass. It's packed body to body and hard for us to squeeze through the crowd. It's even more comical to watch Dex push people out of the way.

Zeal says they always have the VIP room waiting for the Bills, and when I questioned him about how often they come here, he just laughed. This lifestyle can't be good for the team, and it would explain why losing is what they've become good at. I want to change that for them, but I can't do it alone.

We reach a bouncer and a velvet rope that's sectioned off an area with a private bar. There are about five tables in there, and I can see a few people standing around. My heart begins to pound, and I wonder what Avando would be like in this setting. He's this formidable force on the field and a fucking asshole in the locker room, but what is he like when he's having fun?

The rope is opened for us, and we're ushered inside. In here, the music is still loud, but you don't feel the bass in your chest the same way. It's more intimate and doesn't feel like part of the crowded, loud, atmosphere outside. Each table has a few bottles of liquor and a bucket of ice with a server standing in front of it. Obviously girls, because clubs like this need sexuality to be the focal point.

Four girls are standing next to the tables and smile at us demurely as we walk in. Well, all except one. She's currently sitting on the lap of Avando who happens to be occupying the last table with none other than Jameson and Ortiz. So much for hoping they wouldn't show. I scan over their table and see that they look relaxed and are laughing, settling the nervous tension I have whenever I see them.

I follow Zeal to a table and sit down, Dex and Alonso following us. A shot glass is pushed in front of me, and I see Dex beaming as he fills it with Grey Goose. He does the same with Zeal and Alonso, finally holding up his in the air.

"To an amazing year" he salutes, and we all tip our shots back.

It's been years since I've drank. Never being one who enjoyed it, the burn down my throat causes me to choke. The guys laugh, and our server brings us a round of beers on Zeal's request.

"Tell us North," Dex mumbles around a mouthful of beer, "who did you leave behind in Baltimore?"

"My mother and little brother are still there."

"No girlfriend?" Zeal asks. "Or girlfriends?"

They all laugh again, and I join in. "Nah, where I'm from, girls would latch on for a chance to get out, nothing would be real. I had to be careful."

"So no girls ever?" Alonso looks shocked.

"You crazy?" I snort. "Of course, there were girls, just never anything serious. I had bigger and more important priorities first."

"I hear that." Dex acknowledges.

Another shot is poured, and I groan as the guys chant my name to drink the clear liquid. I can already feel the weight of my decision as it coats my throat and stomach in warmth. But whatever… I'm having fun, and it's not everyday I get to let loose and enjoy myself. I push myself constantly to be better, and I know I deserve a break for one night.

I chance a glance over my shoulder and see Avando clearly making out with the girl on his lap while Jameson and Ortiz chat up a few others. I look around the room and see it's filling up fast with players and females they're bringing in from the main room.

I'm still watching Sebastian when his eyes open and land on

me, his mouth still devouring the girl's on his lap. With his eyes still trained on mine, he runs his hand up her thigh then nudges her legs open, giving me a peak of red lace. I know I should look away. What he's doing is wrong, and I know he's taunting me, but my eyes feel glued to his fingers as he toys with that strip of lace. I quickly scan back up to their faces and see Sebastian has once again closed his eyes, still plundering her mouth with his tongue.

Just when I'm about to turn away, I catch his fingers as he slides that red lace to the side and reveals the girl's pink, wet pussy. His fingers spread her lips apart, and his forefinger flicks against her clit, then he sinks it deep inside her. He pumps in and out a few times, then fully pulls out, his finger glistening with her arousal. I watch as that finger moves upward slowly before he sucks it into his mouth, his eyes once again on mine. I startle when I realize I'm still staring, and he fucking caught it, turning quickly in my seat. But the damage is done. I can hear his raucous laughter behind me, and I berate myself for my lack of decency. I need to slow down on the drinking.

"It's always the same with those three," Zeal says to me. "Whether it be girls or fighting … I try to keep them in check, but at the end of the day, they are their own men."

"Does Coach expect you to keep us all in check?"

"Not anymore," Zeal shakes his head. "He's a lot more lenient on them for some reason, and I realized the more I went to him about the problems they caused, the more Coach ignored me. So I stopped."

"Makes sense."

"I know they've fixated on you, and I know they can be a lot to handle." Zeal looks over his shoulder at their table. "Don't give up on us as a team because of a few rotten apples. They grew up rough."

"I grew up rough" I clasp my hand to his shoulder. "The hood doesn't make criminals or gangbangers, the system does. I was lucky enough to see that at a young age."

"One day, when I haven't been drinking like a fish, you'll have to explain that to me." He smiles, and I nod.

"You got it." I'm always willing to educate others if they're open to it.

"Let's hit the dance floor and grind on some bitches." I hear Ortiz shout behind me and turn in my seat.

Jameson and Ortiz are heading out of the VIP area and onto the dance floor, but Sebastian is nowhere in sight. I quickly scan the room and find the girl he was with, standing behind the bar taking orders from the growing crowd in here. Where did he go?

Why the hell do I care? I turn back to face the others and listen in on their enthusiastic conversation about our chances this upcoming season. They're excited, and I can't help but let their excitement settle inside me too. I want to win, and I will do everything in my power to ensure we do. I know what that means … I need to somehow mend my fucked-up relationship with the man who raped me and his little minions. Do I have to like him? Fuck no, but we need to work as a team.

My bladder screams at me, and I lean into Zeal "Bathroom?"

He points to the corner of the room and grins at me. "We get our own over here, no pissed-on toilet seats."

I grin back and get up out of my seat. The room spins a bit on its side, and I blink rapidly to right it. Yeah, no more drinks. It takes a while to get through the crowd, and I stop constantly to say hey to my teammates. By the time I hit the restroom, my bladder is threatening to release in my pants. I storm through the door and sigh in relief when I see the two urinals and two stalls, one of which has someone inside.

"Who's there?"

I halt at his voice and almost groan in frustration. Of fucking course he would be in here. The stall opens, and Sebastian steps out, a little bit of white powder dusting his right nostril. I stand there and stare at the spot until he sniffs and runs his sleeve under his nose.

"What the fuck you looking at, Rookie?" His voice is rough, and his pin-sized pupils narrow on me.

"I just need to take a piss." I start for a urinal. "Am I safe to drop my pants in here?" I look over my shoulder at him.

"I'm not a fucking homo," he snarls.

"Could've fooled me."

"I was putting you back in your place, like a good little bitch," he utters, his voice low with warning.

I open my jeans and pull myself out, finally letting my bladder go and almost moan in relief. I can still feel him watching me, and I would be uncomfortable if I wasn't so drunk and if my bladder wasn't on the brink of exploding before. Of course, this time my piss continues for what feels like hours, and the longer I'm standing here in silence with him watching me, the longer I feel exposed. Finally, I finish and tuck myself away, flushing the urinal. I get to the sink and wash my hands, looking at him watching me through the mirror's reflection. I dry my hands and break the eye contact, heading to the door.

"I bet you enjoyed it, though," he says as I pass him.

The rush of anger that consumes me is fast and powerful. Before I can stop myself, my fist is slamming into his mouth, and I watch as he hits the wall. He raped me and thinks he can make light of it? I don't fucking think so. I grab the front of his shirt and throw his back against the wall again. He grunts from the impact.

"What the fuck did you just say?" I snarl into his face, and the piece of shit starts to laugh.

"That's the second time you've punched me now." His tongue swipes up the drop of blood on his lip. "I'm starting to think you got a thing for me, North."

Not Rookie, not little bitch… He called me North, and I can't explain why that pleases me. We're face-to-face, my fists still gripping the fabric of his shirt and his eyes roaming over my face.

"I see you watching me all the time," he continues, his voice taunting. "Did you enjoy the pussy I showed you out there? Or is that not your thing?"

Those last few words send my rage to a boiling point, and I rear my head back then spit all over his fucking face. The surprise and shock registering in his features are almost comical, but there's nothing I can laugh at right now. I slam my fist one more time into his cheek then let him fall to the ground.

He looks up at me with rage boiling in his eyes, but it's the other emotion I see in their depths that makes me back up and grab the handle, pulling open the door.

As I head back to my table, I scrub my hand down my face, wincing at the pain radiating in my knuckles.

What game is Sebastian playing? And why did it look like he enjoyed being hit by me?

CHAPTER NINE

Sebastian

Last night was a write off, so I'm happy we have today off. I know I had way too much to drink and that getting behind the wheel to get home was stupid, but I'm home in one piece. Or somewhat one piece.

I feel a hand skim across my chest and turn my head to look into a pair of bright green eyes. The girl from the club. Her leg is wrapped across my waist, and I can feel her wet pussy begin to rub along my thigh. I might've been into fucking her last night, but I sure as fuck don't remember it, and I'm not even feeling it this morning. I want her out of my house and right now, preferably.

"I'm gonna need you to call someone to come get you, or I can call an Uber." My voice sounds like grating sandpaper. "But I need you gone like ten minutes ago."

She gasps at the harshness of my words, but I really don't give a shit about her feelings. She's nobody to me. She pulls away from me and hops out of the bed, her tits bouncing with the motion. Again, nothing. My dick is soft, and that's saying something since it's morning and all.

"You couldn't fucking get it up last night anyway," she huffs as she pulls up her red, lace panties and tucks herself into her black dress. "This was a waste of my time."

"You and me both, sweetheart," I say as I sit up and search the floor for my boxers. "But I'm happy my dick won't fall off, at least."

She flips me the finger and storms out of my bedroom, her heels clicking against the wooden stairs. I hear the front door open and slam shut, cursing my drunk self for my stupidity. I shouldn't be bringing anyone back here with me, and I wonder where the fuck Ortiz and Jameson were. They know what the deal is and how I get when I drink… I want pussy, and I don't think beyond that. They're supposed to be the ones who stop me from bringing these hoes back to my crib.

My body reeks of cheap perfume and alcohol, making me think I must've dropped a drink or had a drink dropped on me. Either is a possibility. When I'm drinking liquor, I lose all common sense and act purely on instinct. Those instincts aren't always appropriate, though. In certain circumstances, they're fine, but out here, I need to watch myself. It was the anger I felt after Rookie spat in my face. It wasn't solely focused on him. No, I was fucking pissed off at myself too. That part inside of me that I bury so deep, the dark little speck that fucks with my head … that part actually enjoyed it, and I get why I hate him so much. He toys with that part of me, and I find myself forgetting to hold it down. After that, I remember hitting the bar and the liquor hard.

My bathroom is another mess and I groan when I see the shattered Grey Goose bottle on the floor, dropped while someone was taking a piss, which they didn't flush. Probably me since the seat is up, but who knows? Those two fucks let me leave the club with a whole ass bottle of vodka and let me drive home with it? Fucking idiots.

I start the shower and step inside, letting the water cascade down over my head. I feel out of sorts, and my body is beginning to protest this lifestyle. The covered-up injuries, concussions swept under the rug, and the people paid to care for you seeing you as nothing but a huge, motherfucking dollar sign. I get it … it's a business, and I am an asset, worked over until I am of no use. That's why I don't give them everything. I live the life I want, and I suck just as much out of this industry.

Once I'm done showering, I head downstairs, leaving the mess for when the maid comes by later and throw myself on the couch to watch TV. I order in some food then scroll through my phone, trying to see what the hell happened last night. Nothing hurts, so I know I didn't fight. Except that hit I took from Rookie, but he's a bitch, so I hardly felt it. No videos, no pictures, and no text messages. All good signs that I still had my head somewhat together through the drunken haze but doesn't explain where the hell my boys were.

I send them both texts, telling them to get the fuck to my house when they get up. I need to find out every little thing. After I came out of that bathroom last night, North was gone, and Zeal and his crew left soon after. The rest of the night is a blackened blur.

With nothing else to do, I lie on my couch and think over all the shit I want to do to mess with North. I'd never admit it to anyone, but the fucker's stats are good, and yes, he's also an asset. But that doesn't mean I have to make his life easy. Seems like the little bitch has had too much easy, and for the money he'll be pulling, he could stand to have a bit of trouble. I could turn some more of the guys on him, making him feel unwanted, and the locker room would be his personal hell. I could get him tackled hard on the field and have him looking like the weak bitch he is. I could also corner him in that shower stall again.

My dick hardens at the memory, and I curse at how it pulses from the images in my mind. How he felt excessively tight and how badly I wanted to shoot my load up his ass. I slip my hand under my track pants and groan when my cock jerks in my palm. I remember the feel of him struggling and his asshole squeezing my dick as I forced my way inside. I begin to slowly jerk myself off to the thought of fucking North into that shower stall, pounding into him, both of our moans loud over the spray of the water. I come long and hard all over my lower belly, shock coursing through my body. It doesn't really mean anything, it was a tight hole. I'm not a fucking homo.

I get up and clean myself off just as the doorbell rings, announcing the delivery. My stomach rumbles at the thought of food, and I shove down everything I was feeling about what I did to North. It all just means I need to get laid, and I need to do it soon. With camp and training, I haven't had time to do shit. Last night was our first night out, so it's no wonder I latched on to the first chick who noticed me.

I pay for my pizza and wings, giving the guy a tip that makes him smile wide. I love doing that stuff, helping people who are in mundane, everyday jobs, temporarily making it worth their while. It's not easy dealing with customers. Most of the time they tip you so little you want to spit in their food, and other times they're complaining about you being a minute late, making you still want to spit in their food. When I was a young teen, I tried my hand at a food delivery position. Using my bike, I made deliveries all over Rochester. It was especially stressful. People yell at you when the food is bad, and they blame you for everything. None of them ever understood I was just the delivery kid, and I quickly learned that my temperament wasn't suitable for customer service.

As soon as I'm sitting on the couch, my doorbell rings again. I get up, expecting to see the delivery guy again, but when I open the door, I am faced with a scowling Jameson and Ortiz, who's sporting a black eye. Neither look very happy.

"What happened to you two?" I ask as Jameson pushes himself inside.

"You," he snarls, Ortiz right behind him. "You happened to us."

"What?" I look at them with a raised brow. "What are you talking about?"

I shut the door and follow them as they stalk into my house. I don't know what the fuck is going on, but I'm about to lose it, and then they'll regret pissing me off today. I am not in the right headspace to deal with them like a normal person would.

"I need you to start talking." I can hear the threat in my tone, the underlying anger laced in, and my body becomes rigid. "I'm about to shoot you both in the fucking head and worry about the consequences later."

"Yeah, sounds exactly like what you said to us last night, only you pointed a fucking gun at our heads," Jameson snarls, and I try to wrack my brain for that instance, trying to remember it. Regardless, it is something I would say and something I would do. That's just facts.

"What did you do to deserve it?" I ask, and Ortiz scoffs.

"I was trying to get you into a cab with me," he points to his blackened eye. "You hit me for it."

"Then when I pulled on your arm to get you away from the girl, you pulled a gun on me," Jameson adds. "Right there in the middle of the parking lot, you pulled a gun and pointed it in my fucking face."

I breathe through the want to pound their disrespect back down their throats, and I try harder to remember anything from last night. It's not that I don't believe them, these are most definitely things I would do, but only when provoked. I can sense that these things did happen, I just don't know why, and I'm having a hard time believing I'm the only one to blame.

"All because you were trying to get me in a cab and away from some bitch?" I give them a disbelieving look.

"You told us we were jealous you were getting pussy, and we were to either hop in your Hummer with your bottle of Grey Goose or leave. When I tried to pull you away, you pulled the gun, and I was staring down that barrel." Jameson looks at me with disappointment.

Again, all these things sound like me, but I can't understand why I went to those extremes, and I can't see how them trying to make me see reason had me threatening them with my piece. Speaking of, if I had my gun on me last night, where the fuck is it now? I run my fingers along my short, shaved hair and try to remember, my head thumping harder in the process.

"You got into the car with it," Ortiz reads my thoughts. "And the bitch had the vodka."

I turn on my heel, and I head outside. My neighbors can be the nosy type, but I pay enough for my house to warrant me my much-needed privacy, so if I want to walk to my vehicle with my dick swinging in my track pants, I fucking will. I open the door and look into the front seat, my heart pounding, thinking about having a chick in here as I was swinging a gun around. I open the glove compartment and the center console but find nothing, my heart now jammed up into my throat. Did the bitch take it with her? She couldn't have, because after the shit I pulled on her this morning, I'm sure she'd wanted to kill me, so I'd have bled out by now.

Just as I begin to back out, I see the glint of metal on the passenger side floor, and I groan as I reach in. Why would I just toss it to the floor like that? Was I really that crazy reckless? If I had been pulled over and the cop suspected me of drinking alcohol, there would've been a search. This piece has the serial number removed, and that alone is jail time. I grip the gun in my hand, the cool, smooth surface a contrast to the hot skin of my palm as I look behind me to the street. It's quiet, so I take the chance and tuck it into my waistband, closing the vehicle door. I sprint to the house and hurry inside, once again face-to-face with Ortiz and Jameson.

I feel bad for the shit I pulled; I don't like that I threatened them in such a way, and I wish it were possible to apologize. But I can't do that. It's not something I will ever do. Apologizing admits you were wrong, and I can never be wrong. I sound like a piece of shit, but that's just the way it is when you're a leader. Apologies are weaknesses.

"Listen…" I begin, "I appreciate you having my back last night."

They look at each other then back at me wearily. I know it's hard to determine where I'm going sometimes. That's life, though. You never know how the people around you are going to be in the future, how the relationships you make will weather storms, and what their true personalities are until it's too late.

"I ordered food after I kicked the bitch out of my bed this morning," I chuckle, and they join in with a few shakes of their heads.

"I can't believe you let her stay that long," Jameson says, and I grin at him.

"I apparently had too much to drink because my dick refused to work. Probably a good thing," I muse.

"Yeah, considering you were nearly fucking her in the club," Ortiz snorts.

"Nah, that was just my fingers." I wiggle them, and they both laugh. "Let's go eat."

As I follow them through the house, my mind wanders back to last night, having that girl's legs spread on my lap, watching North watching us. I can't explain how primal my reaction was, like my body disconnected from my mind, and I was consumed with giving him a show. I wanted to see if he was just as into it because it was me, or if he wanted a piece of the pussy I had on display for him.

I scrub my hand down my face and growl into it. I really need to stop with these thoughts. I don't want anything to do with the rookie bitch, so it's back to regular programming next week. I won't stop until I've broken him, and then he can suck my long dick to make it up to me. You don't become a part of my team and act like you actually own it. Plus, my dick needs a good deep throating.

"Rookie left really early last night," Ortiz snickers. "He's such a little bitch."

"Yeah," I chuckle as we all settle in and turn on the TV. "He really fucking is."

We get halfway through the movie we're watching when my phone rings, startling me out of my food induced coma. I let out a pained groan when I see the name that's flashing on the screen.

"Fuck," I get up and hold up my phone. "I gotta take this."

Both snicker like the assholes they are.

"Tell her I say 'sup," Jameson calls out then laughs when I flip him the finger. I swipe open the call and huff as I bring the phone to my ear.

"Hey, you."

CHAPTER TEN

"You sound sick, Dixon." Mom's voice floods my ear, and I cringe. "Are you pushing yourself too hard?"

"I'm fine, Ma," I try to placate her. "I'm just waking up."

"Just waking up?" she squeaks, and I cringe once again. "It's noon!"

"It's my first day off in a long while," I groan and hold the phone away from my ear. "I have been trying to rest."

"Oh, I see." She sounds better, but I can't help but hear the slight tone of disappointment.

That used to really set me on edge growing up because I had the drive and worked my ass off while Danny was a troublemaker. I would be reprimanded for enjoying my downtimes, but he would be coddled when the police brought him home by the scruff of his neck. It's always been this way, and even though I'm used to it, I still feel the resentment I've kept hidden away.

"Well, what time do you plan on getting up?" she huffs. "It's Sunday. Do they not have a church near you?"

She knows there's a church near me, and she also knows I

won't ever be stepping inside. No matter how often I tell her I don't believe, she lets it go in one ear and out the other, hoping one day I'll repent. I take a deep breath and exhale into the phone, my frustration with her evident.

"Where's Danny?" I ask, knowing he's probably not home and hasn't been all weekend.

"He went out with some friends last night," she answers quietly.

"Then maybe he's the one you should be calling and asking what it is he'll be doing today, hmmm?" I know it's harsh, but now that I've hit my life goals, I think her attention should be on the son who's struggling.

"He rarely picks up his phone to me," she sighs, and I roll my eyes.

"Because you let him get away with too much." I roll out of bed and grab my wallet from the side table. "Ma, I gotta go. I'll call you later."

I hang up and open my wallet. I grabbed Danny's old bus pass before coming here. It shows him on the cusp of changing from a troublesome boy into a dangerous teenager, and I keep it as a reminder to get my family out of the streets of Baltimore. I scan through the cards, and when I reach the end, my heart begins to pound. It's not here.

I look on the floor by the bed, underneath the bed, and open the drawers in the table… Nothing. It couldn't have fallen out of my wallet. I know that because it's been in there for almost a year, and it was tucked into the tight sleeve in the back. I know I haven't pulled it out since I've moved into this house because life has been busy as hell, meaning I haven't had time to sit around to reminisce. It should be in my fucking wallet.

I wrack my brain yet still come up with nothing. There's no way it's missing. I try to think of all the places my wallet has been, and I come up with here and the camp. My locker there locks though, and I've been locking it because I don't have any trust for a few of my teammates. That leaves this house. I don't always lock it when I go jogging, but really, I don't have much of importance in here. And besides, why go through a man's wallet to steal an old bus pass? It makes no sense. No, I must have dropped it somewhere, maybe when I was paying for something or in my car. It's not like it's the end of the world, I just wanted to have something that reminded me of where I came from and what I must work toward.

I try to shake off the feeling that something is wrong, like someone has come into my space and changed just enough to be noticeable but not enough to cause panic. Luckily, all my financial records and personal documents are locked away in a safety deposit box at the bank. I was raised to never trust a lock and that if someone wants into your space, they can do it. That's why I live minimally, and I don't care if this place was broken into.

It's just extremely weird that someone would steal an old, expired bus pass when my brand-new Amex Black Card is sitting in the same wallet. Something just doesn't feel right. The only explanation is that I've misplaced it.

I pull up to the Buffalo Bills home stadium and beam. I'm finally here. This week we'll be practicing on the field, then our first NFL game will be on Sunday. I am so fucking psyched to be running out on that field as a part of the first string. I feel stronger than I've ever been, and my body is in top form. I'm ready to work some magic. I'm ready to start racking up those wins so I can shove them into a certain someone's face.

Just thinking about the man who took advantage of me brings back the flurry of emotions I try to keep buried. Sebastian Avando has created this reaction inside of me, and I fucking hate it. It's not so much the fear that flickers there because I know that's normal after everything he's done. It's not the anger because I know that's warranted, and it's not the lingering shame because I'm intelligent enough to know that comes with being a victim. No, it's none of those feelings that worry me. It's the confusion I feel when I see him.

The hatred is the most prevalent, and it burns exceedingly hot, the force of it sometimes scorching my insides when I see him. The fear mixed in just makes me angrier, and that stokes the burn further. But then when I'm alone and the fire burns out, the confusion seeps in. Why is Avando like this with me? Why does he go out of his way to attack me personally? How the fuck did I appear on his radar, and why am I still there? I've proven myself, and I've shown I am worthy of being a Bill. So why is it he's still so quick to knock me down? Another cause for my confusion is how often I think about the man. I know it's due to the fact that he took advantage of me, making me a victim in a place I should be comfortable in, like a second home.

He just seems to worm his way into my mind, and I need it to stop. I want to be able to play the sport I love without having all this contention connected to it. I drop my head to the steering wheel and let my mind ease, drawing in a deep breath. I hold onto it and will my heart to slow down, letting the air out of my lungs in a quick rush. I give myself a quick nod, pull all my doubts and fears back deep inside me, and push open my door. I don't want my first day here to be clouded with thoughts of him.

I jog across the parking lot and hit the steps, taking two at a time before I throw open the door. This place is huge with multiple vendors and a circular walkway to take you around the stadium to the appropriate seats. I remember being a kid and begging my mother to take me to a game, any game really. I would've watched hockey or basketball, as long as I got to experience the hype. Of course, it was never something we could afford, so the first time I saw a live game was watching college football. I was eleven, and after that, I knew I wanted to be a player.

"Mr. North?" An attractive woman appears from a side door

and smiles. "This way to the locker room."

I was told someone would meet me at the front, and even though I'm excited to get down below to the locker room, I really wanted to look around. She must see the flash of disappointment on my face because she chuckles.

"Not everyone is here yet. You have about fifteen minutes before Coach arrives. Did you want to meet me back here then?"

"Yes!" I answer quickly, and she chuckles again. I don't care how I look right now. This is the epitome of my dreams all coming together, and I don't want to forget a single thing.

I take an immediate left and head down the center walkway, scanning the different vendors and imagining what it will smell like in here on a game day. Popcorn, corn dogs, and beer, most likely. As disgusting as that combination sounds, I can't wait to fucking smell it for myself and watch as fathers hold their little son's hands, guiding them toward their seats. That's all I ever wanted for myself, to have a father who would show me those things and praise me when I succeeded. Our father passed away when Danny was three and I was eight. He had a heart attack and died on our kitchen floor. My mother never remarried, so Danny and I grew up without a man around us. It's water under the bridge now but being here brings those longings back. My only consolation is that I'll one day be able to do that for my own child.

I take the first set of steps upward and come out on a platform overlooking the large field below. Rows and rows of seats surround the arena. Imagining them being filled with screaming fans, I can't stop the excitement that bubbles in my chest, the feeling working its way up and over my face. I'm beaming into the early morning sun, and the feeling reminds me why I'm here. This euphoric feeling and the rush of adrenaline it brings… This is the exact reason why I've worked myself so hard for the past twelve years. I give myself ten minutes to stand here, feeling that excitement while letting the warmth of the rising sun soak into my skin.

Before I leave, I make myself a promise that I won't let anyone ruin this for me, and that includes Sebastian. His issues are not mine, and if he continues down this path of fighting me, I will fight back. I won't let him or anyone else take what is rightfully mine.

I get back to the front, and the lady is there waiting, just as she said. I notice she gives me an appreciative once over, and I grin. Maybe it's time I get out a bit.

"What's your name?" My eyes trail down her body and come to rest on her dark eyes. I watch as a pink blush coats her cheeks.

"Danielle," she replies, her voice smooth but shy. "My friends call me Dani."

"Can *I* call you Dani?" I smile at her, and that pink blush turns red. Fuck, she's beautiful, and her features tell of an exotic mix. Maybe Asian and white.

"I don't know," she bites down on that full bottom lip, her teeth sinking into the flesh, capturing my full attention. "Are we friends?"

"Not yet, Danielle." I toss her a wink as she leads me toward a large set of red double doors, "but I want to be." My voice drops an octave. She's tall and lean with curves in all the right places. Her ass is plump but looks firm as I watch her take long strides. I bite into my lip when her calves flex with each step. She's fit.

"Okay," she whispers. "This is your locker room, and the Coach's office is right across the hall.

"Thanks," I tell her, looking around the space. "Do you work here?"

"Yes," she smiles wide. "You'll see me around."

"Perfect. Later." I head inside.

Zeal is standing in the center of the room as I walk in, and I grin as I watch him. He has his hands on his hips as he looks from left to right. I watch as he inhales deeply, his back widening and his shoulders lifting. When his body deflates with his exhale, I chuckle, the noise making him look at me over his shoulder. His face breaks out with excitement, and he shakes his head.

"I think I smell victory this year," he says as I come to stand beside him.

"There's no thinking about it," I grab his shoulder and give him a squeeze. "I know it."

I walk along the lockers, and when I spot my locker and Jersey number, my heart triple beats out of my chest. Number eighty-eight. I've had it since high school… It's been with me through my struggles but always had my back. I run my fingers along the smooth engraving and smile. We fucking made it.

"Offense is always on the same line," he remarks quietly, and I look to my right, seeing Avando's name on the locker right next to mine. Like fate just can't stop laughing her ass off at me.

"It's all good," I shrug. "Everything is fine."

"They'll come around," he repeats his sentiment, and I refuse to burst his bubble, knowing they may never come around.

I nod instead and open my locker, gazing inside. The royal blue color gleams back at me, telling me this locker room was given a fresh coat of paint, and just like me is starting over. Camp experiences aren't going to affect my game here and I can feel how ready I am to be a part of this team. I want the fucking championship.

The quiet moment is short lived as the doors slam open and our teammates begin to pour in. I grab my practice uniform hanging on a hook under my locker and toss my duffle bag inside. I want to get down to the field and run a couple laps before everyone gets there. It's a tradition I've maintained for years.

My head is down, but I see his shoes as he walks by me, slowing in front of the locker beside mine. I'm shocked when he says nothing. I finish tying my shoes then stand to close my locker door, feeling his eyes on the side of my head. I don't look at him, and I don't acknowledge his presence. I won't let him be a part of my first experience here. I turn on my heel and head back for the doors, clapping Zeal on the back as I pass.

"I'm going to run a few laps, see you down there." I watch as he beams.

"See you there."

I step through the double doors and out into the wide hallway. To my left is the set of stairs we came down from the entrance, and to my right is another set of double doors. I know those lead to the field. I hear talking straight ahead and see Coach sitting at his desk, talking to Danielle, her face a mask of determination. I jog across the hall and rap my knuckles on the door, catching both of their attention.

"North!" Coach booms as he stands up. "How are you feeling?"

"Great," I feel amazing. "I was just about to head out to the field for a couple laps."

"Dani," Coach grabs her shoulder, motioning toward me. "This man here is The Human Flash."

I shake my head with a grin, feeling good under his praises and hoping like hell it convinces Danielle I'm worth her time.

"I can't wait to see that." Her husky voice hits me in the stomach.

"This is my daughter. Danielle." As Coach introduces us, my body feels like it's being doused in ice water. *Daughter?*

"We've met," she beams at my expression. No, Danielle, we actually didn't. If I'd known that she was Coach's daughter, I wouldn't have flirted with her, and now shit is about to get awkward.

I give them a quick nod and turn to head out to the large,

imposing, steel, double doors. The sunlight is streaming in through the cracks, and I can already feel the energy spreading through my legs. I want to claim this track with my feet. I throw open the doors and step out onto the concrete ramp that ascends to the field, the walls climbing on either side filled with seats. I jog up to the top of the ramp and stand there, my toes grazing the green grass.

The goal posts stand tall, gleaming a bright yellow, the paint fresh. The grass is a crisp green, and the lines have been freshly painted as well. And then there's the Buffalo Bills logo painted into the center, prominent and proud. I dig my feet into the grass and fly forward, pumping my legs as I circle the field. This feels like home.

CHAPTER ELEVEN

Sebastian

Dani has not taken her eyes off Dixon the whole practice, and it's fucking pissing me off. I'm not jealous. I fucked the bitch last season, and she wasn't that great of a lay anyway. But the pure desperation I see in her eyes makes her look pathetic. I hate pathetic people. Dixon has noticed her, I've seen him glance a few times, but he hasn't really acted on it, and that makes me want to laugh in her face. She's twenty-three, acts demure and innocent, but she's fucked almost half the team. Her ass has been around this field as much as the ball.

Dixon has a quick word with Coach, then he's heading off the field toward the locker room, Dani running to catch up with him. I watch their interaction closely, and when she talks to him, he barely acknowledges her, just giving her a tight nod. I laugh out loud before I can stop myself, and Jameson cuts me a curious look. I clear my throat and shrug, guzzling down a mouthful of Gatorade. I look back to the double steel doors and see Dani walking back, looking dejected and rejected. Dumbass whore. I bet she thought she had a chance with Dixon, but even I know that guy has higher priorities. He has a little brother and mother he needs to pull off the streets. I think of the scuffed, old bus pass I still have tucked into my wallet and grin while I take another drink. I fucking like that he ignored her advances.

I grab my towel and dry my face as I follow the guys back inside. I need a shower, and then I need to smoke the blunt waiting for me in my car. It's been a long ass day, and my body is dog-tired. The guys all rush for the showers, but I hang back, not really in the mood for small talk today. Jameson crooks an eyebrow at me as I sit on the bench, and I wave him off, watching as he and Ortiz hit the showers. To be real, chilling with them is becoming a mundane chore, and all I crave lately is to be alone. Besides, my plans for Rookie no longer require their help, and I can't trust that they'll keep their big mouths shut. I watched him out there on the field, running his times and beaming like a little bitch every time Coach praised him. He must have some serious daddy issues if he needs that constant approval.

What are the odds that North's locker would be right next to mine? I look up at it and roll my eyes. It's like someone is getting the last laugh on me. Not that it matters… He's doing real well pretending I don't exist, and that alone is irritating the hell out of me. I still haven't dealt with him for punching me and then spitting in my face. That he can't get away with. I see the red light on the outside of the sauna and my eyebrows crash together in confusion. None of us really use that thing, preferring to use the ones we all have in our houses. Except one of us doesn't have an extravagant home with a sauna. I bet he would prefer to save his money and use all the team's facilities instead.

I head toward the light, hearing the showers running in the next room, all the guys talking animatedly. I open the door, and the steam cascades around my head, blocking my vision of the inside, effectively blocking me as well. But I know he can sense me just as well as I can sense him, the atmosphere in here plummeting.

"What do you want?" He sounds perturbed, and that makes me grin. I affect him, no matter how much he tries to ignore it.

I drop my clothes to the side and grab a hot towel off a hook, wrapping it around my waist. I step farther into the heated room, my muscles already loosening and the tension in my chest disappearing. He's sitting in the back right corner, watching me warily as I move straight ahead, sitting in the middle of the bench, about three feet from him.

"Are you saying I can't use the sauna now, Rookie?" I sneer at him, and he scoffs.

"I know you have one at home," he retorts. "Zeal told me no one uses this. So what the fuck do you want?"

Zeal has a big fucking mouth.

"I saw you talking to Coach's daughter," I say as I lean back against the warm wood behind me.

"I didn't talk to her." He sounds defensive, and it takes everything in me not to laugh.

"Why? Not your type?" I dig at him. "What would Dixon North rather have in his bed?"

"Why is Sebastian Avando so damn interested?" he snaps back, and my head swings to look at him.

"I'm actually concerned for Dani," my lips curve upward. "She is Coach's daughter after all, and what do we really know about some punk kid from Baltimore?"

"There's no need for your concern," he says, his voice relaxing as he lays his head against the wall. "I'm not interested in Coach's daughter."

His eyes are closed, like he's so sure I won't do anything, and the sight of his relaxation in my presence bothers me. The fact that the skin on his face is smooth and free of imperfections also pisses me off. What hardships has he endured? My gaze falls lower, over the beating pulse in his neck and then to his swollen chest. North is stacked, and his abs are perfectly defined. He must work out hours every day. My eyes land on the towel he has secured around his waist, and I see that it's damp with his perspiration, the beads running down between the ridges of his abs then soaking into the fabric.

"Now who's watching who?" His voice is quiet as my eyes

skip back up to his. He's wearing a smirk and looks smug, like he caught me tripping.

"You can never know your enemy too well, Rookie."

"That's what I am to you?" he scoffs. "An enemy? Why? What the fuck did I ever do to you?" His voice begins to rise.

I snicker as I get up out of my seat, happy I can pull a reaction out of him and proving I'm not being ignored, despite his best efforts. "You were fucking born."

I step down from the wooden platform, but before I can take another, I feel his hot body near my back. He turns me around and slams his fist into my cheek then shoves me against the wall. I snap out of my shock quickly, anger growing hard and fast as I grab him by the throat and switch places, slamming him into the wall. He shoves me off him, and I take that opportunity to smash my fist into his cheek, watching as his head cracks to the side.

"The fuck is wrong with you?" I growl as he shoves me again, his chest heaving. "You have a motherfucking death wish." I point into his face.

He slaps my finger away and growls, making me once again grab his throat, slamming his head into the wall. Both of our chests heaving and hatred shining bright from our eyes, my fingers curl tighter. He doesn't react and I hate that about him. He works so hard to be unaffected by me. I hate it so much. I squeeze tighter and that anger once again burns hot, just as his hand comes up and wraps around my throat, hauling me into his face.

"What the fuck do you want?" He growls around my grip on his throat.

Maybe I need a reaction, or maybe I'm out of my fucking mind, but I slam my mouth onto his. His hand twitches around my throat, but he doesn't move. He doesn't react either which has me growling into his mouth, preparing to force his lips open with my tongue. And then shock courses through me when he opens them without a fight. His tongue clashes with mine in a rough battle of teeth and lips as his hand releases my throat to skim around behind my head and yank me in closer. My growl ends on a groan, and I'm kissing him like I'm starved for the very air he's breathing into his lungs. I suck his tongue into my mouth and step into him, our bodies flush. His chest pressing against mine, his hard cock digging into my groin.

He's hard, and so am I.

Finally, something inside me wakes the hell up, and I push off North. I look into his face and see shock plainly coating his features. Our gasping breaths mingle, my heart is thumping, and my insides begin to quake, uncertainty making me volatile. I curse as my fist slams into the wood beside his head before I yank open the door, quickly putting distance between us.

I wanted a reaction … I guess I got one.

"Fuck!" I scream into the steering wheel.

What the fuck was that back there? Why does he bring out the worst in me? It's taking everything I have not to storm back in there and beat him to death. My need to one up him is getting out of control, and I crave his fear like an addict. I don't know what happens to my head when he gets close, and I can't control my actions when he's in my personal space. I punch the side of my head, the pain skating across my skull, and still, it's not enough. I need to go home and soak my brain in powder and just forget what happened today. Because if I don't, I will end up killing North, and my whole life will be over.

I slam the vehicle into drive and burn my tires as I speed out of the parking lot. I weave through traffic and cut people off, their horns sounding at my back. I don't care. There's something rattling loose inside my head, and the more I try to avoid it, the more it's fucking me up.

My tires squeal as I turn onto my driveway. It's a miracle I made it home without killing anyone. I rip myself out of the Hummer and tear into my house, slamming the door behind me. My body is shaking with an energy I can't release, and my head is consumed with a fog and *him*. Why did he kiss me back?

No.

I scrape my fingers over my scalp, and when I feel the skin underneath grow wet with blood, I moan in relief. Everything is fine as I close my eyes and try to breathe. I'm not actually gay. Then I think of us in towels, pressed together, and our cocks…

NO!

I turn quickly and slam my head against the wall, causing the sheetrock to crack. I'm not fucking gay! I know what I want, and it's a woman under me. I've had so much pussy, free pussy. It comes with the sport. I turn quickly and pull my phone out of my pocket. That's what I need. It's been too long, and my body needs a release that only a *woman* can give me. That only a soaking wet pussy can give me.

I dial Jameson's number, and he picks up after two rings.

"'Sup?"

"I need to chill." I can hear the tight, anxious tone in my voice. "Get over here with some girls."

"In your house, Avando? We can hit up Neon Girls—"

"No," I cut him off from suggesting the local strip club. "Here."

"All right," I can hear the grin in his voice. "Give us about an hour."

"Make it thirty minutes," I growl and hang up the phone.

Sure, I could take myself over to Neon Girls and grab my

regular, she knows how I like my dick sucked. But I know that won't be enough today, not after what happened. And besides, I need more than a blow job. I need to sink into a hot, wet pussy and pound the shit out of it. I get upstairs and take a shower, feeling the sting of the shampoo as it seeps into the scratches on my head then glare down at my hardened cock. Why the fuck did it betray me like that? Getting hard for that little bitch rookie.

I have yet to soften since the sauna, and I know it's because I've gone too long. Maybe I should've tried to fuck the bitch from the club. Maybe then my brain wouldn't have shut down and what happened with North never would've happened. Because that's my real problem … I have certain needs, and when they aren't met, bad shit happens. I ignore my cock as it pulses, begging me for relief as I grit my teeth against the temptation. I step out of the shower and wrap a towel around my waist, not letting myself think of the towel I wrapped around my waist inside that sauna. I swipe the steam from the mirror and look at my face critically.

I have scrapes on my scalp, but they're turning pinker and less red. I have a small cut on my forehead from the wall. It looks a little bruised, but all in all, I'm ready to let myself go today. I can't end it with what happened in that sauna… I need it to end differently, I need to wipe that shit out of my head.

Nothing works better than coke and pussy.

Dixon

What the hell was that? I don't even remember the drive home, and the memory of what happened has my body going another round with the shakes. Did Avando kiss me? Did I actually kiss him back? I press my trembling hands to the back of my neck. I'm so fucking confused. I'm not gay. Not even a little bit. There has never even been a moment of confusion in my life. I have always been attracted to women, dating a man wasn't an option. I don't like men. I mean, I don't think so.

I growl and stand up from my couch. Why the fuck did he do that? Is this another one of his mind tricks? Like he owns me or something? He rapes me, taunts me constantly, and now he's kissing me like I'm all he thinks about. What kind of game is this? All I know is I failed miserably because I kissed him back, and I know in that moment, I would've gone further. But why? Why would I want to do that? Put aside the not being gay part, the guy fucking raped me! I don't understand what's happening with me, and I can't pinpoint the exact moment when I began to see him differently. But I do, and it pisses me off. He's fucked-up and a bully to the extreme. He looks and acts like a gangbanger, and he's a fucking rapist. There's clearly something wrong with his head, and I just fell again into one of his games. That's the only explanation.

Now I have something else I need to push down and ignore, pretend like it never happened, and it's all thanks to Sebastian. If my mother ever found out what has been happening, she would die of a heart attack then somehow come back to haunt me. She's an active member of the African Methodist Episcopal Church in Westport. She believes in revivals, fellowship, and First Sunday. Homosexuality is frowned upon, and same-sex marriages contradict their teachings. I've never really heard her opinion on it, and it's never been spoken about in our house. Not that I'm a homosexual, but if this ever came out, I don't know how'd she react based on the fact that she's very involved with the church. I'm so fucked.

Is he going to pretend like it didn't happen too? Or were his sidekicks somewhere recording it? Oh my god, is that shit on video somewhere? I begin to sweat as I pace my small family room. Is that his endgame? To somehow blackmail me off the team? That can't happen. I would say I was gay if it came down to it because I've worked so hard for this life, and I won't see it disappear because of him.

I need answers.

I grab my keys and head back outside. I know where he lives… It was something Ortiz said the other day, mentioning the street name. I know exactly where it is because soon after, I Googled it. I don't even know why. It all ties into these confused feelings I'm having … I need to look him in the eye and figure out what it all means. What the fuck does he have planned?

I drive through the streets, my GPS telling me where to go, all without knowing his house number. I'm guessing I'll see his vehicle. I don't know how he'll react to me pulling up to his house. I may very well get a gun in my face for it, but I can't ignore all this shit. It's eating me up inside, and the self-doubt is slowly attacking my mental state.

That kiss couldn't have been staged. Again, the conflict in my mind is like an illness, and I can't get rid of it. It couldn't have been staged… I know the way he kissed me, and it wasn't something he did for an audience. It was rough and angry, filled with absolute fury. It was passionate, and we were both affected. I *felt* it. He wanted it, and I can't deny that in that moment so did I. I don't know what that means, but I need to hear it from him. I need to know what he's doing and just what he expects from me.

I turn onto his street, and I can hear the thumping bass as I move forward. I can't tell which house it's coming from, but I assume it's his. Sounds like he's trying to ignore shit. too. Or maybe he's celebrating a win. I don't know. I slow down when I see his vehicle in the driveway of a large colonial style home, spotting a few other vehicles too. This is the house that's vibrating with the force of the loud music, girls spilling out of its front doors. He's having a party? On a Monday afternoon? I spot Ortiz there, dragging a woman inside and laughing as she tries to adjust her too short skirt. I don't see any other teammates, but I would bet a lot of money that Jameson is also inside somewhere.

I don't see any others from the team, nor do I see their vehicles. My heart begins to hammer again as my mind flies through the different reasons why those three are throwing this party. Am I about to be exposed for something I didn't do? I know I did it, but I had no intention of doing that, and I'm starting to feel like everything was indeed a plan. I begin to feel lightheaded, resting my forehead to the cool steering wheel. I hate not knowing. It feels like my world is crumbling under my feet after I've worked so hard to build it. I thought I'd built it to be immovable, unable to break, but I'm learning that in reality, it's so fucking weak.

The foundations of my beliefs and the work I've put into my future are now crumbling out from under me. All because one man couldn't just leave me alone. I can't help but ask why? It goes to show that no matter how stable you feel at any given time, it can be ripped away from you, and the decisions you make determine the fallout. One decision, one act, can completely destroy your life's work, and I'm not sure how to prepare myself for the outcome.

I pull away from his house and the rager of a party he's having only to pull onto my own driveway. My mind is blacking out all extreme emotions, and my overwhelming panic is one of them. I don't know what I'll face when I show up for practice tomorrow ... I just know I'll have to be prepared for the worst.

It's always the worst when Sebastian Avando is involved.

CHAPTER TWELVE

Sebastian

He looks sicker than I feel, and I feel like someone stomped my head into concrete.

He comes into the locker room with deep hollows under his eyes and his skin dull, like he's legit sick. He stands stiffly beside me unlatching his locker, and I stare at him openly, willing him to look at me. But he doesn't. I don't know why that pisses me off, but it does. It makes me want to punch him, again, and demand that he look at me.

He grabs the back of his sweater in both hands and pulls it up over his head, his muscles rippling with the motion. I see the tats he has all over his back, and I clench my fists to stop myself from reaching out. I see skulls and snakes, all things that tell of death, and I try to imagine who Dixon North really is. He has a large tribal design that climbs his shoulder and reaches his neck, the lines intricate.

"What are you looking at?" His voice is rough like gravel.

"You look like shit."

"So do you," he retorts, giving me a side eye.

"I have an excuse," I grin, not at all feeling as brave as I sound. "Did I keep you up all night? Were you thinking about me, homo?"

He slams his locker door shut then steps into my face, the air escaping his nostrils hot on my face. His eyes are almost black and right now have murder written in their depths.

"Is that it?" His lip turns up into a sneer. "You want to lie and tell everyone I'm gay?"

He has a slight dimple in his right cheek, and it deepens as he scowls, waiting for my answer. Fuck him, though. I like that he's scared, and it means he'll keep his mouth shut too.

I spy a large blue star in the center of his chest and press my hand to it. His skin is hot to the touch, and I can feel his heart beating a mile a minute. He's so scared. I shove him lightly out of my face then step around him, giving him a small smirk. I don't say a single thing and throw him a wink, his brow lining with perspiration. His chest rises and falls rapidly, his muscles bunching tightly.

I quickly turn away and sit on the bench beside Jameson, not letting myself fall too far in to my own thoughts. Coach says he has to speak to us today, and I know it's about the annual sponsor's gala, it's always at the beginning of the season. It's a way to thank those rich old cunts for tossing us some money and letting us run around with their logos on our uniforms. Last year, Jameson, Ortiz, and I triple teamed Dani in the bathroom while our dates sat at the table waiting for us. It was a great fuck you to her father who had been annoying us for a year. That's what he got for his suspicions and frequent surprise drug tests. She fucking lapped it up.

Dani is like the welcoming committee for all new players, her pussy waiting to greet them before she moves on to the next piece of fresh meat. I know her sights are now set on North, but after watching them yesterday, I don't know how successful she'll be with him. For some reason, that brings me a twisted type of pleasure.

Coach walks in, and I fantasize about smashing in his smug face with my fist. I look to my right and see Jameson's jaw is tight, probably thinking the same thing. Coach is the type of guy who likes to be all up in his players' personal lives, and he has zero tolerance for drugs. Like any drug, even weed. He's a nosy prick.

"You guys know what time of year it is," he begins, looking pointedly at Jameson and me. Sponsors love us because we're the powerhouses of the team. "The annual Bills gala is in two weeks. We are all to be there, and we will all be enjoying ourselves. But not too much enjoyment." Another pointed look at me. *Fuck off, old man.*

"Your plus ones need to be given to me by this weekend to prepare plate counts. Bring a plus one." He claps as he looks around the room. "It gives off family vibes and makes us look less like a team of partying bachelors."

I look over my shoulder at North and watch as his brows fall together. I wonder who he'll invite. Will it be someone from Baltimore? Does he have anyone? I have yet to see his family or friends visit. Speaking of… I need to go see my boys this weekend. It's been weeks since I've been back in Rochester. Time away from here and the pressures of football are needed sometimes, and there's no better place than with my boys back home.

Dani slinks just inside the locker room door. She's not allowed any farther, so she leans against the wall to listen to her father. I don't miss the looks she continues to throw over my shoulder, and I know she's looking at North. The desperation pouring off her reeks, and Jameson snorts beside me. I look at him and cover the grin on my face with my hand as he stares at her. We know what she's about, and we know why her sights are set on North. I toss him another look over my shoulder, and this time my eyes clash with his. He's already looking at me. I turn back around and swallow thickly, a weird feeling gathering in my stomach.

I need to get the hell away from here.

Coach claps his hands again then turns his back, barking at us to be on the field in fifteen. North, already dressed, heads for the double doors, and I know he's doing his morning run. I stay in my seat, not moving from my spot, and watch as Dani reaches her hand out to grab his arm. He stops and glances down at it, his back tight and his jaw flexing.

"He looks pissed," Jameson murmurs from beside me, and I nod.

She says something to him, and he turns his head a bit more, throwing me a look over his shoulder. Yeah, I'm watching you. I give him a smirk, and he pulls his arm from Dani's grip but leans in, his big body crowding hers as he whispers something in her ear. My teeth crash together, and anger burns bright in my chest. What the fuck is he saying to her? Her eyes widen, and her cheeks grow rosy, pissing me off even further.

"Looks like Rookie will be getting his dick sucked soon," Jameson declares as he stands, chuckling all the way to his locker.

She peers up at him when he pulls back, and he gives her a tight smile, nothing that looks genuine, though. Then she watches him as he walks out into the hallway and out of sight, her desperation seeping into the room. Fucking slut. She must sense my eyes on her because she turns and looks straight at me, her brows crinkling in the center. She wanted me not too long ago and did everything I asked, even fucked my boys in an attempt to secure me. In the end, it was never meant to be, and I know I broke her heart.

Her lips turn down into a sneer, and she turns her back, walking across the way to her father's office. Yeah, she's still not over it, which makes me chuckle. She can try to replace me with North all she wants. He and I are nothing alike, and eventually, she'll be looking for the next dick to suck. Maybe by then I'll be willing to break her heart all over again.

I can see the sweat dripping off his brow as the same happens with mine, both of us panting heavily. Our uniforms are grass stained, our helmets caked with dirt, and our faces filled with determination. Practices can get messy and oftentimes painful because we are competing internally. Second string is always trying to up the first, and Coach is always watching for potential breakout players.

It's been different playing with North on my side of the field, but I will admit—only to myself—that he's been an asset. He does work hard, and he focuses on nothing else but the game. He's still a little bitch, though.

"First string, you're done for the day," Coach yells out, and the second-string groans. They'll be kept behind to do extra runs. He does this every practice to the side that slacks the most.

North is already halfway back to the locker room when I start toward the large double doors. I like that he doesn't like to be anywhere near me and rushes to get out before anyone else. I like that I affect him.

"What's going down for this weekend?" Ortiz asks, and I shake my head.

"I'm goin' home for a few days. I'll be back Saturday night," I answer him.

"Damn," he groans.

"Neon Girls Thursday night?" Jameson slaps Ortiz's back.

Our first game is this Sunday which means we get Thursday evening to Saturday evening off. Perfect time to go home, fuck some shit up, and come back revived. Plus, I got a little someone there waiting for me, and I can't disappoint her. She's my anchor to home and knows exactly what I need to bring me back when I feel like life is slipping.

Jameson is a fucking whore who can't keep his dick to himself. Ortiz tags along, but for the most part, he doesn't fuck just anything and attempts to keep a good rep, despite his closest friend's behavior. I respect him for that.

The locker room is noisy as everyone strips out of their dirty uniforms and heads to the showers. I lag behind as I see the red light is on for the sauna. I know I shouldn't, and I really hate that I don't listen to my internal warnings. Once the locker room is cleared out except for a few guys lingering about, I slip into the sauna and snicker when I hear him curse.

"Fuck this," he grumbles, and I hear him get up from his seat. Understandably.

"Chill, man." I stand in front of the door and block his exit. "Truce?"

"You're gonna keep your hands and face to yourself?" I love that he wants to be here no matter how hard he fights it.

"Promise." I smile wide as he stares into my eyes. When he takes my word for it, he turns back around and sits in the same spot he was in yesterday.

I follow him and sit in the same spot as yesterday too, leaning my head back against the wall. I should use the sauna more often. I can feel the tension leaving my muscles, and the steam gives me a lazy haze, relaxation settling bone deep.

"I saw you talking to Dani," I break the silence.

"I know."

"She's like a shark," I snicker. "She's attracted to fresh blood."

"I came on to her first." I see the slight shrug of his shoulders and I don't understand why his admission has me grinding my teeth.

"So that's your type," I say more to myself.

"Why are you always at me about my type and shit?"

"I like to get to know my teammates," I counter.

"By sticking your dick in their asses?" he retorts, and I swallow down the panic that threatens to rise.

"That was just a reminder of where you're supposed to be."

"Oh, yeah?" I can hear the anger simmering hot in his words. "And where's that?"

"On the bottom."

"You'll never get the chance to try it again," a threat I know is the truth.

"We'll see," I grin when he turns his face from me. "Anyway," I steer us away from that topic, "what did she say to you?"

"Why do you care?" he throws back.

"Just curious if she's running the same game on you that she did on me."

"I can't see her running shit on you," he snarls. "More the other way around."

"Nah, girl's got game." I close my eyes and let my mind take me back to the first day I met Danielle. "It was my rookie year two years ago, and I wandered out to the field. Excitement had me amped."

I can feel the heat of his stare and complete attention as I continue. "She found me out there and called me Mr. Avando, her cheeks turning this sexy shade of pink when I turned to look at her. Did she do that to you?" He doesn't wait for me to respond, his jaw locking.. "Yeah, bitch got game," I chuckle.

"It doesn't mean shit," he spits out. "It's just a gala."

My head snaps to the left to look at him as shock courses through me. "You're bringing her to the gala?"

"Why not?" he shrugs.

"Be careful," I warn him. "That's Coach's daughter. Unless you're looking to get into the family. What? There aren't any girls in

Baltimore?"

"There are enough girls in Baltimore, but none I'd bring here."

"You mean none you'd wife up," I correct him, and he shrugs.

"This has been weird as fuck," he mutters and stands. His towel slips a bit, and I get a peek of the top of his ass crack. I squeeze my eyes shut tight, clenching my fists and try thinking of anything else. But it doesn't work. My cock begins to swell, and I only release my breath when I hear the door shut behind him.

What the hell is going on with me?

CHAPTER THIRTEEN

I think I'm fucked in the head. No, I know I'm seriously fucked in the head.

I bang the back of my head against my headrest and look out of my car window. His vehicle isn't in the driveway, and this is the second day in a row. Yes, I am sitting in my car outside of Sebastian's house, and I am hoping to talk to him about shit. Try to smooth out the waters further and maybe make this whole experience less tumultuous. But he hasn't been home since Thursday, and it's now Friday night without any sight of him. Our first game is on Sunday.

I could ask Zeal for his number, but then he'd have mine, and that's not something I'm comfortable with. Besides, what the hell would I say? I'm stalking your house, where the fuck are you? Hey, I know you raped me not too long ago, but I'm hoping we can talk? Yeah, see? I'm fucked in the head. I don't like the fact that he hates me for no reason… I can't seem to wrap my head around it, and there's something in me that needs to fix that. That's not to say I've forgotten about the rape, but it's something I work hard to forget, and I don't want to be reminded of it whenever I see him.

Is that typical victim shit? I don't know. I just know myself, and I'm over it. I've learned what I can from the situation. I won't ever be taken advantage of again, not without killing someone, and that's just facts. I don't want to feel like a victim, and I'm not weak because of what happened, I just want to move on. Does he deserve consequences? Yes. Will I make sure he gets them? I don't know.

I pull away from the curb and head back home. I wish there was something besides working out that could take my mind off shit. I haven't taken the time to really get to know my teammates yet, and my family is back in Baltimore. A heavy ache takes over, and I feel the loneliness start to seep in. This is new. I've never been one to feel alone. I like being alone, and usually I have a hard time forming bonds. My life has been work on top of hard work, grind only to grind harder, and long-term relationships take time. Something I've never had much of.

I guess this all means I'm lonely, and for once in my life I'm craving connections. It's in this moment that I wonder what a relationship with my brother would've been like or if I did have that one best friend who lingered throughout high school until now. Danny also sees me as a threat. He despises my need to ensure he's safe, instead calling me a mama's boy. My high school career consisted of me playing football, training for football, and sleeping. No time was spent on fostering lifelong friendships. Now that my life goal is resting in the palm of my hand, I realize I've done myself an injustice.

I pull onto my driveway and pull out my cell phone, scrolling until I find Zeal's name way down at the bottom of my list and hitting send before I change my mind.

"North!" his voice booms. "What's up, man?" I can hear voices in the background, and it sounds a lot like a few of the players.

"Nothin' really." I swallow down my pride that's begging me to hang up. "I just need to get out of my head about our first game."

"Get your ass over to my place!" he laughs. "I would've sent you a text earlier, but I didn't get the vibe that you were a poker guy."

"Poker?" I ask. "Oh, no. I don't play cards, but fuck, I'll

watch."

"Sounds good," he chuckles. "Grab beer too!"

After grabbing beer, I punch his address into the GPS and head over to his place. Zeal's house is a different scene than the party at Sebastian's. I can hear the music, but it's at a lower decibel, and there are no half-naked ladies falling out the front door. I pull up to the curb outside of his house and whistle low under my breath. The house is actually a mansion and about three times bigger than what I'm staying in right now. Fuck, it's ten times bigger than what my mother and brother are living in right now, and that's after I got them out of the projects.

I get out of the vehicle and walk up the driveway, the beat of the music becoming louder with each step. The sun set about an hour earlier, but the sky is still lined with reds and oranges, that cast a nice glow over Zeal's beige stucco exterior. The door opens before I even reach the top step, and a grinning Dex stands there with a handful of cards.

"I told the fuckers to call you."

"What's up, man?" I clasp his free hand in mine. "You winning?"

"Nah," he laughs. "I'm telling you, Zeal and Alonso are fucking cheating."

I laugh along with him as I follow him to a large dining room, the table lined with football players. The tabletop is covered in chips and beer bottles, the center pot looking large.

"Whoever wins that," I point at the pile, "is taking me out on a date."

The guys laugh and catcall as I dump the beer into an iced cooler at Zeal's feet. I pop one open for myself and watch as the guys scream at each other over bets. Finally, it comes down to Zeal and Dex. I can see the three of a kind in Zeal's hand. Zeal is sure of himself and shoves the rest of his chips into the center, keeping a smug grin on his face. Dex gnaws on his bottom lip and looks between his hand and the chips.

"Give it up, man," Zeal taunts.

Dex slams down his cards and screams at the top of his lungs, "Flush, motherfucker!"

This is exactly what I've been needing, and I wipe the thought of Sebastian Avando from my mind.

Sebastian

"That's him?" I ask Delano sitting in the passenger seat. I point out the guy leaving the convenience store.

"Yeah," he nods, his eyes hardening in anger. "That's Johnny."

When I got here, I heard that Delano's little sister had been drugged and raped at this Johnny bitch's house, and that shit doesn't fly around here. You don't mess with our family, and when you decide to ignore the warnings, you deal with the consequences.

"That guy too?" I point to another guy sitting in the driver's seat of a car Johnny is getting into.

"Yeah, that's Carlos. He's fresh out of the pen."

"He's gonna wish he stayed in," I growl as I pull off the curb to follow them.

The streets are quiet this late at night because people know once the sun goes down in Edgerton, they should stay in their homes. I grew up here, watched my mother suck dick on the streets here, was raised by those very streets. There are only two rules to abide by: mind your business and don't disrespect. It's easy.

Delano and I were brought in at the same time when both of us were real young. I decided I liked money and a lot of it, so I went off to make something of myself. Delano decided he liked dealing drugs and running the streets. I don't judge him for that. It's what I would be doing too if I didn't have the skills to play football. Around here, you do what you can to survive, and you make sure you're never on the bottom.

Delano's little sister just dropped out of high school. It's a shame, but it happens to many here, especially when there's no prospect with a diploma, and money is needed more than reading a book. Jayla decided that becoming a prostitute was easy money and a great way to help her family out. Again, no judgments. She worked a party for Johnny, and he decided that she and another girl would be fun to rape.

Delano and his family are my family, and these fuckers disrespected that. I have a reputation to uphold, so I can't let this slide. The streets of Edgerton know me well, and they know I'm ruthless. This is my home, and if these pieces of shit think they can come into it and disrespect me, they got another thing coming. The light ahead of their car turns red, and the car stops as I bring mine up to a roll beside it. I roll down my window and lean my arm out, my gun tapping on the metal.

Johnny looks from my gun to me, and I must give him credit, he barely flinches.

"'Sup?" he juts out his chin.

He doesn't know me, I know that, but it still pisses me off. These are my motherfucking streets.

"Shit," Carlos leans over and chuckles. "You're that football player, from the Bills, right?"

"Yeah," I smirk.

"We should get autographs," Carlos says to Johnny who's trying to see farther into the interior of my car. If he spots Delano, he'll know what's up.

The light turns green, and both cars stay still. We're the only ones on the street anyway. I look at Johnny as I continue to tap my gun, waiting to see the move he makes, and hoping I get to see his blood tonight. The blow I had earlier is starting to wear off, so I can feel the numbness receding, my anger taking its place. These two wannabe gangbangers think they look tough, but they don't know what it's like to be chased down, and I would bet they have never had a gun held to their heads. That changes tonight.

Finally, Carlos points out a parking lot just beyond the light—which has turned red again—and he still has a weird goofy smile on his face. The fucker is not bright at all. I pull through the red, still no cars in sight, and Carlos follows suit. We pull into a plaza parking lot, and I recognize the laundromat as one of the first places I ever robbed. I park across three spots, and Carlos parks a space behind me. I roll up my tinted windows and look at Delano.

"Stay in here for about two minutes. If they see you right away, they'll know what's up and ditch out," he nods, his eyes wide. I snort at him. "You scared?"

"Nah." He is.

"I want this done fast and clean. We got a party to get back to."

He nods again, keeping an eye on his side view mirror as Carlos and Johnny get out of the car. Johnny is tucking something into the back waistband of his jeans, and I grin knowing he'll never get a chance to use it. The man is at least smarter than his friend by carrying a gun, but it won't help him tonight.

I get out of the Hummer, tucking my own piece into my side before pulling my jacket closed to hide it. Both guys are sitting on the hood of their car and Carlos pops out a doobie, readying up for a chill session.

"What brings you back?" Johnny asks me, and I can't help but chuckle.

"You do know me."

"Yeah." I see his eyes shift to the side. He knows exactly who I am.

"Came back to see my boys." I lean against the back of my vehicle, facing them. "It's going to get busy soon."

"You gonna win something this year?" Carlos laughs, and the sound makes me want to cut his throat open.

"We'll see," I shrug.

It takes a few seconds, but I see the perfect moment when Carlos lights his joint, and Johnny turns his head to watch. I snap forward, smashing my fist into Carlos's face and pulling my gun on Johnny in the same beat. Johnny's eyes are wide as he begins to stand.

"Don't move," I snarl. "I have a few questions for you two."

I hear my passenger door open then Delano's footsteps as he comes toward us. Johnny watches him, his eyes narrowing as Delano gets closer.

"You know my boy, Delano?" I ask Johnny while keeping an eye on a moaning Carlos. He's clutching his bleeding nose, laying on the car's hood.

"Yeah," he sneers. "Why'd you guys put the jump on us?"

"You know his sister?" I cock my gun. "Jayla?"

"Nah," he answers quickly. A little too quickly.

"You sure?" I nudge his temple with the barrel and watch him swallow. "I heard you threw a party for your boy here for getting out of the pen." I jut my chin toward Carlos. "Thought maybe he'd want some pussy, am I right?"

Johnny just shrugs, but his pallor is a tad bit green.

"What were you inside for?" I kick Carlos's foot, and he glares at me.

"Aggravated rape." His voice sounds nasally from his broken nose.

"Well, that's interesting." I look at Johnny with my brow raised. "Delano, tell them what you told me."

"My sister Jayla was asked to do a job, a party at your place." He stares at Johnny. "She told me that you held her down and let him," he juts his chin toward Carlos, "and a few others rape her. Then you raped her after."

Johnny's jaw tightens, but he keeps his mouth shut, his eyes on my gun.

"Her face is bruised, and she can barely walk!" Delano screams, and his voice echoes around us. No matter what noises are heard tonight, no one will come to investigate, they know better.

"She's alive, no?" Carlos yells back, and that snaps my patience. I swing my gun to his head and pull the trigger. He falls backward onto the hood, his chest not moving, and I exhale my tension. So much better.

Johnny hasn't taken his eyes off me. He knows what's about to happen, and I must say, he's fucking braver than I gave him credit for. I toss my gun to Delano and fix my jacket.

"Quick and clean," I remind him as I turn my back and walk to the driver's door.

I can hear Johnny trying to talk Delano out of it, but the sound of the gunshot has me smiling as I get inside the vehicle. Delano rushes inside, and I can see sweat all over his forehead.

"Relax," I tell him as I pull out of the parking lot. "Give me my piece."

He drops my gun into my hand, then I drive us back to the party we were at when he told me what happened to his sister. I pull up to an old, run-down building, the music loud and people loitering around the place. It's an old, abandoned school that we've turned into our party spot.

"We should've taken them somewhere else. I've never done that in the open before," he says to me, and I nod. I get it, he's worried about going away.

"Everything is okay." I roll my eyes and hit his shoulder. "Have I ever lied to you?"

"No," he smiles. "I owe you one, brother."

"Nah, that's what family's for." Then I remember there is something small he can do for me. "Do you know anyone from Baltimore?"

"Nah," he shakes his head. "But Chappy might." Chappy is better known as Roger Chapman, a drug runner who operates between here and Detroit.

I reach into my pocket and pull out my wallet. I search through it until I find the scuffed-up card. "Can you ask him if he knows this kid?"

"Yeah," he nods. "He looks tough."

"He probably is. I need info by this week, and don't lose that. I'll want it back."

"No problem." He tucks it into his pocket.

"A'ight." I wave for him to get out. "I'll be in in a bit."

I watch as he gets out of the Hummer and walks up to the building, his shoulders a bit straighter. I handed him back his balls tonight. I knew he was starting to feel complacent here. Our turf is protected well. and we haven't had to do shit like we did tonight in a long time.

With my rage settled once again, I get out of the vehicle and head to the party. I bet North is sitting at home, jacking himself off to the thought of me.

CHAPTER FOURTEEN

Dixon

He went home to Rochester for the weekend. I heard him talking to Jameson and Ortiz about it, and I couldn't help but listen. He said he got some shit done and reminded people of who runs Edgerton's streets. I've heard of Edgerton and how rough those streets are, so I can see why Sebastian is the way he is. He needs to be the one running shit, and he likes reminding people that he's at the top. It makes me want to dig into his life and find out what he was like as a kid.

I've been watching him during warmups and practice, but he has yet to look my way. I don't know why I care. I shouldn't, yet even though I keep telling myself that, my eyes wander back to him.

"North!" Dex calls out, and Sebastian's eyes finally land on mine. I quickly look away and nod at Dex. "Poker tonight?"

"You know I can't play that shit," I laugh. "And you still owe me a steak dinner."

I've been watching him all morning and wondering why he wasn't looking at me. Now I can feel his eyes boring into the back of my head.

"Tonight, baby!" Dex hollers and claps his hands like he's

making it rain.

There's a nervous energy throughout the team, but for the most part we're calm and anticipating a good game. I know I'll be tired as fuck tonight when the game is over, but if we win, that adrenaline will take over, and a party will be great for morale. If we lose, it'll be a great pickup.

"I'm in," I laugh.

A breeze kicks up across the field, and I can smell autumn coming in. It's in the air, the smell of damp leaves and freshly mowed grass. I love autumn for the cooler weather and the football season. This was always my favorite time of the year because it got me out of my house and out of my troubles. I never focused on the rent being late or Danny not turning up at home, and I never had to think of what we would be scraping together to eat that night. It was just me and the field every day.

Coach yells at us to begin our stretches so that we're limber for this evening, so I cross to center field. I need a bit of alone time to sink into the proper headspace for the game. I like to reach inside and grasp that need that's always simmering just below the surface, and let it consume me for that short period. The crunch of grass sounding behind me has me pausing and looking over my shoulder to find Sebastian following close at my back.

He gives me a small smirk, and I roll my eyes, continuing to center field. I can't deny how my heart begins racing, and my stomach is swirling, knowing he's behind me. It's silly and completely confusing. These feelings are all so foreign to me. I'm not sure what it is, fear … uncertainty, wariness, and yes, even excitement. I don't know how this one man can bring out so many emotions, and I can't fucking figure out what that means. It perplexes the shit out of me, and when I'm in those lost, confused moments, I can't seem to control my actions.

I sit down on the grass and stretch my legs out in front of me. I concentrate more on my legs, considering how much they're used throughout the game. Sebastian plops down beside me and mimics my stretch, bending forward to touch his toes. He ditched his shirt halfway through practice, so I watch as his back muscles, completely saturated in ink stretch, the exposed parts of his skin a dark terracotta.

"I heard you played poker with a few of the guys this weekend." His voice startles me out of my thoughts as I bend forward to touch my toes.

"I watched," I correct him.

"Don't play poker?" He turns to look at me, and the sun catches his irises, making them look like pots of amber honey.

"Nah," I quickly look away and swallow. "I didn't see you there."

"I was in Rochester visiting family," he replies as he pulls a foot into his groin for another stretch.

As wary as I am of him, I'm also liking that we can have some sort of small talk. After everything that's happened, maybe this is a sign we can somehow learn to accept each other.

"Your parents?" I ask, and he snorts derisively.

"My mother is dead, and I never knew my father. He could have been one of many who spent a few minutes between her legs in exchange for crack."

Wow.

He watches me closely for a reaction, and I can't figure out if it's true or another Sebastian riddle.

"I went to see my boys," he explains, switching out his foot for the other. "My real family, the ones who took me in."

Took him in sounds like a gang, and again, another puzzle piece falls into place in the makeup that is Sebastian.

"I see." I murmur.

"What about you, Rookie?" He stops stretching to look at me. "Will your family be here tonight?"

I don't want to tell him that my mother would love nothing more than to come watch me play, but she has to work, and she would never leave Danny in Baltimore alone. I tried to convince her to quit her job, but she refused then lectured me about things that never last.

"No."

"You don't have a family?" he questions, his eyes still on me, watching for any reaction.

"I do," I huff and lean forward, "they just won't be here."

"A'ight," he chuckles and stands. "I love a good mystery." Then he jogs off to Jameson and Ortiz who are watching me with confused faces.

Same fuckers. I'm extremely confused as to why the man who raped me is trying to have small talk.

"North!" Coach grabs the carbon steel of my helmet and drags me into his face. "I need one more from you, kid. Can you give us one more?"

I can barely see through the sweat that's dripping off my brow and hitting my cheeks, but I nod because I fucking can. We need one touchdown to bring us ahead by a point to win this game, and I will do anything physically possible to bring this home for us.

I look at my teammate's faces. We're all tired, yet we're all still hungry. Zeal throws his arm over my shoulder and gives it a squeeze. "One minute, three seconds left." I give a quick nod at his words "Get to the sweet spot, North, and I promise to find you." He bounces his helmet off mine, and I inhale a large breath. Our team needs this win.

We get into formation, and I try to envision the play he's asked us to do. I can see it, step-by-step, and it plays in my mind in slow motion. We've practiced the hell out of this one, so I could do it in my sleep. I stare into the faces of the guys crouching across from me, exhaustion showing clearly, and I know I can take advantage of that. I need that second wind to kick in, and I will run laps around these guys.

I hear the whistle blow, and I take off, twisting out of the reach of one, making a run for where I know Zeal will want me. I skid to a stop and jump out of the way of a defensive end, looking to the sky. I see the ball spinning, the leather reflecting the stadium lights, and reach up, feeling the stretch all the way to my shoulders. I touch the leather, my fingers gripping for purchase and my heart pounding in my ears.

I fumble the ball, and I watch in horror as it bounces, my heart sinking into my stomach. I just fucked this up for us. Avando appears out of nowhere and scoops up the ball, turning to run toward the end zone. I run behind him, his speed a match to my own, and watch as we near that thick, white line.

It's sudden when a large defenseman rams into Sebastian, effectively knocking him to the ground two yards from the end zone. I dodge out of the way and curse when I not only see but hear the impact of his head and shoulder hitting the ground. My actions are instinctual as I pull the man off him and see Sebastian still has the ball clutched to his chest. But he's unconscious. I step back as medical runs on the field, and the Bills are given a timeout with thirty seconds left in the game.

Avando comes to, and he looks around, clearly disoriented. Medical helps him to his feet as players stand around, watching them slowly make their way off the field. I want to follow behind them. The way he hit his head was scary, and I have an overwhelming need to make sure he's okay. He saved my fumble, and it cost him. I know he did it for the team, but it also feels like he did it for me. It feels like he took that hit for me.

Zeal rushes up and shakes me out of my thoughts. "North, we

need to win this. Are you good?"

My eyes are still trained on the two double doors Sebastian went through, and my mind is no longer focused on this game.

"I don't know," I shake my head.

"Two yards," Zeal squeezes my arm. "Then we can see what's going on."

I pull my eyes away from the doors and look at him, seeing the desperation on his face. I promised this team I would do my best to help them win, and I can't back out now, no matter how much I want to. I give him a tight nod, then we huddle, listening to the play he wants. We break apart and we line up, Zeal calling out the positions. My body is on autopilot because my mind is on the other side of those double doors.

I do the one thing I know well which is run. Instead of going forward though, I run along behind Zeal, and he passes me the ball, the opposing team momentarily stunned. I take advantage of those few moments and avoid two defensive tackles, my strides growing longer.

My feet glide over that white line, and the crowd is roaring, but I'm already running for the doors that will lead me to him. I hear Coach calling my name, but at this moment, I couldn't care less about our win. The team can celebrate all they want on that field, but I need to be inside. I push by the few medics and throw open the doors, my heart thumping loudly in my chest. I can't hear anything as I storm into the locker room, and growl in frustration when I don't see the doctor anywhere.

"Avando!" I yell into the room, but there's no response.

"They took him to the hospital for a routine checkup." I turn to see Dani leaning against the door. "It's his third concussion."

Concussion. It's common for us to rack up concussions, especially offensive players, and it's also common that people shrug them off. I have had one concussion during my football career, and luckily, I had a great doctor who warned me about the consequences of repeated blows to the head. Three concussions are a lot and could be a career ending problem, not to mention what it could be doing to his health. I rip off my uniform just as the guys start piling in. They're loud and obnoxious about the win, and I can't bring myself to be on their level.

I rush over to the showers. I can hear them talking about the after party, and I can't help but be pissed off that not one of them has brought up Sebastian. I take the shortest shower then pull on my clothes, rushing back out into the main room.

"North!" Dex screams. "You were fucking amazing tonight."

I give him a tight smile and grab my duffle out of the locker. "I'll catch you guys later."

"Are you coming by my place?" Zeal calls out.

I don't bother to answer as I toss him the peace sign over my head. I'm nearly out front when I hear hurried steps behind me. I instantly turn, not liking my back to anyone, and see both Jameson and Ortiz rushing to the exit.

"He's at the hospital," I say to them, and they stop suddenly to give me a once over. "I was going to head over there."

"Why?" Ortiz asks.

"He's a teammate, and he's been injured," I shrug, and Jameson slowly nods.

"Respect for that," he says and darts around me. "He's fine, though. The doc said he shouldn't drive, so we're on our way to get him now."

"Oh," I chew on my lip. "Okay, yeah, cool." I sound like a sniffling idiot.

"See you around, North," Ortiz nods, respect shining in his eyes as they both hurry out.

Of course, he would call them. Those are his boys, not me. I fall back against the wall, the sounds of my teammates celebrating behind me and my confusing emotions chilling right here in front of me.

Jameson drives his car onto the driveway. Ortiz jumps out of the passenger side, opening the back door. I lean forward and watch as Sebastian slowly gets out of the car, his skin looking a little too pale. I watch him closely as he walks to his front door, Ortiz and Jameson waiting by the car. I can't believe they're going to leave him alone tonight ... he has a fucking concussion.

He waves at them then opens his door, going inside without a backwards glance. It's like he knows he's alone and that there's no one who will be with him. The thought has me feeling terrible.

Jameson and Ortiz pull out of the driveway, their music blasting loudly as they drive back down the street. I watch as Avando closes the front door slowly, then I sit here, debating what I should do. Maybe they're going to pick up some stuff for him, and they'll be back soon. I can't imagine his closest friends leaving him behind.

When thirty minutes goes by, I know they're not coming back, my stomach sinking at the realization that Sebastian has no one. I shouldn't care, I tell myself as I get out of my car, and I shouldn't even be thinking of helping him. I growl inside my head as I jog up his driveway. I stand on his porch and look up into the top right corner. A red light blinks back, letting me know I'm being recorded. Can't turn around now. I ring the doorbell and wait, my stomach slowly working its way up into my throat.

A few minutes later, and still, he doesn't answer the door. I ring the doorbell and shuffle from foot to foot. Maybe he sees me and doesn't want to answer the door. He hates me after all. I don't know what compels me to turn the knob, and I gasp when it opens, revealing his foyer to me. Why didn't he lock his door? Is he expecting someone? Like an idiot, I step inside his house and close the door behind me.

"Sebastian?" I call out and hear nothing. Only silence greets me.

I step out of my shoes then walk in farther, finding the kitchen and then the family room. Still no sign of Sebastian.

"Avando?" I yell out a bit louder and hear a creak above my head.

I head back out to where I saw the stairs and take each step slowly, unsure of what I'll find or how I'll be received. He could very well be loading a gun to shoot me with as soon as I get to the second floor, and he would be in his rights to do so. I am an intruder.

There are plenty of doors up here, and as I stand, looking between each one, I hear a slight noise to my left. I head toward it and stop in front of a messy bedroom. This has to be his room.

"Sebastian?" I call out again, and when there's no answer, I enter his room. The bed is unmade, the sheets hanging over the side, and he has clothes thrown everywhere.

I get to the center of the room and hear the faint sound of running water. I follow it to a closed door and press my ear to it. There's no other sound, just running water. My worry gets the best of me as I open the door and rush inside.

CHAPTER FIFTEEN

Sebastian

The feel of the cold water spraying on my face brings me back to consciousness. I groan and push myself up from the floor, the tile as cold as the water. I know the routine after a concussion, so as soon as I felt myself getting drowsy, I came into the shower. It's worked before, but this time, I must've blacked out.

The doctors asked me to have someone here with me for this exact reason, but I don't want Jameson or Ortiz in this house right now, not while I look weak, and I am not calling someone here. I can deal with it. I know the drill with concussions, this being my third one, and I was sure this one would be like the others, but I was wrong. I feel more disoriented, my body is heavy, and my mind is slow. I need to hide this shit though because I can't let Coach know the extent of my injuries. I'll be benched. And I don't have an injury clause in my contract, so they could eventually let me go if they really want to, and then I will be out of a job. That can't happen.

"Sebastian?"

Why am I hearing North's voice? Why does this shit keep happening? The doctors said I was asking for Dixon while I was in and out of consciousness, and now I'm hearing his voice in my home? That shit is impossible. I step out of the shower and grab a towel, wrapping it around my waist.

"Avando?"

It sounds like he's right there on the other side of the door, and I groan as I slap my hand to my forehead. Fucking stop. The hit makes me dizzy, and I fight to keep the blackout at bay. I'm afraid to be here alone with how weird my head feels. I open the bathroom door and stumble into my bedroom, the room swaying and out of focus. No, I rub my palms against my eyes. Stay awake.

"Sebastian?"

"Fuck!" I scream. "Why do I keep hearing you?"

"Because I'm here?"

"No, you're not!" I scream again and turn toward the sound.

I blink as my vision greys, but I do see North standing there, his arms outstretched and wearing all black. I shake my head and stumble against my bed, the movement making the pounding in my skull worse. Why am I seeing and hearing North? I fucking hate the pussy.

"I think you need to relax." How is he still talking? What the fuck is wrong with my brain? "Do you want something to drink?"

I fall forward on my stomach across the bed. "Please stop talking." I slap the top of my head. "Why is it always you?"

"Why always me what?" he asks.

"Inside my head, making me think things and feel things that aren't real." I may as well confess to the fake version of him. "That's why I did what I did to you, I needed to somehow get you out of my head. Now it's getting worse."

"Worse how?"

"You're stuck in my head, I think about what I did to you all the time." I roll over onto my back, the towel opening, and falling to my sides. "I'm not gay," I ground out just as I feel myself hardening.

"I'm not gay," he says as his towel falls open, and his cock juts out, long and thick. He's had that inside me, and I can't seem to take my eyes from it as he groans some more, his arm thrown across his face. Is he hard and thinking about me?

I'm not gay either, but my dick is hardening in my own pants at the sight, so I turn away with a curse. I don't know why Avando has this effect on me, and it's frustrating as fuck. I don't even completely understand what the fuck I'm doing here. He's not my friend, and he would never do this for me. I hear him groan again from behind me and turn to see him grab a pillow and hug it in close to his chest.

"Don't leave, Dixon." He sounds so fucking broken.

I take a deep breath and walk back to him, grabbing the blanket that's on the floor. I cover his naked body then sit at the end of the bed. I know I have to stay and wake him every half hour. No one else cared enough to do it.

"I'm here," I answer him as he begins to snore softly.

Thirty minutes comes and goes, and I haven't moved from my spot at the end of the bed. He's been talking in his sleep, and a lot of it is about me. Him begging me to stay with him, asking me why I'm here then cursing me for being here.

"Sebastian," I nudge his shoulder. "Hey, man, time to wake up."

His eyes open slowly, still glazed over and unfocused, and it begins to worry me.

"What's your name?" I ask him.

"Why are you still here, North?" he moans, sounding a bit more like himself.

"Someone has to make sure you're alive," I retort as I help him to sit up. "Here, drink this." I hold the Gatorade to his mouth.

He watches me as he drinks, and when I pull the bottle away, his eyes remain on mine. Still not completely focused, he sways as I release him, falling back onto the bed.

"My head hurts," he complains.

I lean over him, reaching to grab a pillow for under his head when I feel him fist my sweater, hauling me down on top of him.

"Why are you still here?" His breath fans my face, and I swallow thickly.

"I told you—" I begin, but I'm cut off when he grabs my face with his other hand and drags my mouth to his.

It's not a sweet kiss, nothing you'd expect from a lover. No, this kiss is infused with hatred, and it burns as he plunders my mouth. His tongue takes no prisoners as it rips through my lips, and his teeth draw blood as he bites onto my flesh. His groan sends my blood pumping fiercely through my veins as I match his hatred with more of my own. I don't know what's happening with us, but right now, it feels so damn good. Then all thought leaves me as I ground my cock down onto his naked body.

"The things I do to you," he whispers as I run my tongue down his neck, "have to stay inside my head. No one can know, Dixon."

He's said my name twice now, and each time sounded reverent, like a prayer. My mouth travels down farther, and I latch on to his nipple, biting into the small, hardened nub. His fingers curl around my hair, and he moans my name again as I continue downward. I reach his belly button and dip my tongue inside, grinning when he hisses. His hips come up, and his cock bumps under my chin, forcing reality in that moment.

I am about to fuck a man. Not just any man, but a man who has raped me. I rest my forehead on his muscular lower belly and take a deep breath, trying to figure out what my mind and body are saying. Is this what I want? Is Sebastian the person I want to have this sort of relationship with? I've never ever been with a man, never crossed my mind, and I have never even held an attraction for one.

He makes the decision for me. When his soft snores hit my ears again, I lean up to look into his face. He's sound asleep with a small grin on his face and a hard dick that's digging into my ribs. I push off him and grab his blanket, covering him once again.

"Don't leave," his face contorts with distress.

"I'm here," I whisper as I lay down beside him.

"North?"

His voice shatters through my dream of running laps around the field, and I open my eyes to see his face above mine.

"Hey," I croak out and notice he looks clearer, his eyes once again focused.

"What are you doing here?" He sits up and looks under his blanket, realizing he's naked. "I remember the shower." He sounds confused but keeps looking back at me.

"That's all you remember?" I ask as I sit up beside him.

"There are snippets of other shit, but I can't tell what's real and what's not." I can see him staring at the side of my face, and I'd bet those snippets are us making out. "You just came inside my house?"

"Yeah." I stand and turn to face him. "I was told you were at the hospital with another concussion. So I came by here to check on you. I rang the doorbell, but there was no answer, and your door was open. You shouldn't be alone with a concussion."

He nods and looks up at me, uncertainty shining in his gaze. "Thank you."

"You're feeling okay now?" I ask and look to his bedroom door, the need to escape becoming overwhelming.

"Yeah." He clears his throat and rubs his hand over his nipple, the one I bit into. "I'm good now."

"All right." I walk slowly to the door. "I'll check in on you tomorrow after practice."

"Nah," he says, and I look back at him once again, the confusion so clear on his face, his hand still covering his nipple. "I'll have Jameson and Ortiz."

"Right." This awkward situation is only growing worse by the second. "I'll see myself out."

He doesn't say anything as I slip out of his bedroom and rush down the stairs, my mind a tangled web. I guess I will have to forget everything we did in that room and face that it died the second it was over. I open the front door and shut it behind me, then I jog across the street to my car. I slip inside and take a deep breath, trying to control the wild patter of my heart. He doesn't remember anything we did. He doesn't remember those heated kisses or how I almost had him in my mouth. That should be a blessing for me since I'm not sure what's going on and what my actual feelings are, but it's not.

It's somehow making me feel like I've had my heart pulverised then handed back to me a pile of mush. I look back up to his second story, knowing his room faces the back, wondering what he's doing now. Is he trying to figure out if what we did was real? Does he hope it was? Do I want him to realize it was real? Am I gay?

I bury my face in my hands and try to imagine any attractive man, judging my feelings for them. As I flip through the images in my mind, I feel nothing, and then Sebastian is there. I feel fucking everything, and it has me sucking back a sob, my emotions no longer in my control. I just made out with a man. I would've even gone further, and I can't figure out if I'm gay or not. I don't want any other man, I don't find any of them attractive, and the one I do have feelings for happens to be the one who took advantage of me.

I am completely fucked in my head. There's no other explanation.

CHAPTER SIXTEEN

Dixon

It's been a week, and he's supposed to be back today. We have our next game tonight against the Giants, and Coach said Sebastian would be here but not playing. I've stayed away from his house, and I tried my hardest all week not to think too much about what happened. I've boiled it down to me being in the moment, and he was not himself. I'm not gay, and I don't want to sleep with Sebastian Avando.

I blame my lack of close friends in life, and I'm confusing worry for his well-being with romantic notions. It's a relief because now I don't have to worry about telling my religious mother about my sexual orientation, and I can rewire my brain to realize I just want to make sure Sebastian is okay. If it weren't for my fumble, he'd be okay, and these feelings of guilt manifested into something I can't explain. If he somehow remembers what we did, I will deny it until I'm blue in the damn face. Besides, who's going to believe a concussed person over me?

Once practice is over, which I spent watching those double doors for him, I'm relieved to have some time to myself before the game. The guys usually head to the weight room, but I go to the sauna. I need to relax my legs before the game, plus it gives me time alone to get into the right headspace.

We won our last game by a point, and yes, it's a win, but I know we can do better. We need to be in top form for playoffs, and that means I can't make any more stupid mistakes. That means I need to stop obsessing about *him* and start putting in the hours for training. I strip down, tossing my practice uniform in the bin, then head for the sauna. I turn the dial to the temperature I want and sit on the wooden bench, same spot as always. I rest my head against the wall and let the heat seep through me. Fuck, it feels so good.

As I relax, my mind begins to wander, and I end up back in that bedroom with Sebastian, my dick starting to harden at the memory. I want to fight it, think of anything else and move the hell on, but I can't.

I know I have this place to myself, no one ever comes in here, and when I do find myself no longer alone, it's always Sebastian. I reach beneath my towel and stroke my hand along my length, groaning when I squeeze roughly at the tip. Lately, I've been worked up frequently, yet I've been denying myself the release because I always had him on my mind. It was proof to myself that I wasn't gay, that if I could ignore the arousal and pretend it never happened, then I was fine.

I stroke back down to the base, picturing his mouth around me, Moaning his name as I envision him bobbing there, sucking roughly at the tip. I'm fine, I convince myself as I imagine Sebastian gagging on my length, his throat tightening around me and my cock jerking in response. He deserves to choke on my cock, to have his eyes burn with tears as I deprive him of air, and he deserves to swallow every drop of my cum. The detailed imagery in my head has me tipping over the edge and coming in hot squirts all over my stomach. I stay where I am and absorb the sensations still flowing through me. I'm fine, none of this means I'm gay.

We're playing amazing tonight. The third quarter comes to an end, and I nearly stumble over my feet when I see Sebastian sitting on the bench. I didn't think he would show when I failed to see him for most of the game, and now that he's here, I'm not sure how to feel. I jog to the bench with a few minutes for break until the fourth and grab a Gatorade. We're up by a touchdown, and I have to make sure it stays that way.

"North," his voice runs through me like the sweetest melody, and I grit my teeth. "Looking good tonight, keeping that ball tight."

He's taking a dig at me, but unlike previous times, this one is a joke. I toss him a shrug and gulp down the Gatorade, my stomach a mess of nerves with him so close. He comes to stand beside me, and I can feel his gaze on the side of my face, so I turn to look at him.

"You're quick," he looks straight at me, "but you're not the best. Remember that."

"What are you fucking talking about?" I growl at him.

"Don't go out there thinking you run this team, let them do the work too." He shakes his head and backs up. "Play as a team, Rookie."

I slam the helmet back on my head and jog back out to the field. Zeal is already there with most of the first string, and I listen as they discuss plays. I try to wipe my mind of Sebastian and his words, but I can't help getting pissed off. I am a team player, I always have been, and when have I ever said I was the best?

"North," Zeal grabs my shoulder, "you did awesome this game. How about Dex takes home this next one for us?"

I open my mouth to argue, to assure him I can do it. But instead, I hear Avando's voice in my head, telling me to play as a team.

"Yeah, man," I nod. "That sounds good."

It's our power play and one we use when we really want to confuse our opponents. It's not common to have your defensive tackle running for the end zone unless they're tackling the opposition. We get into our formation, the same one Zeal would call to have me run to catch the ball or for Ortiz to catch the ball. The Giants line up across from us. The defense have their eyes on me and Ortiz, the two most likely runners to end up with the ball. The whistle blows, and we take off, the defense crowding me, waiting for that throw. Only it doesn't come.

Dex is halfway down the field, and we watch as he catches the ball, both Ortiz and I getting in front of the defensemen running to catch him. It's enough, and we watch as Dex gets ahead and plows over that white line. All of us are screaming his name with pride.

We all jump on Dex, the crowd screaming behind us as we crush the huge motherfucker into the ground. He really did it. Maybe I should've believed he could from the beginning. No matter how much I despised Sebastian's words, maybe he had a point, and I'll have to watch myself. I don't want to project to the team that I don't believe in them or that I'm the only one who can run the ball into the end zone.

After team handshakes, we all head back into the locker room, and I rush to the showers as the guys get a bit rowdy. I have never been one who stuck around to get drunk or party, and right now my body is begging for relaxation. I turn the shower on hot, keeping my back to the wall as I begin to lather up. Just as I'm finishing, a few of the guys trickle in, and they begin chanting my name, making me laugh.

"You've been a really good addition for our team, North." Dex claps me on the back.

"Thanks, man. I'm glad to be here."

I head out of the showers and find Sebastian sitting on the bench talking to Jameson and Ortiz. He doesn't spare me a glance as I head to my locker.

"When are you back?" Ortiz asks him.

"Next week. When we're in Cincinnati," he answers.

"Yeah, those pussies are easy to knock out," Jameson answers, and the words make my insides crawl.

Do they refer to everyone as pussies? Probably just the ones they hate or want to rape. My anger is fresh tonight, and I don't know why. Maybe having Sebastian here is messing with my mindset. The farther away I get from him the better. I debate whether or not to use the sauna when the three of them stand and make their way to the doors to leave. Fucking perfect. I get inside the sauna and close the door, setting it to my usual temperature. I sit in my spot and rest my head on the wall, groaning when the heat settles into my muscles.

There was something different about Sebastian today. His demeanor was quieter, and he seemed calmer. It's a relief he didn't remember what transpired between us, and maybe now we can push forward as teammates. I am done with the shit that's been hanging over us.

"It's amazing, the dreams you have when your brain gets knocked around." His voice startles me. and I bang my head against the wall.

"The fuck?" I sit up and watch as his outline comes closer through the fog.

His face appears right in front of mine, and I suck in a breath at the sight of his light brown eyes. They flicker between my mouth and my eyes, watching me closely for any reaction. I can't help the pounding of my pulse nor the rising of my dick at his proximity, and the heat in here is not helping. I watch as a bead of sweat escapes his brow, and that's when I realize he's still fully dressed.

"What do you want, Avando?" My voice sounds low and raspy, not at all authoritative.

He leans in, his mouth brushing along my jaw and settling at my ear. "I'm not fucking sure."

My cock pulses with my heartbeat, and I bite into my lip to stop the moan, the copper taste of blood flooding my tongue. He presses his mouth to the column of my throat and sucks on my skin, sinking his teeth into my flesh. I can't hold it in any longer, so I groan long and deep. I feel his mouth turn up at my reaction, then he releases my skin from his mouth, brushing back along my cheek.

He stares at me once again and grins. "Funny dreams indeed."

Then I watch him turn away and slowly disappear through the mist. Did I just imagine all that?

A few days later, Coach gathers us around for a meeting to discuss the upcoming gala on Saturday evening. He lectures us on not drinking too much since we have a game the next night. And we have to travel to Cincinnati, so he wants us in top form. To be honest, I've completely forgotten about the gala and haven't even seen Danielle to confirm our date. It feels weird taking her when I don't know where my head is at with Sebastian.

Obviously, I can't go with him, I know that, but still, it feels wrong. What if she thinks this is a real date? That afterward she'll expect us to continue dating? I don't think I can commit to anything right now. She doesn't deserve a confused man who can't decide what the fuck he likes. I do know for sure that it isn't her, so I need to make sure she knows that. If she's upset about it and decides not to come with me, I will understand and fly solo. No biggie.

I don't even want to go near the sauna today … it seems to be where I get cornered the most by Sebastian. And I don't know when it'll happen, but an explosion is on the precipice. I feel like we're hitting a point of no return that's going to fuck everything up. I must avoid him. As Coach drones on about the rules, I slip my head into my hands and think of all the shit I'm going to need to buy. A new suit, some shoes, and I need a haircut. I press my fingers into my coarse hair. Yep, I'm going to need a nice fade for the event.

"You good?"

I want to scream as I feel him sit beside me, but instead, I give him a casual grunt, not bothering to even look at him. I'm so tired of him and the emotional rollercoaster we're on. Is this just a game to him? Does toying with me give him some type of twisted pleasure?

Coach finishes up his speech, then I stand, grabbing my duffle bag.

"No sauna today?" His voice is mocking, and I grind my teeth.

"Nah." I take a breath and look down at him. "It's not as satisfying as it used to be."

He shocks me by throwing his head back and laughing, sounding genuine. I shake my head, fighting my own grin as I head to the doors. Standing there is Danielle, looking slightly uneasy.

"Hey," she says and bites down onto her plump lower lip. That's something I would usually find attractive, but today, there's nothing.

"Hey."

"So … ah … what color dress should I wear?" she asks nervously.

"Pardon?" I raise my brow, and she giggles at me. It's a cute sound coming from her.

"I thought we could match for the gala? What color will your tie be?"

"Oh, shit," I scratch the back of my neck. "Right, I haven't bought the suit yet. I'll do that tomorrow."

"Oh, okay," she nods, and I realize how damn awkward this is. "What's your favorite color?"

"Green," I reply, and she gives me a shy smile. She really is so cute.

"Okay," her hand comes out and squeezes my forearm. "I can't wait."

I give her a smile, then I hurry away from her to exit the building. After this gala, I need to start to distance myself from Dani.

CHAPTER SEVENTEEN

Sebastian

I am a little obsessed with making Dixon uncomfortable. I don't know what happened exactly at my house because I can't decipher what was real from what I dreamt. After his reaction to me in the sauna though, I have a feeling we did at least some of the shit I remember, and he's beat up about it.

As for me? I don't know what the fuck I'm feeling, but I like it. And regardless, it's not going to go anywhere. So why not have some fun? I'm not gay, but there's something about him that I'm drawn to, and I don't feel like exerting the energy to fight it. I wouldn't mind getting him on his knees to suck my dick. Those lips he has are perfect for wrapping around a dick, and fuck yeah, I want it to be mine.

I cut out my lines on the tabletop and look over at Ortiz as he screams Spanish into his phone. He's been fighting nonstop with his girl lately, and I find it comical. I'm glad I don't have those issues. I snort my first line and groan as the dizzying effect takes hold. Blow's been the only thing that's helped with the side effects of my concussion. I also blame it for how I've been feeling toward Dixon. As soon as I'm healed, I'm sure they'll go away, and then life will resume as normal.

"Fucking whore," Ortiz yells as he hangs up the phone. "She saw pap photos of me leaving the strip club with Jameson."

"Just tell her she's lucky you didn't fuck any of them," I shrug then snort the next line.

"She's Latina, man," he moans as he slumps on the couch. "She wouldn't care, and the next time she sees me, she's gonna rip my balls off."

"On to the next," Jameson chuckles around a spliff. "The girl I'm bringing to the gala has a sister. You in?"

"Fuck yeah," Ortiz perks up as he takes the spliff.

I'm interested to see how Dani and Dixon will be during the gala. I watched them today, and their awkwardness actually cracked me up. He's just not that into her, and someone needs to let her know that. Maybe it should be me. I know how he is when he's into someone, the noises he makes when he wants something he's been denying himself… I wouldn't mind telling her what's up. My dick begins to swell with the thought of him sitting in that sauna, so I slip my hand inside my pants, giving it a rough squeeze. I've been wanting to jack myself off to the thought of him and the shit I suspect went down in my bed, but I've been waiting. I want to come all over his face instead.

I withdraw my hand and cut out my next line. Patience is a motherfucking virtue.

Today I'm waiting for him in the sauna. It's been three days of ignoring him, and I know he's wondering why I haven't spoken to him. I like throwing him off guard and doing the unexpected with him. I can see why he likes it here… It's soothing, and my muscles are growing more languid the longer I'm in here. I should use the one I have at home.

I know he's going to see the sauna in use, and I know he'll know it's me, but I'm hoping his curiosity gets the better of him. I've been purposefully avoiding him, and if I'm starting to get to know him as well as I think, he'll want to ask what's up with me.

As if on cue, the door opens forcefully, and he's standing there, a towel around his waist. The scowl on his face is comical, and I chuckle before I can hold it in.

"Why are you in here?" he growls, anger so potent in his tone.

"It was a rough practice today," I feign innocence. "I needed a moment to relax."

He doesn't say anything as he stomps over to the bench, stopping to see that I'm even sitting in his usual spot. He moves down to the far side of the bench, away from me.

"What's your problem?" I ask.

"My problem?" he scoffs. "You! You're my problem. Why do you keep calling me a fucking pussy?"

Oh, right. Maybe I wasn't completely ignoring him. I did throw in a couple jabs here and there, but I can't let people see how far my feelings have changed for the guy. That's something I wouldn't come back from, and I'd be known as the gay boy on the Bills team. I can't have that.

"Stop acting like one," I shrug.

His anger gets the best of him, and he's across the bench in record time, his hand around my throat. I struggle to swallow around his hold and wrap my fingers around his wrist, squeezing him just as hard. I know how precious his hands are, but even so, he's still gripping me. That's how angry he is.

"What are you fucking doing, Sebastian?" he snaps.

"Seb," I choke out.

"What?" his hold loosens, and he drops his hand. "What the

fuck did you say?"

"Call me Seb." Why the fuck am I saying this to him? Only the boys I grew up with call me Seb.

"No thanks." He stands and tightens the towel around his waist.

"Wait," I tell him before he has the chance to leave. "I thought we could get to know each other."

"Why?"

"Because we're teammates?" I answer his question with one of my own.

"Now you care about that?" he looks at me critically. "You didn't seem to care a few months ago in the shower—"

"Can we move past that?" I cut him off.

I'd like to say I'm just pulling his leg, and I don't care if he forgives me or not, but that would be a lie. I know why I did what I did. He needed to know his place, and it was always going to be underneath me, like a bitch. I still feel that way, I just know I went too far, and I don't want that hovering over us forever.

"I don't know." I can see the turmoil in his features. "That shit was fucked-up."

I shrug. My nonchalance is evident, but I tried, and if he ever wants to hear it again, that'll be too bad for him. That's as close to an apology he'll ever get because I just don't do them. I make my decisions, and I stick by them, right or wrong. Life is too short for regrets, and I'm not wasting mine on them.

I stand up from the bench, my towel falling from my waist. I watch as he looks down at my hard cock. I'm shameless, really, and I can't help but be hard whenever he's around. Maybe it was the time in the shower that changed everything. I got a taste, and now I want more.

"What are you doing?" His voice drops a few octaves, and

he visibly swallows. I can see the sweat gathering at his temple, and I know it's not just from the steam.

I like this feeling, being in here alone with him, knowing at any moment someone could walk in. The towel at his waist tents, and I snort at his reaction. He wants me too.

"Tell me what happened at my house," I demand as I take a step closer.

"What do you think happened?"

"Dixon," I chastise as I step into him, our chests brushing. "I wasn't asking. Tell me what happened at my house."

His breathing accelerates, and mine follows suit, my eyes dropping to his tattooed chest. He's inked as much as I am, and that says something; I have a shit ton of tats. He licks his lips and stares at my mouth, tempting me to grab him, but I won't. I need to hear what happened at my house so I can separate my dreams from reality.

"You kissed me," he whispers.

I remember that. "What else?"

"Nothing much after that because you fell asleep." He rolls his eyes, and I grin because he murmurs it with disappointment.

"So you didn't suck my dick?" I stare into his eyes.

"No!" he exclaims, lowering his gaze. I watch as his chest heaves, and sweat beads between his pecs, skating down between his cut abs. Fuck, that's hot.

"Did you want to?" I'm so close to him that my lips brush his with my words.

"I don't know." He's being honest, I can tell.

I lean in and bite his lower lip, pulling on it until it snaps back into place. His eyes darken, and he sucks the lip into his mouth, tasting me on it.

"I wanted you to," I tell him, and he shakes his head.

"You passed out."

"I dreamt you choked on my fucking dick as I came down your throat." I run my fingertip down over his Adam's apple. "Fuck, I really want to choke you with my dick, Dixon."

For the first time, he's the one who grabs my face and drags me in to kiss him. It feels unsure, like he's struggling with what we're doing, so I grab the back of his head to deepen it. I'm not sure what all this is either, but it feels good, and I don't want to waste time fretting over little shit. It is what it is, we want each other for some damn reason. I still love pussy, though. I pull his towel off and wrap my arm around his waist, lining our cocks up.

The smooth, velvet feel of his dick against mine feels foreign but so amazing, and we both moan simultaneously. I want his mouth wrapped around my cock, and I want to watch his eyes tear up as I fuck his throat, but I have to go slow. He's scared and confused, it's emanating from every pore in his body. I know not everyone is like me; they all question their existences and need to know their purposes. For me, I like what I like when I like it, and I have it while I want it. I have never wanted another man before and that's how I know I'm not gay. I just want Dixon.

I reach between us and grab his cock, giving him a firm stroke. He breaks away from my mouth and stumbles back, his face shocked.

"I can't do this." His voice shakes in fear as he bends to pick up his towel.

I can't force him … yet. So I sit back on the bench and lazily stroke my cock as he rewraps himself. He stares at me and my movements, the hunger evident in his eyes. He can say he can't do it all he wants, but I can see he wants to. I can work with that.

"Why are we doing this?" his pained voice fills the room.

"Because we feel like it," I shrug.

"I'm not gay."

"Nor am I," I shrug again.

"This feels fucking gay, Sebastian," he retorts.

Is it weird that I hate him calling me by my full name? I want him to call me Seb, but I can't figure out why. The people I grew up with call me Seb and that's all, not even Jameson and Ortiz call me that. So why do I want to hear him say it so badly?

"Because you're too much in here." I point to my head. "But go ahead. Be afraid, *pussy.*"

His eyes narrow at my words, and he takes a step forward, growling. Instead of taking the bait, he turns abruptly and leaves the sauna as I chuckle. I lean back and let go of my cock, not giving myself the release I crave. I won't until I can have it squirting down the back of his throat. I don't know why he's so worried about his sexuality. Doesn't he fuck females? I do, that's how I know this is just a one-off.

Dixon

I decided the only way to get Sebastian off of my mind was to go shopping for a suit. I haven't done this in years, and the stress of finding the perfect one was enough to shut him out. My phone starts ringing in my pocket, and I pull it out to see my mother's name on the screen.

"Hey, Ma."

"Dixon." She sounds stressed, so I leave the store and stand outside to talk to her.

"What's up?"

"It's Daniel," she sniffs, and I steel myself for the news. "He's been expelled from school. I have to send him to the public school."

I knew there was a high chance of this happening because

Danny doesn't know how to stay out of trouble.

"What happened?"

"He got into a fight, and the cops were called." She takes a breath, and I know that's not going to be the worst of it. "They searched his locker and found drugs, Dixon. Not just weed, he also had cocaine and pills."

Clearly, my brother has become a drug runner. "Okay… I have an away game this weekend, but I can be home for Monday."

"No, Dixon." She sounds defeated but firm. "You have to concentrate on your career. I will handle Daniel and his schooling."

"I think it's time to do something more, Ma."

"Like what?" she asks.

"Maybe one of those reform schools."

"I can't do that to him," she says with sadness. "He will hate me."

"Better he hates you than die on the streets selling drugs, right?" I know I'm being harsh, but it's the truth, and sometimes it takes harsh words to wake someone up.

"He has a court date in a month. I'm hoping this will make him change, that he can prove to the judge that he will do better." She bypasses my question, so I know talking to her will be futile. I need to speak directly to my brother.

"Yeah, okay."

"You have a good game this week, okay? I'll be watching as always." She hangs up, and my heart breaks for the woman who was left to raise two boys alone.

My brother and I grew up without a father figure, so I get what's happening. I know he's looking for the acceptance of his peers instead of looking within, and that's a sure path to destruction. Not only is he selfishly thinking of himself, but he's putting our mother in danger, and my career in jeopardy by association. I tried the easy way by showing him the type of life he could have with hard work and dedication, but like most kids his age, this lesson must be taught differently. I don't want to go above my mother's head, but I know there's no saving my brother the easy way.

It's time to give him a taste of the future he will have if he continues selling drugs and running the streets. Maybe a bit of bootcamp will straighten him out, and if it doesn't, then I will have to cut ties with him … completely cut him off to show him what his decisions could cost him.

I walk back into the store, Sebastian completely eradicated from my thoughts, and look over what the salesperson picked out for me. It's not easy finding the perfect penguin suit being this tall and wide. Without much thought, I grab the suit on the very top and ask for it to be rang up. I don't care enough about this gala at the moment. It's the least of my worries, so any damn suit will do. Three thousand dollars and a mini heart attack later, I'm getting into my car and heading home. Only then do I let myself think of him and what we did in that fucking sauna … again.

I should stay out of there, but I know I won't. Sebastian Avando has this hold over me, and I'm unable to escape it.

Chapter Eighteen

Was it wrong that I told Danielle I would meet her at the venue? I mean, her father is going to the same place… Is that such a big deal? She sounded disappointed, but I couldn't bring myself to care. I don't even want to go, and her sounding upset before even getting there cements that. I just want this night over with and then get on the bus that will take us to Cincinnati. Yes, right after the gala, we are all piling into a bus and hitting the road. It's not ideal… Having to sleep on the bus then practicing for the game sounds like a terrible idea.

I pay the taxi that drops me off, then I grab my duffle bag, spotting the bus in the parking lot. I'm a bit late, but whatever. At least I made it, and that's saying something considering I almost changed my mind. I hand my bag to the driver then head inside the convention center.

The decorations are lavish and ostentatious. The large silver garland with bright red roses in their centers, large chandeliers, and the smell of rich people. You know what I mean…. Their colognes and perfumes smell like they're worth more than my mother's yearly salary. I hate that I'm here, this isn't what I signed up for. I wanted to play a game I love and provide for my family, not schmooze with rich folks because they gave us some of their money.

"Dixon?"

I turn and see Danielle standing by the stairs, and I cringe because it's obvious she was waiting.

"Sorry I'm late—"

"You could've texted," she butts in, annoyance clear on her face.

"I'm sorry," I try again. "I hate crowds, and shit like this makes me uncomfortable."

I guess she feels the honesty in my words because she steps forward from the shadow of the stairs. Her dress is a bright emerald green, making her skin pop, her radiance on complete display.

"You look beautiful," I say with awe because she truly does.

The blush that coats her cheeks makes her even more so as she steps closer to me, fingering my black silk tie.

"I thought maybe you would do green as well, when I asked you…" she trails off, and I groan.

"Was that why you asked? Is that why you're wearing green?" I scrub my hand over my face. "This is all new to me, I'm sorry." More apologies.

"It's okay," she chuckles. "You look dashing, Dixon."

"Thank you." I feel myself flush, and she laughs again.

"Have you ever been to anything like this?" She looks up the stairs to where I presume the gala is being held.

"Never."

"I'll give you a run-through so you're not surprised." When her lips curve up, I decide she has a beautiful smile. "So there are a bunch of rich assholes up there who think that because they donate money to the team, they are entitled to know shit about you."

I laugh out loud which earns me a wider smile.

"They'll be intrusive with their questions, and they will look down on you because they see you as their investment. Some even going as far as viewing you as their property."

I know this already, I gathered that when Coach told us how many zeros were on the checks we received, but I let her continue.

"They're not here for you guys tonight. They're here for themselves, and they want flattery. You don't have to do that, of course," she rushes out. "But you being the rookie, it'll be expected."

"I have to kiss rich asses is what you're telling me," I grin at her.

"Yeah," she giggles and shrugs. Yes, she is absolutely gorgeous.

"What else should I know?"

"Don't be offended by their ignorance," she explains. "They are only acquainted with their own way of life."

"Got it." I nod and hold out my arm. "Shall we?"

"You just want to get this over with, huh?" she grins.

"I'm sure you'll help me enjoy my time tonight." Her eyes heat at my words, and I realize too late how presumptuous that sounded. "I don't mean … like that…"

"I would love to help you enjoy your time, Dixon." Her husky voice is a direct hit to my dick, and I feel it start to swell.

Well damn, I guess I'm not gay.

The aroma of rich perfumes and foods that I'm not accustomed to assault my nose. The large room is scattered with tables that are covered in sparkling lace. There's what looks to be a dance floor in the center, and to the far back is a platform with a podium on it. A live band is up there now, playing instruments I could never name and songs I have never heard before. There are servers gracing the floors with trays of long-stemmed glasses filled with bubbling liquid topped with raspberries. Everything screams extreme wealth.

"North!" Coach exclaims, and the group he's standing with all turn to look. I guess that's what I get for being late. "Come here, and meet a few people."

"Here we go," Danielle murmurs beside me. "Smile."

I plaster a wide, fake smile on my face and let her lead me toward the group. It's a group of older men—I would guess in their fifties to sixties—and some have wives with them. They have friendly enough faces, so I release the breath I was holding, letting go of the anxiety with it. This is a first for me, and I don't want to fuck it up.

"Guys, this is Dixon North," Coach says as I come forward. "Our newest addition."

I give them a small smile. "Nice to meet you."

"How does it feel to be playing on an NFL team?" one of the men asks with a smile on his face.

"Amazing," I answer honestly. "I'm honored."

"This is a big change for you," another adds. "What college did you play with?"

"Clemson."

"Oh, Clemson!" a woman exclaims. "They are a great team."

"Thank you, ma'am."

"Your life must be very different now," another woman states, and I look at her in question.

"How so?"

"I know how much money an athlete receives," she chuckles and pats what I assume is her husband's arm. "It's life changing."

"Yes," I agree because it's true. "Currently, my life is the same in the sense that I'm still catching footballs and running toward an end zone."

"Oh!" she laughs. "I like that."

I smile and give her a nod. They're not so bad. Maybe a little pretentious, but not rude.

"You're a great addition to the team, Mr. North."

"Thank you very much." I smile, and Danielle tugs on my arm.

"Do you mind if I steal him away?" she bats her lashes, and a few of them chuckle. "I've been eyeing those fancy drinks."

"It was great to meet you all." I give another nod as Danielle steers me away.

"Impressive, *Mr. North,*" she teases. "I believe they liked you."

"I'm a likeable person, Danielle." I smile at her, and she sucks in a breath.

"Dani." She looks up at me through her lashes. "Call me Dani."

"I guess that means we're friends now, huh?"

She laughs as I grab us two glasses from a passing server. "Dixon, I have no interest in being your friend." Again, her eyes heat up, and my cock twitches in response.

I give her a slow once-over. She's wearing fuck-me stilettos, her form-fitting dress with a slit running up the side to the top of her thigh. Her brown hair is down her back, hitting her waist.

"Like what you see?" she asks quietly as she sips her drink.

"Yeah, I do." I really do. "Green *is* my favorite color."

She giggles again, but our moment is interrupted when Dex calls out to me from a nearby table.

"North! Get over here. You're sitting with me and Zeal." I turn to look at him over my shoulder, and my eyes land on the table behind him.

Sitting there are Sebastian, Jameson, and Ortiz, of course, and each of them has a woman sitting next to them. I knew they would bring dates, it's expected that we do, so I brought someone too. But seeing Sebastian sitting beside an attractive woman with dark, curly hair, piled high on her head, has me feeling some sort of way. She has the most illuminating bronzed skin. She looks regal and poised, her face looking young, but her dark brown eyes are filled with wisdom. Seeing her leaning into him, then the annoyance in his eyes when he looks at Dani and me, pisses me off. Except, I feel it too … the annoyance of seeing him sitting with her, whoever the fuck she is. Maybe she's a hot stripper he pulled in and stuffed into a dress last minute. Whatever.

I pull my eyes away and wrap my arm around Dani's waist, giving it a slight squeeze as we walk to our table. I feel the intensity of his glare, but I ignore it as I sit in my seat, thankful that my back is to him. Dinner is seven courses of pea-sized portions, and by dessert, I'm still hungry. Hopefully, there will be a way I can get the bus driver to stop at a burger joint on the way to Cincinnati. The heat on the back of my head hasn't let up, and I can't understand how I can feel him. How is that even possible?

"Sebastian is looking grumpy tonight," Dani says into my ear, her mouth grazing the lobe.

"He has a beautiful woman next to him, I can't imagine why." I lean on my hand and turn to stare at her.

"Did he tell you what happened with us?" Her cheeks grow pink, and this time it's from embarrassment.

"A little."

"I thought I was in love with him," she scoffs, and I'm surprised by the shot of jealousy that courses through me. "I would've done anything for him, and I did."

"You did what?"

"Unimaginable things, anything he asked me to do, and then one day I was shocked to learn he has a wife."

I hear her words, they sink inside my brain, and I understand what they mean, but I'm frozen. She must be mistaken, there's no way. And I'm sure someone would've mentioned it by now, right?

"Married?" I feel my mouth moving, and I can hear my voice, but I can't seem to focus.

"Yeah, with a daughter too."

My body feels as though it's doused in frigid water as I abruptly stand. "Sorry, I need to use the restroom."

She gives me a confused look, but I don't stick around to find out why. I have no idea where the damn bathrooms are, and I don't care who's watching as I rush out of the room. I head back down the stairs and shove my way outside, sucking in the cold air.

Married?!

Daughter?!

I fall against the brick wall behind me and bend over as I try to catch my breath. She must be wrong, there's no way he's married. And he has a daughter? It can't be. I try to take in deep breaths, but the little bit of food I just ate is working itself up my throat and burning my esophagus.

"She told you." His voice hits me, and I lose my battle with the food, spewing it all at my feet. "Fuck, North. What's wrong with you?"

I look up at him, anger threatening to boil over as I bare my teeth. "The things you did with me, the things you did *to* me, all while you had a wife?"

"And?" he smirks like this is all a joke to him. "What did you think this was?" He swings his finger between us. "Did you think we would run off together into the sunset? I'm not fucking gay."

"Fuck you." I shove him out of my way. "Don't ever come near me again. You're a fucking cheater."

"A cheater?" he throws his head back with a laugh. "There has to be feelings for it to be cheating. You were just something warm until I saw her again. Easiest *pussy* I've had yet."

I leave him at my back as I stumble inside. I grab the first person I see and ask them to direct me to the bathrooms. This is what I get for getting involved in shit I have no idea about. How did I ever become attached to Sebastian? I get inside the bathroom and splash my face with cold water. After toweling off, I see a small box of toiletries, and relief washes over me when I see mouthwash. Once I pull myself together, I stare at my reflection and make myself a promise.

Sebastian Avando will be forever wiped from my memory.

Sebastian

I turn to chase after him, but my phone rings in my pocket, and I can't ignore it. I pull it out and see Delano's name. Knowing he would only call me if it were important, I swipe the screen to pick it up.

"'Sup?"

"Hey, man. I got some info on that kid."

I can feel the corners of my mouth lifting because this is some good news. Just when Dixon thinks he'll get rid of me, this will be what brings him back. And this time, I'll have my way with him before he tries to escape again.

"What is it?"

"He's a low-level drug runner and likes to boost a few cars, just had his first run in with the law. Got kicked out of school a few days ago, and word on the street is his initiation is coming up," he grunts.

"Interesting." I scratch at my chin. "Little North is a wannabe gangster."

"Soon to be an actual gangster," he chuckles. "From what I heard, he's tough, and he doesn't mind doing the dirty work."

Dirty work. I know what that means. There was a time when I didn't mind it either since cleanups meant I was working my way in. Not too long after that, I was fed daily, clothed, and had a warm bed to sleep in without strange men trying to touch me after fucking my mother. But why would Dixon's brother need to be in a gang? Why was he choosing that life?

"I need another favor."

"Sure, bro," Delano is quick to appease me.

"I need info on his family, specifically his home life."

"You got it." He hangs up, and I stand here, staring out into the parking lot.

I knew tonight would happen the way it did. Dani can't keep her mouth shut, and she's still hurting from me breaking shit off with her. It was just a matter of *when* not *if* she would tell him I'm married. What shocks me, though, is Dixon's reaction to it and how upset he was. But why? I shake it off and head back inside, the hall still buzzing with chatter. I enter the room and walk back to my table, Paola's eyes firmly on me.

I will say one thing about my wife … she doesn't play when it comes to me, and she won't hesitate to gut someone. I sit back in my seat and stretch my arm out, placing it on the back of her chair.

"Everything good?" Her thick Ecuadorian accent makes me smile.

"Si, Mami." I run my fingers along her shoulder. "All good."

She goes back to scrolling through her phone, and I watch Dani, her eyes flicking back to me every so often. Thirsty ass hoe. Dixon comes back into the room. He probably looks normal to everyone else, but I see the truth. His eyes are red-rimmed, the corners of his mouth are turned down, and his shoulders are tipped downward.

"Is that the new one?" Paola asks.

"Yeah."

"He's handsome." I look at her with a smirk, and she tosses one back.

"Watch it," I tease her.

"I know," she chuckles. "Same area code."

I laugh heartily at that, and Dixon's shoulders tense at the sound. He can try to let me go, but I won't let that happen. I'm not done with him yet, and just like my wife said, soon we'll be in different area codes.

It's hard for people in regular relationships to understand the dynamic I have with her. I grew up with Paola because her older brother Alejandro was the one who took me in. Jandro died a few years after he made me promise to take care of Paola, and I don't go back on my word. I love her, but there's always been something missing, and she feels it too, so we're discreet. At least she is. I get photographed at strip joints and shit, but if I'm not flaunting a mistress, she's good about it. Plus, I know she's fucked every pool boy in New York.

"I'm tired, Seb." She curls her fingers around my bicep. "I think I will head back to the hotel now."

"Let me get the driver." I stand and help her up from her seat. "Did you call to check on Carla?"

"Si," she nods. "She's behaving."

We have a beautiful daughter named Carla, and in a few

months, she will be three years old. I married Paola when she was eight months pregnant even though the child was not mine. We don't fuck, never have. Like I said, it's not like that, but that little girl is mine. My blood may not flow in her veins, but I'm the only papi she will ever know. She's my number one.

After texting the driver, I walk Paola downstairs where she looks up at me with a smile.

"You look like you need a friend." Her hand cups my cheek. "Call me when things get tough, okay?"

I respect her, and I love her, but I would never dump my problems on her. For years, she has been trying to get me to open up more and talk to her more, but I'm not that type of guy. Sometimes her nagging gets annoying, but I deal with it. She's the mother of my child, so no matter what, she's my family.

"*Buenas noches.*" I lean in and kiss her softly on the lips. Then I watch as she sashays to the waiting limo. Only the best for my wife. She waves and tucks herself into the back, her scent lingering beside me.

It's not too long after when people start to leave and head home. Thank God. If I had to talk to one more sponsor about his charity to us, I was going to break a nose. Ortiz and Jameson have been doing shot for shot at the bar while their dates have been huddled together at the table, giggling over wine. It's a good thing they know each other because they've been ignored by the guys for most of the night. Coach keeps looking at them like he would like to break their noses. Dixon has remained in his seat for the whole night with Dani by his side, and even though she's been shooting me looks over her shoulder, she's been attentive to him. He's been stiff and quiet since we had our conversation outside, giving Dani one word answers.

I watch as Dex starts bringing the rounds of shots to their table. Dixon slams each one back, the glasses adding up in front of him. He's an emotional person and works hard to hide that, but I can see beyond his hardened outside layer. He's a mess right now, and he is drowning himself in alcohol to feel better. I like that he feels that way over me. I mean something to him… The moment I saw him spill his guts outside, I knew for sure. Dixon wants me, and there's no amount of convincing himself otherwise that will change that. He's so fun to toy with.

As Jameson and Ortiz begin to get louder at the bar, Coach starts to wrap shit up. He's strict about our lives outside of football, and he won't stand for those two to fuck up the game tomorrow. Not over free booze anyway. He approaches them first and asks them to make their way to the bus. They listen but grumble as they head away. Next, I notice as Dani tugs on Dixon's arm, motioning for him to follow her outside. You better believe I'm following as well. I want to watch her make her move, and then I want to watch as he shuts her down.

They walk out of the room, Dixon slightly stumbling and Dani giggling at him. I wait a few minutes then rise from my seat, walking slowly out of the room. I can still hear Coach behind me, winding down all the conversations and starting with the 'we better get on the road' spiel. We'll be out of here in about a half hour, and I'm hoping to sit next to Dixon. I want him overwhelmed with me and on the verge of snapping… That's when shit is the hottest.

I step outside and look around. I don't see anyone, but I do hear Jameson and Ortiz being rowdy in the bus. I round the corner and startle when I see Dixon leaning against Dani's car with her standing in front of him. He's looking at her with a goofy grin on his face as she laughs at him, slapping his chest playfully. What the fuck is going on here?

My feet won't budge from their spot on the asphalt, and my eyes can't look away from them. They look happy, and it's really pissing me off. She reaches her hand up to touch his cheek, and he grabs her wrist. Okay, this is it, he'll push her away now. Instead, he hauls her in close to his body, wrapping his other arm around her waist. He guides her hand up behind his neck and smiles down at her, his eyes glazed. His tongue slips out and runs along his bottom lip, looking like he wants to ravish her. He's never looked at me like that, and I know he fucking wants me more than that slut.

His hand slips down her back and over her plump ass, his fingers digging in. He hauls her in even closer, grinding her into his dick, and then he swoops down, kissing her with a hunger that makes me both hard and infuriated. Her left leg comes up and presses into his hip, the slit curtaining open, revealing her smooth skin. I want to rip her off him and show her just who he really wants, but I can't move. My eyes stay trained on them even though my heart is about to break through my ribs and my stomach threatens to empty itself. His hand moves along the skin of her thigh as his other hand snares into her hair, tipping her head to a better angle and deepening the kiss. Movement at her thigh draws my sight downward, and I watch his fingers skim up and under her skirt, pushing it aside. Half her ass is on display, and I want to choke the whore for not having any decency.

His hand moves down her ass crack, slowly dipping under her thong before disappearing between her legs. Her groan has my eyes snapping back up, and I come face to face with Dixon as he stares me down, his finger moving in and out of her pussy. Then with his eyes still on me, he devours her mouth once more, his thrusting fingers picking up their pace. I know what he's doing… It's reminiscent of the night at the club with the waitress. But doesn't he realize how far we've come since then? This is ridiculous.

He pulls away from her mouth and removes his fingers from between her legs, bending to whisper something in her ear. She nods up at him then moves around to the driver's side of her car. He stands there with his arms crossed against his chest, watching me with a mocking smirk on his mouth as he turns, opening the car door. What the fuck is he doing? We have a game tomorrow. He needs to get on this bus, and I need to watch him.

The door slams shut, and Dani pulls out of the parking lot, the taillights teasing me as they fly down the street. He really has no clue how much he just pissed me off.

CHAPTER NINETEEN

Dani lets me sleep the six hours it takes to get there, and I can see the exhaustion on her face. I start to feel guilty but then remember she practically begged me to ride with her, telling me she didn't want to go alone. We park in front of the hotel, and I groan when I realize my bag is on the bus, which doesn't look like it has arrived yet.

"Don't worry," she says, reading my groan, "I texted my dad and told him to grab your bag."

"Thanks." I'm not sure how much I like Coach knowing I'm with his daughter.

"Can I stay with you?" Her voice is small and her eyes pleading.

"I have a game later. I really need to rest."

"I know," she chuckles. "Just to sleep. I don't want to sleep alone right now."

I should refuse her, but as I stare down into her eyes, I can feel myself giving in, even though we're not dating. Why aren't we dating, though? If shit hadn't started up with Sebastian, I would've been down to date her, and I'm attracted to her. Fuck it, I'm wiping my mind of *him* … right?

"Yeah," I nod and smile at her. "I would like that."

We get inside, and I get the keys for the room booked under my name, both of us still so exhausted. We ride the elevator up, and it dings on my floor, sliding open to reveal a long corridor.

"Dad usually books out the whole floor for the team," she says as we walk to my door.

"Is this going to be a problem?" I ask her, referring to us being together.

"I spoke to him, and he knows how I feel about you," she answers as she follows me into the room.

"How you feel about me, huh?" I grin. "And how do you feel?"

Her eyes slowly blink, and her small smile is so damn cute. "Right now? I could sleepwalk and get in that bed." She unzips her dress, the zipper running down the side. She shimmies it down her hips and steps out of it, the fabric pooling at her feet like glistening emeralds. She's wearing a black lace bra and thong, and my mouth waters at the sight. I need to sleep. I scrub my hand down my face and chuckle when I hear her laugh.

"You're gorgeous," I haul her into my body and kiss her softly. "I want to do so many things to this body right now, but Coach will kill me if I'm not in top form later."

"I couldn't anyway," she smiles, resting her head on my chest. "I am exhausted."

I nudge her toward the bed and remove my suit, leaving my boxers on. I crawl into bed beside her. As soon as her head hits the pillow she's out. I pull her in closer, resting my head on top of hers and feeling content as I drift off to sleep.

"Get up." I feel cold metal press into my temple, and my eyes pop open quickly.

Dani is sleeping soundly beside me, her small snores filling the room and her lace bra on display.

"Get the fuck up, or I'll blow her brains all across this fucking room." Sebastian growls, and I do as he says. I can feel rage rolling from him, and I don't doubt his words for a second. He has a gun to my head.

He shoves me into the bathroom, and I hit the small counter, hissing when my hip bone bangs against it. He shuts the door, and I look up at him in the reflection of the mirror. His eyes look haunted.

"What are you doing?" I ask him as he holds the gun to the back of my head. "You gonna kill me?"

"I fucking want to," he growls through his teeth, "after the shit you pulled."

"Me?" I begin to chuckle because this is actually crazy. "The shit I pulled? Bro, you're married. Go talk to your wife."

"That's why she's laying in your bed?" he grins maniacally. "So you can try to get over me?"

"Get over you?" I turn to face him and smack the gun out of my face, no longer able to hold my temper in. "I never had a thing for you."

That grin stays on his face as he steps closer. He's still in his dress shirt and slacks, the top four buttons undone at the top. His eyes are bloodshot like he hasn't slept at all, and the dark bags under his eyes make him look sinister.

"I think you do," he leans in, his hands and gun resting on the counter at my sides. "And I think it scared the shit out of you. But you felt something, Dixon. Why else would you spew your dinner when you found out I was married?"

"Because I was disgusted." I try to sound disgusted, but my voice drops an octave and instead sounds raspy.

Our noses brush. I bite the inside of my cheeks to hold in a moan, but I lose that battle as soon as his tongue snakes out, brushing along my lower lip. His scent—something that is uniquely him—fans my face, and I cave, giving into a craving so fucking strong, it's stealing all logic. I grab his waist and grind my cock into his lower belly, slamming my mouth to his. His lips open instantly, and our tongues glide together, turning our heated exchange into something sensual. We've never been sensual … it's always been aggressive, and right now it's like we're feeling something more than anger.

He thrusts his cock against mine, and then his hands are at the waistband of my boxers, pulling them down over my hips. I should be thinking of the woman sleeping soundly in the next room. I should be thinking of the woman he's married to, and I should just shove him away from me, but I can't do any of it. I've never seen myself as a weak man, but right now in this moment, as his hand wraps around my throbbing cock, I am powerless. Our mouths break apart, and both of us are panting when he finally strokes my cock, the feeling of his hand so different from a woman's.

"Did she make you come, Dixon?" he sneers as he squeezes me.

"No." The word tumbles out before I can even think of lying to him.

"No?" his voice smug. "Is this only for me?"

I grit my teeth to hold back the word vomit that wants to admit everything to him—how I'm feeling and what I want him to do—and he chuckles at my tightened jaw.

"Don't worry, Dixon," his tongue runs down my neck, "I already know." He gives my cock a hard squeeze and continues stroking me.

My balls tighten, and my head falls back as I begin to feel the euphoria spreading throughout me. His grip is sure, and I can feel the callouses scraping against my sensitive skin.

"Come for me," he demands before he sinks his teeth into my neck.

As much as my mind wants to fight him, my body listens well, and I come all over his fist, making the most embarrassing noises as I do. I haven't been with anyone like this, where the hatred and need are on par, and my heart is constantly fighting my brain. I can't deny I've been wanting this moment—constantly thinking about it—but now that it's happened, I just want to take it all back. Now we're stuck in a place where we can't go back, and moving forward is impossible.

"Stop thinking," his fingers—soaked in my release—curl around my chin. "Don't do that."

"Sebastian, what are you doing?" I whisper. "You're married."

"You don't know everything." He releases my chin and steps back, looking at my cum on his hand.

"I don't want to know everything," I shake my head and pull up my boxers. "This is it, Sebastian."

He pushes me aside to wash his hands, and I watch as his jaw flexes, anger creasing his forehead. Once he's done and has dried his hands, he picks up his gun.

"It's over when I say it is." He makes me look down the barrel. "And not a moment sooner."

Sebastian

Maybe that was extreme, getting into his room and holding a gun to his head, but I was so damn mad. I was stewing in that anger for over six hours. He's lucky I didn't shoot them both on sight then walked back out. I fucking wanted to. I saw her curled up on his chest in just her underwear, and I saw red.

Practice is shit since half the team is hungover, and the other half doesn't look like they've slept. We're going to lose tonight, and there's nothing this practice is doing to improve that. It's always different during away games… The field isn't ours, the fans aren't the same, and our determination isn't as strong. Today, it's just me and Dixon giving it our all, and Coach is ripping the other guys a new one. It's so funny to watch, and I heard Dixon snort at something Coach said a few times.

Dani is sitting on the bench watching practice today, and I can feel her attention mostly on me. Dixon is a real idiot for entertaining her because she's only out to get me. She wants me and always has. She's like a rabid squirrel chasing a nut. My fucking nuts. She's been bringing him his Gatorade or handing him a towel, and the whole time, I'm growing more and more heated. He came for me last night, not her. That's the only thought keeping me sane right now.

"Fuck this!" Coach throws down his clipboard when Dixon literally skips and jumps around the useless guys on the field. "Go to your rooms! Use the gym!"

Dixon storms off the field, and I look at Dani with my brow raised. Of course, her eyes are already on me. "Shouldn't you go check up on Daddy?"

"My man needs me," she shrugs and tosses me a smirk.

"Your man?" I laugh heartily and shake my head. "Girl, I see what you're doing." I lick my lips slowly and watch as she stares transfixed. "Like I said, I see what you're doing."

I hear her growl behind me as I grab my helmet off the bench and head inside behind Coach. What the fuck does she mean 'her man?' My fingers clench around the helmet's cage, and my teeth practically crack as I grind them. She better watch her attitude. Maybe I need to show her a thing or two about her *man*.

I hate locker rooms in other stadiums; they fucking suck, they just aren't home. I grab a quick shower and get the fuck out of there before I have to see Dixon and Dani together again. I don't think I could refrain from shooting them this time. Once we're dropped back at the hotel, I hit the weight room. I'm tired, but a nap won't do shit for me now. Regardless, sleep is hard to come by at the moment.

Jameson and Ortiz show up around an hour later, both looking like death and guilt raging in their eyes.

"Coach is fucking pissed," Jameson mutters as he sits on the weight bench.

"Naturally," I snicker. "You looked like a pair of dogs chasing your tails out there."

"Looked like Dani hooked herself another rookie last night," Ortiz says as he rubs his temples.

See what I mean? She's the team pass-around, and we all know it. Fuck, we all rode that ride. Dixon was supposed to be different. I saw how he avoided her, and I didn't think he was one she could get to. Goes to show that every man is weak for pussy.

"He'll learn," I shrug.

We are dragging ass and down by two touchdowns in the fourth. Dixon and I are trying our best, but it's not enough. We're going to fucking lose to Cincinnati. I don't care how much Coach wants to rag on us, he should've realized what that gala would be like. Open bar with unlimited booze and a bunch of guys wanting a good time equals hangovers.

"Fuck!" Dixon curses as we gather around Zeal to hear our final play. He's tired, and I know how he feels because I am just as dead. Zeal sees it when he looks at the both of us.

"I want to win," he starts, looking around into all of our faces. "But I know when I'm kicking a dead fucking dog."

The guys look guilty, but they also look really damn green in the face. Even I know this game is done. So do the Cincinnati fans who are here, screaming in victory. I don't think I have another run in me, and when I look at Dixon, his face tells me he feels the same.

Zeal tells us a play that fakes out throwing me the ball, and instead, he'll throw to Dixon. It's tricky, but if done right, sometimes it can be pulled off. I want to disagree, to tell him that the other team knows we've been relying on North this whole game, so why would we switch that up now? I don't though because I'm tired, and arguing about the final play is energy I can put into winning this game.

Maybe it's because my eye follows North, or maybe it's like I thought, and they just know that Dixon will be the one to run that ball, but they crowd him. Zeal has no other choice but to throw it to me, and I know without a doubt, I won't get far. The defensemen are closing in on me, so as soon as I have the ball, I'm running. I try avoiding the defense, running around them and then turning back, but I waste too much time. The whistle blows when I am twenty yards from the end zone. Game lost.

Dixon storms into the locker room, throwing his helmet into

the wall and cursing loudly. It should've been an easy game to win, yet we threw it away. I feel his anger. He rips his uniform off, and I lean against the locker watching him, he's hot when he's this worked up. He curses again as he heads to the showers, the rest of us remaining silent. I can feel the shame pouring from the guys, and I feel the need to up the morale.

"It's one game, guys," I clap my hands. "We're better than we were last year. Let's not have this game hover over us. We'll get the next one."

Zeal tosses me an appreciative look, and the guys all get up, making their way to the showers. He lingers, waiting for the last one to shuffle in. Then he turns to look at me.

"Thank you for that. I know I should be saying it, but fuck…" his hand drags through his hair. "I'm fucking ashamed too."

"You played well," I shrug. "I didn't see you pounding them back last night."

"I should've stopped them last night." He claps me on the back and goes for the shower. "Thanks again."

I watch as he bypasses an angry Dixon coming back into the room, his body dripping wet. My dick perks up, and I groan into my fist as I stick my head in the locker. I have seen hundreds of naked guys, but I've never had a reaction so primal, so damn visceral.

"Fucking bullshit," he mutters, and I can hear the rustling of clothes as he changes.

"We can't win them all," I say without looking at him, knowing the temptation would be too much.

"Sure, we can," he growls and slams the locker.

He brushes by me, and I turn to watch as he leaves the locker room, throwing open the door with force. We're getting on the bus from here and heading back to Buffalo. He better be on that bus.

CHAPTER TWENTY

Dixon

"Do you want to ride with me, hot stuff?" Dani calls out, and I cringe. I like her, but she's becoming clingy, and I haven't made any promises to her.

"Nah." I turn and look at her. "I should stay with the team. We're all feeling a bit down."

"Right." She looks disappointed, and I stuff down the frustration. I know I'm reacting like this because my emotions are still running high from our loss.

"I'll see you later." I give her a nod.

I turn, but she suddenly appears in front of me and wraps her arms around my neck. "I had a good time last night." I open my mouth to speak, but her lips press into mine, and her tongue jams inside. It's a weird kiss, a little too forceful and a lot fucking strange.

I hear a snort behind me and break the kiss—if you want to call it that—to look over my shoulder. Sebastian walks by with a small smirk on his face, and all I can see is both of us in the bathroom, with my cum on his hand. I look down into Dani's face and see her eyes trailing him as well, probably with similar thoughts as mine. It dawns on me then… She did this so Sebastian would see. Is there something she knows about him and me? My heart thunders in my chest, and I can feel my mouth go dry in utter fear. Was she awake last night?

We both watch him as he walks to the bus, and when he gets to the door, he tosses us a wink. She quickly turns back around, and I see the blush on her cheeks. She wants him. She's with me and kissing on me to make him jealous. But why? She knows he's married. Not that I can say much. I know he's married too, yet that didn't stop me last night. It didn't stop either of us. I should be hurt that she's using me to get to him, but instead, I'm thinking maybe I can pull the same shit, only my intentions would be to turn him away. If he thinks I'm dating someone and if it looks serious, he'll know he doesn't stand a chance.

"How about dinner tomorrow night?" I ask her, and her eyes brighten.

"Sure."

I lean down and kiss her softly. "See you then."

I step up into the bus and see Sebastian sitting at the far back, his hoodie obscuring his face. I like the back too, always have, and I'm not letting him take that from me either. I walk down the aisle, and he looks up, his golden eyes twinkling with humor. I sit in the row in front of him and lean my head back, closing my eyes. I'm so tired, and my body feels drained. I need rest. The physical exertion and the emotional drain are becoming too much.

The seat beside me dips, and I know without even looking that it's him. His scent is as familiar to me as my own, but I keep still, my eyes remaining shut. He doesn't say anything either. Once everyone gets on the bus, I steal a look at him from the corner of my eye. His head is also back, and he has earbuds in his ears. I don't know how—maybe he senses my watching him—but without looking at me, he takes an earbud out and offers it to me. I take it and pop it in my ear, curious to find out what he listens to. I'm shocked when I hear the subtle notes of a classical symphony. I turn to look at him and find him smirking, like he knew I'd be fucking shocked.

Fingers brush along my cheek and down my neck, the calloused tips making me shudder. I slowly wake up, and the sound of the orchestra floods my senses once again. I turn my face, and Sebastian is right there, so close. I look down to his lips, watching as they turn up in the corners as I lick my own.

"Watch it, North," he whispers. "People might see."

I doubt it. The high seat back provides cover, and both of us are slouched down even farther. So without much thought and with my senses still half asleep, I lean in the few inches that separate us. I press my lips to his, softly, and nip his bottom lip with my teeth. His hand lands on my cheek and pulls me in closer, his tongue licking across the seam. I open for him, and our tongues glide against each other's, the sensuality of the kiss taking my breath away.

"Fuck, North," he whispers against my mouth. "What the fuck are you doing to me?" He grabs my hand and places it on his cock. He's hard and pulsing, just as I am.

I pull away and let my head fall back against the seat. "I don't even know," I answer truthfully and close my eyes.

I don't sleep for the rest of the trip, but I keep my eyes closed. I don't know what's happening with us, and the constant feel of his heat beside me is driving me insane. I need to get out of this confined space so I can think clearly once again.

It's about an hour later when we're pulling up to the convention center. Most of our vehicles are still parked in the lot, so everyone begins to file out. We stay in our seats and wait, Sebastian's eyes flicking across my face. His phone rings then, forcing him out of his head, and he picks it up.

"What's up?" He's still watching me, but a crease appears between his brows. "And the father?" I can tell he's talking to a guy as I stand up out of my seat, needing to get the fuck off this bus. "Thanks, man. Talk soon."

I'm halfway down the center aisle when I feel him close at my back. His scent and the temperature of his body are seared into my brain; I'd know him anywhere without even having to look.

"You should come over," he says into my ear, and I stop walking. He steps closer, his chest brushing my back, and I shudder at the proximity. "We can go for a jog or something."

Or something. I want to say yes, my mouth opens with the word about to spill out, but I stop it just in time. I'm not ready, and I don't think I ever will be. He has a damn wife.

"I'm tired," I say and continue walking.

"Tomorrow night," he suggests, and I look at him over my shoulder.

"I can't. I have a date."

"With her." He rolls his eyes, and I step down from the bus.

I don't answer him because it wasn't a question, and I don't owe him an explanation. Although I do like the fact that he's fuming about it. He brushes past me and grabs his bag off the ground, stalking to his vehicle. I watch as his ass bunches when he steps, his track pants so thin, they're molding to his muscular legs perfectly. I shake myself out of it and walk to my car, my thoughts a jumbled mess. I want Sebastian, there's no denying it. Yet I also want a normal life. For me and how I was raised, being gay isn't normal. It won't be accepted, and I can't give my mother that stress on top of everything else.

I can't be gay, though. It's just one man; I haven't found any others attractive. So I'm straight but lusting after one guy. I don't know what any of it means, and it's so exhausting to always swallow down my needs, so naturally, it boils over sometimes. Like on the bus when

I kissed him. I can't let it go further. He's married, and I know there's no future there. It would all be a waste of time and energy. I can't deny, though … in those moments, when it's just him and me, there's no worry or confusion, and that's why I forget this is just a dead end.

My phone rings, and I see my mother on the screen. I release all thoughts of Sebastian and pick up the phone, preparing for what I know will be bad news.

"Hey, Ma."

"Sorry about your game, Dixon. Was it because of me telling you about your brother?" She sounds worried, and I don't want her to be.

"No, Ma, just a bad day. Where's Daniel?" I ask her.

"Don't worry about that, son." I can hear the worry in her tone.

"Ma, I will come there if I don't hear what's going on," I warn her, and she huffs into the phone.

"He's been gone for a week."

"What?" I sit up. "Like missing?"

"No, people see him around, but he's running with those boys back in our old neighborhood. He doesn't like the new house."

"Then we need to consider a bootcamp or something like that." I exhale in irritation. "His future is flushing down the drain."

"Yes," she sniffs, and her voice shakes. "You're right."

"I'll figure something out, and I'll be home in a few days," I tell her.

"Your career is important, Dixon," she says sternly.

"It was always to make our lives better. What's the point if I have all this money and no family to give it to?"

"One day, you will have a family of your own," she explains.

In that moment, Sebastian's face floats through my mind, and I feel my throat close. I may never have a family of my own.

"I will have enough for that too," I assure her. "I'll call you tomorrow."

My next call is to my college coach. He runs a camp for troubled teens, and I know if there is anyone who can help me, it'll be him. It would mean sending Danny to a whole other state, but maybe that's exactly what he needs. After an hour of sitting in my car, I have a plan, and now all I have to do is execute it. That means going home, back to my old hood and finding Danny, pushing through a group of hardened individuals to get to him.

It's a risk, but he's my family, and he's worth it. I can't let him become another statistic.

Sebastian

I have his number. I found it in the directory in Coach's office, and I've been staring at it for over a day. Coach is punishing us for our loss by giving us brutal practices early every morning, and it's not so bad, only Dixon hasn't been to them. He missed yesterday and today, prompting me to steal his number. Now that I have it, I don't know what to do with it. When Zeal asked Coach where he was, we were all told that Dixon was off, and he'd be back in a few days, nothing else. Is he sick? Is his mom sick?

I found out that she's a single mother who struggled with three jobs to raise her sons. That's how a mother should be, and it explains the drive in Dixon to overcome his environment, something I know all too well. But it also explains his younger brother and the acceptance he's craving by joining a gang. With a mother who was rarely home and a brother working constantly to be great, I bet he was lonely. Probably still is, and I would assume seeing his brother accomplish his goals is not working in his favor, especially if maybe he doesn't share the same talents. I don't know the story, so a lot of this is assumption, but I can imagine his pain. I had it too. My boys became my family, and yes, my life can get crazy, but I'm happy.

Maybe there was an emergency with his brother, and if so, I'm sure I can get that info. I call up Delano and bark some orders for him to get me what I need to know, telling him he has two hours to do it. Then I grab my bag and leave the locker room. I don't get far when I smell her, and trust me, I know her scent because she wears so much of it.

"How's your wife?"

"Where's your man?" I smirk at Dani and walk by.

"He's dealing with some family bullshit right now." Her voice is taunting and smug. "We talk every night."

They talk every night? He's really getting serious with her after everything we've done? I know she's saying it hoping to make me jealous of *him*, but it's the damn opposite. I'm jealous she gets to talk to him when that's all I've wanted the past few days. He feels that comfortable spilling about his family to her? That's where they're at right now? Great.

I don't bother giving her any more of my time, and the sound of her chuckle behind me only has me more heated. I'm fucking calling his ass when I get home.

CHAPTER TWENTY-ONE

Dixon

My Bluetooth rings throughout the interior of my car and I groan when I see it's an unknown number. After the last few days, there's not much more I can deal with, so if this is another one of Danny's 'friends' calling to threaten me, I will turn around and shoot that whole neighborhood up. Fuck a career.

"Hello," I answer, my irritation evident.

"Where the fuck are you?" When his voice fills the car, I suppress a moan at how fast my cock fills at the sound of it.

"Sebastian—"

"You spoke to her, but you couldn't fucking call me?" he cuts me off.

"Spoke to who?" I don't know what the fuck he's talking about. "And I don't have your number, asshole."

"Dani, and I don't want to hear your excuses."

I haven't spoken to Dani since before I left, and that was to tell her we couldn't go out as planned.

"Dani? I haven't spoken to Dani," I snap.

"Then how'd she know you were with your family? Don't fucking lie to me." Fuck, the gravelly tone to his voice has my cock jerking in my pants.

"Probably from her father?" I retort, and he goes quiet on the other end. "Why is Dani telling you she's talking to me?" I muse out loud.

"Because she wants my dick and thinks it's making me jealous."

"You must think everyone wants your dick, huh?" I snort.

"Do you want my dick, Dixon?" His voice drops, and my heart goes with it. "Because I want to give you my dick. Better yet, get the fuck home so I can beat you with this fucking dick."

I think I just came in my pants. His tone and those demands … beat me with his dick he says. That shouldn't sound appealing, right?

"You've gone quiet." Amusement laces his voice. "You're thinking about it, aren't you? Come over here, and I'll give you the real thing, no more thinking about shit."

"You leave your wife or something?" I throw back as soon as I bring myself under control.

"I'll never leave my wife." There. He said it, and maybe that's exactly what I needed to hear.

"I'll see you at practice tomorrow," I say before hanging up on him.

I want to see Sebastian. I've thought of him plenty over the last few days, but he's intense, and I can't handle anything else right now. I'm failing my brother, and I don't think I can pull him back from the life he's living. He's hoping to initiate soon and refuses to come home. He says he has a new family now, and I don't know how to tell my mother without feeling like I failed her too.

He looks different now, and he speaks differently. He's not the

nd. That's exactly what I did… I left him behind, so he

mily to fill the void. I didn't think it was necessary to

as still here and that all the money I was making was for them. Now it's too late.

My fist hits the wheel as I scream, my vision blurring as my eyes fill up. How the fuck do I get him out? I don't know enough about gang life to even figure this out on my own, and I've never been close to anyone in a gang either. That's when Sebastian slams back into my head. Could he somehow help me? Do I want to confide in him? Do I have a damn choice?

I pull onto my driveway and rest my forehead on the wheel. I'm so fucking lost. I feel like I have the weight of a father's responsibility on my shoulders, and I don't know how to carry it. No matter how strong I am, I'm crumbling beneath it, and the people closest to me are the ones getting crushed. I have pride, and I want to be able to do it all on my own, but I'm failing.

I get out of my car and walk inside my house, hoping with the insane part of my brain that Sebastian will somehow be in here, ready to tear me apart. Of course, he isn't. I'm alone and forced to face my problems. My mistakes are heavy, and my accolades are light, redemption seeming impossible. Danny and I were supposed to be all we had, best friends and brothers. I failed because I thought he was strong enough to be alone while I sorted us out, and that's on me. I feel the cool air touch the moisture on my cheeks, sobbing as I step into my empty house, finally letting loose the torrent of pain inside of me.

The amount of stress and pain I've endured and put my body through over the years, it feels like it was all for nothing right now. The nights I ran my ass off around a track and the days I spent throwing a ball until my shoulders ached, all for nothing. I love football, but it was never a passion. I did it because of the privileges that came with it. I made it my mission to help my family, and football was the key to that. I fucking failed.

I no longer want to get up in the morning and go to the

stadium, it feels like a waste of time. I feel like I need to move my back to Baltimore and find a way to get my brother out of the mess he's in, then take care of my mom. She's aged in the few months I've been gone, and even though she's only working one job now, she looks more tired than she ever did. She's worried about her baby, and that's something I will never forgive myself for. She couldn't do it on her own, and I knew that, but I still went chasing after the American dream, thinking my ass deserved it.

With lead feet and a heavy heart, I shuffle to my bedroom. I pull my clothes off and crawl into bed, the blankets cool. I pull out my phone and pull up Danny's number. He rarely responds to Ma or me, but I'm sending him a message anyway.

I love you no matter what, you're my brother.

Sebastian

It's nearly five o'clock in the morning, and my ass is resting against the stadium's brick as I wait for him. I think I've lost my damn mind, but I feel like something's really wrong, and Dixon has no one. I want him to know as fucked-up as we are and after everything that's happened between us, he at least has me. He doesn't want anything to do with me until I leave my wife, but he can't help himself when we're alone, and I need to help him stop burying us.

Finally, his car comes into the parking lot, and he parks in the same spot as always, opening the door. He gets out and stands still, his shoulders slumping forward. I can see the despair pouring off him, and my heart begins to pound. What happened while he was away? I know the brother is fine, my source said as much, and his mother is now in a safer neighborhood. What happened to make him look that sad? He walks toward the entrance, never seeing me and keeping his head down. When he reaches for the door, I grab his wrist, and he looks at me, shocked.

"Let's go for a walk," I gesture around the building, but he stays rooted in place. "Please?"

"For what, Sebastian?" Even his voice sounds ladened down with sadness.

"Just to talk."

"I don't want to talk," he shakes his head.

The door opens then, and Dani sticks her head out. She's never here this early. She steps out and reaches her hand out to brush his cheek, his jaw clenching in response.

"Hey, baby," she croons.

He doesn't say anything but allows her to come all the way out and wrap her arms around his neck. She kisses his cheek, and I clench my fists to stop myself from tearing her off him. Finally, as she buries her head into his chest, her face turning to the side, she sees me.

"Oh!" she exclaims and straightens up. "Sebastian, I didn't see you there."

"I bet you didn't," I sneer sarcastically.

"Come on, Dix." She grabs his hand and tugs him behind her. "Dad wants to have a word with you." Did she call him Dix? That's just weird.

He doesn't give me a second glance as he follows her inside, and I watch as the door shuts behind them. I know she doesn't want him, and all of this is to make me jealous. Stupid, dirty whore. She's interfering with *Dix* and me, pouring gas on an already raging inferno, and she's about to be incinerated. I would never lay my hands on a woman, but she's forcing my hand, and I need to expose her for exactly what she is.

"Bro, let's hit up Sky Lounge tonight," Jameson says as we finish up our showers.

"Fuck yes," Ortiz agrees.

I shrug my shoulders, not really caring what we do, my mind not on the conversation. Practice was shit today, and Dixon was out of it, kind of like he didn't really want to be there. His drive is gone, that swagger he had when he walked on the field that first time is gone, and he looked fucking miserable.

"Did y'all say Sky Lounge?" Zeal grins as he gets out of his shower.

"Yeah," Jameson holds out his fist and Zeal bumps it with his own. "Let's get this team's morale back up with some drinks and titties."

I roll my eyes, but Zeal laughs and nods. "Sounds good. I'll let everyone know."

As I walk back out to my locker, I see the sauna light on. I want to go in there. I want to force him to talk to me, but I can't do that. It's time he comes to me on his own. I can't always be there, waiting for him to do it. If he wants to stick his dick inside Dani, then I'll stand back and let him do that, watching for the perfect moment to rip the rug out from under them. No matter how hard he tries to ignore what he feels for me, it'll always resurface, and when that happens, I'll be there.

I quickly change and watch as Zeal opens the sauna door. I can't help but wonder if he was hoping it was me. Zeal yells out the plans for later tonight to him, and when he comes back out with a smirk, my heart races, knowing Dixon is coming. I can't help but remember the last time we were at the club and what went down between us in that bathroom. The tension was so thick, even then, and the hatred only masked the feelings brewing underneath. It'll be interesting to be back in that setting but with our emotions more tumultuous and the hatred waning.

After I get home, I sit at my table, staring at the lines I've cut in front of me. My head is killing me, so I know I need it, but something is nagging at me. This last concussion has been different than the last few, and I'm still not fully recovered.

The headaches are constant, some less severe than others, and the dizzying spells aren't going away. If I go to a doctor about it, Coach will pull me, and I can't have that happen. I can't fuck up my career because my head isn't right. I need to provide for my family. I snort the first line and groan as immediate bliss permeates my head, the thudding of my brain slowing. I take the next line then sit back, absorbing the relief of having no pain.

My doorbell rings, pulling me out of my trance, and I yell out for them to come in. Jameson and Ortiz are loud the second the door opens, but it doesn't bother me now that my headache is gone, and I'm grinning when I see two large blunts in Ortiz's hands.

"Yes," I reach for one.

"Heads up," Jameson cuts in looking serious. "I heard a piss test is coming up this week."

"Get us clean piss," I shrug.

"I'm on it," Ortiz nods.

Listen, I get the need to knock out performance enhancing drugs, and I agree eliminating them makes the game fair, but coke isn't gonna do shit for the talent I already possess. Piss tests can fucking suck my dick.

"I've noticed Rookie is a bit off lately," Ortiz beams at me. "What did you do to him?"

I can't explain the sudden rush of anger, and it takes me a minute to tamper it down, my muscles trembling from the force.

"I haven't had anything to do with the bitch," I say through my teeth as I light the blunt.

"He was off for a few days, and when he came back, he looked like shit," Jameson chimes in.

"Who cares?" I grind out, smoking the J.

"We thought you were up to something…" Ortiz continues, "we saw you sitting beside him on the ride back from Cincinnati."

"I like making him uncomfortable." Not a damn lie.

We leave after we smoke, and Jameson and Ortiz do a few lines. I wonder if that waitress is working tonight. How fast can I piss off Dixon by having her like putty in my lap again? Or would he see an opportunity he'd want to join in on? The thought of us sharing a female is not as appealing as I thought it would be. I want him to myself, and after I get it, then he can go back to fucking females.

There is a line outside the club that runs along the front of the building and curves around to the side. Thankfully, we don't stand in that shit. As soon as the bouncer sees us, his fist is out, and the rope is opened, each of us pounding our fists to his. The place is packed, and the women are eyeing us closely. We look like sex on wealthy sticks... Our big, athletic bodies draped in designer names, iced out chains gleaming from our necks, and pockets fat with bills.

Jameson and Ortiz grab a group of girls to follow us to the back, and I notice one eyeing me down. She's sweet looking with an innocent flare to her. I like that. She has long braided hair, and her skin is ebony, popping against the ivory, lace dress she's wearing. We head to the VIP, and the rope is lifted, the music dropping a few notches. The room is already filled with the team and the women they've grabbed off the floor. I head straight for the bar, and I'm floored when I see Dani there, tucked under Dixon's arm. She looks content and secure as she runs her hand along his torso while he's chatting up Zeal.

"Avando!" Dex Carver comes up behind me, clapping me on the back. "Shots?"

I startle out of my thoughts and smirk when both Dixon and Dani look our way. "Fuck yeah."

Dani gives me a smug once-over, and Dixon barely spares me a glance. I can already see how this night is going to go down. I follow Dex to the bar, and he orders two shots of tequila. My stomach flips as the golden liquid pours. I can feel Dani's eyes on me as I tip back the glass and take the shot, signaling the bartender for another round.

"Yes!" Dex exclaims. "I love when Avando comes out to play." You bet your fucking ass I'm ready to play.

I want to crush Dani's perfect bubble about Dixon, and I know I can, it's just going to take some time. Unfortunately for her, I've got all the damn time in the world, and he's with me during most of his days. I can feel a plan forming in my mind, but it won't work unless I have Dixon trusting me, it'll take a lot of work getting to that point, especially after everything I've done. How do I make him see I only want what's best for him?

I head to the table with Jameson, Ortiz, and the ladies they grabbed on the way in, the sweet one eyeing me over her drink, her gorgeous brown eyes shining with interest. I can start on Dixon tonight, fan the flames I know are building inside of him, and help him see what he genuinely wants. I hold my hand out for the girl, and when she obliges, placing her hand in mine, I pull her to her feet.

"Name?" I breathe into her ear, and her shudder has me chuckling.

"Nicole."

I wrap my arm around her waist, pulling her in closer while keeping my mouth to her ear, "do you dance, Nicole?"

She nods, and I lead her into the middle of the room just as *Too Close* by Next starts playing. *Too perfect.* I grind my pelvis into hers, and delight runs through me when she matches me move for move. My hand moves to her ass, and I grip it in my palm, moving against her harder. She looks up at me almost shyly, and I look down at her, amused. She is exquisite.

After our dance, I head to the bar to grab us drinks. When

Dixon appears at my side, I hide my grin in my hand and ignore him. I can feel his eyes on me. When the bartender steps up, I ask for two beers.

"I wonder how the last chick you were here with would feel about seeing that display." He sounds jealous, and it makes my heart soar.

"She could join if she wants." I flash him a smile and grab the beers. The scowl on his face has me laughing as I walk back to the table.

I will have him eating out of my hand in no time.

CHAPTER TWENTY-TWO

We're having a surprise piss test today.

I've done this plenty of times but never hungover and pissed off. Last night was a shitshow. Watching Sebastian grind on some female was affecting me more than it should. It still fucking is because he's sitting at the far corner of the locker room with a satisfied look on his face, and I want to punch it off. He took her home last night. I watched them leave together, and now he looks like she gave him exactly what he's been looking for.

This is just crazy. Why the fuck do I even care? Maybe because I still haven't taken Dani home, and the fact that he can fuck any chick is grating on my nerves. I should be able to as well. Maybe it's time I did. Dani has been practically begging me to fuck her, but I have been putting it off due to some misplaced sense of guilt. What the fuck do I have to be guilty about? I know my sexuality, and even though Sebastian wants to convince me otherwise, I love women.

I pull out my phone as I wait for everyone to piss in a cup and text Dani. I ask her if she's free tonight, and when she instantly replies yes, I tell her to pack a bag. This confusing relationship with Sebastian stops today. I'm ready to move on. I have to move on. I breathe out the frustration and wait for Coach to finish up with the testing. I'm tired, and I want to get the fuck out of here.

Coach releases us all with clean tests, and I find Dani in the corridor, a small smile on her face. She's beautiful, knows about football, and she cares about me. It's time I take this up a notch. I tug on her shirt and chuckle when she falls into my chest, a look of surprise on her face. I lean down and kiss her thoroughly, her moan betraying how turned on she is. I can do this… She's perfect and everything I've been looking for. I hear a snort behind me, and I know it's him, but I don't let it affect me. He can snort all he wants. This is happening, and the push and pull with him is ending.

With my arm around Dani's shoulders, I lead her outside to my car and press her up against it with my pelvis. It's getting colder here in Buffalo as fall merges into winter, the cold air making her nose red. I kiss it softly, and she tips her head back, giving me a sweet smile. I can feel the potential we could have, but I can't deny something is missing, and it's not just on my side. I know it could probably be rectified. With a bit more attention, our affection will grow too.

"This week you're playing the Cowboys, right?" she asks as she shivers with the cold breeze.

"Yeah," I nod.

"I've watched your practices, and you guys are strong. You've made us stronger, Dixon."

I kiss her forehead then open the door for her to sit inside, closing it gently behind her. Then I cross around to the driver's side, feeling eyes on me the whole way and knowing exactly who it is. I look up at him standing on the steps only to see he's not watching me at all. Instead, his eyes are on Dani. I get inside and find her staring right back at him, a hint of a smirk on her lips. I don't know exactly what went down, but I can see it's not completely over between them, and I can't seem to muster up an ounce of concern. Fuck, I should be concerned, right? I want a relationship with her, so always finding them watching each other should be bothersome, right?

When we get to my house, she steps inside, looking around. "You need to decorate."

"I don't know how long I'll be here." I close the front door. "I'm trying to convince Ma and Danny to come live with me, and when they agree, I'll have to find something bigger."

"Why don't they want to come?" She looks at me with her brow raised.

I like her, but not enough to tell her my family issues yet. "Long story."

She accepts my explanation for what it is, and we settle in to watch a movie, her eyes constantly moving to my face. I feel like it's now or never to make a move, this one instant will determine where we're going, and I'm ready. I mute the TV and turn to look at her, licking my lips as she watches. I lean in and kiss her, her lips feeling small and timid. I need to give myself a mental shake to stop myself from imagining him. I lock his image away and deepen the kiss, pulling her onto my lap. She straddles my hips and slowly begins to grind down, her hands landing on my chest.

We're going through the motions, but the passion isn't there; the heat that feels so intense and the combustion that teeters just along the edge is missing. It's just not there, and my traitor cock agrees as it lays flaccid against my thigh. I don't want to hurt her, but I can't see this going any further if I don't take it up a notch. I stand with her in my arms, and she wraps her legs around my waist, her mouth still on mine. I settle her on my small kitchen table, her ass right at the edge then guide her to her back with my hand at the center of her chest. Her heart isn't racing, and her breath isn't getting lodged in her throat, all sure signs of what's missing. But I ignore it, desperate to get over him and get her under me.

I pull her pants off, taking her panties with them to stare down into her pink folds. Nothing. My dick doesn't even twitch, and my heart doesn't accelerate. Again, I push down the thoughts and slip my hands under her ass, lifting her slightly off the table. My tongue swipes along her center, and she moans with the motion, finally getting into it. I look up and find her eyes shut, and I wonder if she's imagining Sebastian between her legs. Just the thought of him being here as I eat her out, watching as rage courses through him and his eyes alight with jealousy, has my dick hard in record time.

"Fuck me," she groans. "Fuck me so hard."

I want to tell her to say my name but decide against it, not wanting her voice to discourage my cock further, instead imagining Sebastian asking me the same thing … his legs open and his cock hard against his lower stomach, begging me to fuck him. I haul down my pants in the front, just enough to free my cock, and at the last minute, I remember a condom. That's not something I want to forget. Luckily, I have one in my wallet in my pants, so I grab it and roll it on. Then I'm pushing it inside her. The feel of her warmth, her writhing beneath me, and how tight she is has me groaning.

I spread her ass cheeks wider, and instead of looking up into her face, I watch as my cock disappears inside her, over and over. I imagine this is what it would be like with Sebastian, his ass so damn tight and his moans a mix of pleasure and pain.

"Play with yourself," I grunt out as I thrust harder into her, her walls clenching the second her fingers land on her clit.

"You feel so good," she says as she continues to furiously circle her clit. I'm softening with her words, so I reach up, placing my hand over her mouth.

I imagine it's Sebastian I'm shutting up, and I'm dominating him, forcing him to take my cock. My balls clench, and my breath gets caught in my chest just as her walls squeeze me, milking the cum from my cock. I come hard as she continues pulsing, her screams muffled behind my hand, and Sebastian laying in her place in my mind. Guilt begins to burn its way throughout me, and I chance a glance at her as I slowly lift my hand off her mouth. Her eyes are on the ceiling. She's not here with me either. The guilt disappears, and I can't help but wonder… Was she imagining the same person I was?

Sebastian

I want to call him. I want to disturb whatever the fuck they're doing, and I want to chase her out of his house. I'm going wild with all the shit I'm imagining them doing and I slam my fist through the wall again. Why is he taking it this far? Is he that determined to erase me? Just as I'm about to punch another hole, my phone rings, and my heart soars with hope that it might be him. Maybe he realized his feelings for her aren't there, and it's me he wants instead.

When I see Delano's name, I almost chuck the phone at the wall, taking two deep breaths to calm myself down.

"Yeah," I grit out as I answer the phone.

"Daniel North fucked-up."

I straighten at his words. "Go on."

"He's on the run for botching his initiation," he continues. "He didn't kill his target."

All gangs are different, but what they have in common is an initiation. Some kill, some rape, and some just take an oath. I had to kill, but luckily, my target deserved it. But some don't, they can be random picks.

"Any idea where he is?" I ask.

"Nah, the second we find out, I'd say they will too. He'd be smart to leave the state and not come back."

Leave the state, like maybe show up at his brother's place, potentially putting him at risk.

"Keep an ear out, and the second you hear anything, you call me," I bark out.

"You got it," he says and hangs up the phone.

I have to go keep an eye on Dixon's house. He's not a gangbanger. He wouldn't know the first thing about protecting himself. He keeps his doors unlocked, and that's just begging to be killed. I rush out of my house and jump in my Hummer, my tires burning as I speed out of my driveway. The kid could be on his way here right now, and his gang could be on his tail. I get to Dixon's house and exhale the tension when I see it's quiet, a single light on downstairs. His TV room, if I remember correctly.

I turn off the engine and settle into my seat, waiting for any disturbance. I wonder if Dani is in there still. I bet she's sunk her claws in a bit deeper, and it's going to hurt that much more when I have to rip them the fuck out. I'm about to doze off when I see the porch light come on and the front door open, making me quickly slouch down. He knows what I drive, so if he looks up the street, he'll see me here. Dani appears first, and she pulls a bag higher up on her shoulder, her face looking indifferent. Then Dixon is behind her, leaning on the door frame and smiling down at her. If she has a bag, why isn't she staying over?

She reaches up and kisses his cheek, like you'd do for an aunt or uncle, then she walks to the street, an idling cab waiting at the curb. Why isn't he driving her home? Did they fight?

They don't look like they've been intimate, and the thought cools the rage threatening to explode. Maybe I still occupy his mind. She waves and gets into the cab, then Dixon disappears into his house. I settle in and wait it out. If his brother shows up here, I may just kill the little shit myself.

I startle when I hear the slamming of a car door and groan when I realize I fell asleep. I watch as Dixon starts his car and pulls out of the driveway, heading toward the stadium. I look at the dashboard and see it's four in the morning, meaning I slept for one damn hour. I sit up and pull away from the curb, following behind him at a far enough distance. I'm going to die during practice today, and we have a game tomorrow night.

There's no way I can keep an eye on his house every night like this. I'll be shit on the field, and Coach will pull me. How the fuck is this going to work? If the kid was coming here, he'd either already be on his way or here already, so that means I have to stake out the house this week. The stadium comes into view, and I see Dixon walking up to the entrance, his head hanging. Something is fucking wrong. I grab my extra practice bag that I keep in the Hummer and follow behind him. The locker room is empty save for the two of us, and I watch as he throws on his running shoes, Looks like he plans to keep running laps like he does every day before practice.

"You're quiet," I murmur as I begin to tape my hands. May as well do a bit of weight training this morning.

"I don't have anything to say," he replies.

"I saw you take Dani home. Shouldn't you be in a better mood?"

"Why? Because we fucked?" he chuckles sarcastically. "Some things sex can't fix."

My stomach burns with jealousy. Scorching liquid moves up to my chest, and I can't hold in the growl that escapes. "You fucked her."

He finally looks up at me, his brow raised. "That's what generally happens when you date someone."

"Date?"

"Yeah, seeing someone exclusively on a regular basis," he retorts and stands from the bench.

"I feel sorry for you if you think she's seeing you because she actually likes you," I snort, and he turns to look at me. "Tell me…

While you were fucking her, did she look at you?"

He flies forward and shoves me into the row of lockers, his forearm pressing on my throat. "Stop fucking talking."

"She didn't, did she?" I continue to taunt him.

He pushes off me and slaps his hand against the metal behind me. "You're jealous, and you look stupid for it," he sneers and heads out onto the field.

I am boiling with jealousy, and I'm about ready to strangle Dani. I rest my head back against the cool metal and breathe., I have a plan. I can't let my anger ruin it because it'll need perfect execution. And by the end of it all, Dixon will realize who it is he wants.

CHAPTER TWENTY-THREE

It's been a few days, and little North hasn't shown up at Dixon's house. Meanwhile, Dixon has been growing quieter. He doesn't interact too much with the team, and he looks like he doesn't sleep. I've been watching the house, and Dani comes over every night, but she never stays. It doesn't make the anger any less, and every time she steps up into his house, I can feel my jealousy grow. I'm a damn mess, but I think hiding his feelings is taking a toll on him. Good.

It's game day, and that means light practice on plays we'll be using later then some weight training. I'm fucking exhausted, but I need to push through for the team. We've been on a winning streak, and even though I hate to admit it, Dixon has been a huge help with that. He's fierce out on the field, and he takes no prisoners. He has a single goal, and he pushes himself until he gets it.

Dani has been lingering around us all day, her cloying perfume and her arrogant face starting to make me nauseated. The one thing that's holding me back from flipping my shit is the fact that Dixon is just as distant with her. He doesn't smile while she talks, and his body language is closed off. Just like he is with me, which gives me some comfort. She still hasn't won him over completely, and that means I still have a chance at breaking them up without losing him in the process.

I say all this, but in reality, I don't know what the fuck I want from him. I'm not looking for a relationship, I have one, and besides, I'm not going to be with a man. But I want to experiment and work through my sexual feelings for him … the same feelings he has for me. No amount of ignoring or pushing them away will change that. We have this connection, and ignoring it will only fan the flame.

Am I selfish? Fuck yes, but I always have been, and that's not changing now. I don't care if he wants a relationship. First he'll be with me, and then he can choose a woman who actually wants him. Dani is up to something, and I know it has everything to do with me. She was in love with me, and when I dropped her like a used rag, she didn't take it well. Not that I wasn't completely transparent with her. She knew the deal was to fuck until one of us didn't want to fuck anymore, and unfortunately for her, she caught feelings. Most females do. I warned her not to.

We're lining up to run out onto the field, the crowd roaring, and energy is coursing through us. Dixon is at the end of the line with Dani, and I can hear him telling her not to sit on the bench tonight, he would rather she be in the stands. She attempts to argue, but his continued silence on the matter pisses her off, and she storms off toward her father's office. I can't help but let my mouth tip up. Maybe I won't have to go through with my plan after all.

The stadium erupts into chants and screams as we circle the field, some of them calling out our numbers. It's a feeling that never grows old, no matter how long you play, and it gives us that extra bit of strength to push through to the end. I can't seem to take my eyes off Dixon as he circles the field. His hand is up waving, but his face is a mask of indifference. I don't know what's wrong with him, he never gives me the chance to find out. He's been so distant and cold.

By half time, I can feel the repercussions of lack of sleep, and my body is becoming sluggish. We're up but not by much, and Coach is looking a bit tense. We're used to losing, our initial reaction is to expect it, but with how hard we're working this year, we can start to change that. It's not changing yet, though… All of my teammates look defeated and tired, all except Dixon. He looks fucking livid. I want to ask him what the fuck is up, but I don't think I'd receive an answer.

Even behind the helmet he looks murderous, and I can't help when my dick twitches in appreciation.

Dixon

We can't find Danny.

Ma says she's called everyone, but no one has seen him. He missed his weekly call-in twice now, so it looks like I'll be heading back home after this to find him. It really pisses me off that I have to do this at all. He's nearly grown now and needs to start minding his responsibilities. At seventeen he's still a minor, so I'm having Ma sign the papers to put him in a program for troubled youth. He'll have no choice, so I can only hope he comes out of it a changed man, otherwise the consequences will be dire when he's an adult.

This game has been a blur, and even though we're up, my spirits are so damn low. Football isn't the same driving force it has been for me all these years. I can't do that if I no longer have a family who needs me to.

With half time over, we head back out to the field, and Zeal stands there with his hands on hips, ready to call the shots. I've been feeling Sebastian's eyes on me constantly, but I can't deal with him and his warped mind right now. Same with Dani. She's trying hard to be the understanding girl, but I can't help it that I don't feel a strong connection with her. I jumped into something to avoid something else, and that's my mistake to fix. I just don't know how to do it. Breaking up with her feels sudden. It's only been a couple of weeks, so saying I'm just not that into her would be rude. I want to be into her. Without a connection forming and all this stress on my shoulders, it's been hard to do that.

Zeal calls the play, and it's the same one we've been practicing all day. I could do this shit in my sleep. The whistle blows, and I'm off, my feet digging into the grass. Throughout this game, the Cowboys' defense has been trying to crowd me, but it's been to no avail. I am either too fast, or our offense takes them out. I lose my focus for one second, my eyes up on the ball sailing toward me, and just as I reach for it, a body slams into mine. The air rushes from my lungs in one fell swoop, and I'm hitting the ground hard on my knee.

The pain that rips through my leg is intense, and I scream as my vision blurs. It's the same injury I had before, so the pain is all too familiar. I wrap my hands around the knee, holding it at a bent angle. Straightening it out would be excruciating, and the tremors wracking my leg muscles are agonizing. I can't concentrate on what's going on around me, but I see two medics appear above me.

"Can you stand?" one asks, and I grit my teeth.

"Yeah." I can stand, but putting any weight on it will be impossible.

I'm hoisted up, and as soon as my toes touch the grass, the pain courses up my leg, causing me to cry out. My arms are slung over each medic, and I'm walked off the field to a roar of boos. I don't care about anything else right now aside from the fact that I am injured again, and a reinjury is always worse than the initial.

I'm laid out on a stretcher inside the locker room as the medics haul off my pants and shoes.

"It's swelling fast," one of them says. "Get an ice pack."

It's like being transported in time, back to the beginning of my third year at Clemson when I laid on another table, ice sitting on my knee.

"Dixon?" Dani's screech hits my ears, and I can't decide what's more painful. "Oh my god, are you okay?"

The fuck does it look like? I continue to stare at the ceiling and the fluorescent lights, eerily reminiscent of when I fucked her on my kitchen table, only reversed. I can see how she was distracted enough to imagine a whole new scenario as another reality plays out.

The ice pack is placed on my knee as I can hear Dani asking the medic if I hit my head, probably because I'm not answering her. I don't really care right now. I'd be happier if she just went back to wherever it was she came from, permanently. That's not nice, I know it's not, but I'm in pain, so I feel justified. I want to be left alone.

One of the medics appears over my face again, and this time I get a good look at him. He's got a thick beard on his face, but it does nothing to cover the long scar stretching from the center of his top lip and over his nose. Cleft palate.

"According to your file, this knee was injured fifteen months ago, correct?"

Before I can confirm it, Dani is whining about needing me on the field and how pissed off her father is going to be. That pretty much sums up my usefulness to her, and I can't even be mad at it… Hers is even less for me. Just pisses me off that I'm laying here again, my knee propped up to drain, and all for reasons I can't seem to remember. My body goes through degradation and stress, all for dreams I see disappearing before my eyes.

I hear the crowd outside roaring in triumph, and I know that means we won the game. I try to dig inside and feel something … pride, anything. But right now, I just want to go home to be with Ma and to find Danny.

"Where is he?" I hear Sebastian say as the doors to the locker room bang off the walls. "Dixon!" His face appears over mine. He's sweaty, and streaks of dirt line his cheeks. "Is it bad?" He looks to someone to his right.

"Looks like a strain. Hopefully it's not a tear," the medic explains. "We won't know more until the swelling is down."

"Oh, fuck. A tear? That means surgery, right?" Dani's panicked voice soars. "That's the end of this season for him."

"Will someone get this whore out of here?" Sebastian demands, and I snort, the first thing I've reacted to. He looks down into my face, and when he sees my smirk, he responds with one of his own. "You're dating an annoying whore."

I shrug and hiss air through my teeth when the medic lifts my leg. "I think an x-ray would be better so we can determine the damage," Coach says from somewhere down near my feet. He appears in the spot Sebastian was just in and lays his hand on my shoulder. "You need rest. We'll check up on it in a few days."

I give him a nod, and then I'm being wheeled out through the double doors, depression hitting me hard in the gut. How the fuck can I find Danny if I'm stuck to a bed for days?

"Where are you taking him?" I hear Sebastian asking the medics. They tell him which hospital, but I don't care to hear which. I don't have anyone here with me to tell anyway.

Four hours later, the result of my x-ray says it's a sprain. I should be relieved, but I'm simply happy to get my ass out of there. I'm prescribed anti-inflammatories and some pain meds then wheeled out into the waiting area. I see Dani sitting in a chair, her hair dishevelled and her makeup a mess.

"Hey," she gives me a tentative smile. "I'm here to take you home." I can see she's a bit nervous and looks slightly ashamed.

I give her a small smile and decide to forgive her. It was a stressful fucking moment for all of us. Plus, she's here, right? She cares enough to be the only person here with me to make sure I get home. The doctor hands her a pair of crutches and tells me to stay on my back for a few days, doing the bare minimum, reminding me to schedule a checkup.

I take the crutches from Dani—not at all a stranger to them—then let her lead me out to her car.

"I'm sorry for my behavior earlier," she whispers into the silence of the car.

"It's all good," I shrug. "Emotions were running high."

My left knee begins to throb, the pain meds wearing off and exhaustion rolling over me quickly. I need to get home and call Ma, then I need to figure out a way back to Baltimore. No matter my injury, Danny is still missing, and I can't shake the feeling he needs me.

CHAPTER TWENTY-FOUR

Sebastian

I followed behind Dani to the hospital and watched as she went inside. I was expecting her to come out alone, having witnessed Dixon's disregard of her, so I was surprised when they came out together. I watched as she tucked him into her car, and then she took him back to his place. When he let her inside with him, I knew I would have to go to extremes to show him the truth.

The sky darkens, and when that bitch doesn't come out as usual, I know she's staying the night. That actually bothers me more than I want it to, given that I'm not planning anything serious with Dixon. I just really want to watch him suck my dick. I get out of the Hummer before I can fully think through my actions and approach the house. I know he's not one for much security, so I head to the back door and hope it's unlocked.

I stand in front of the glass door that doesn't even have a curtain covering it. I can see straight through the house to his front door, and there isn't even a light out here that turns on with movement. He's a dumb fuck. I need to get all this rectified for him, to make sure he's safe when my ass isn't pulling all-nighters to do so. I grab the handle of the door and give it a tug. It slides open a few inches. I wait to hear an alarm or beeping, and when I don't, I curse the idiot under my breath.

I step into his kitchen and close the door behind me. I look around, screwing up my face when I see a few open cans of soup. Sure, when I was dirt poor and begging on the streets that shit was gold. I wouldn't touch it now if I was starving. Leave it to Dani to make canned soup for him… Useless damn female. At least she has nice tits.

I walk through the kitchen slowly and stand in the middle of his TV room. It looks nearly unused, and for some reason that makes me snort. I creep up the stairs, one at a time, and thank the fact that the house is new because nothing creaks. I pause at the top of the landing and see that all doors are open except for one, Dixon's bedroom. I wait and listen for any sounds. I really don't want to storm in while they are having sex, but I will. They should be having sex. Sure, his leg is injured, but his dick isn't, and I'm sure a girl like Dani has ridden more than a few in her day. Again, I'm hit with satisfaction, knowing they aren't fucking when I hear no noises.

The door isn't completely shut, so I ease it open with the toe of my boot and step into the room. They're laying in the same bed, both on their backs with not even an inch of skin touching. I used to sleep in bed with my boys like this, there's nothing intimate about it, yet I can feel my body begin to vibrate with unrestrained emotion. Why does she even get to sleep beside him? And in his t-shirt as well. It's pure instinct that makes me reach behind my back and grab the cool metal of my gun. I want to shoot her in the head. I walk around the end of the bed and up along her side, gently pulling my piece from my waistband. I stand over her head, her brown hair spread over the pillow and her mouth open slightly. She looks like she's at home, but she fucking isn't.

I run the barrel of the gun along her forehead, brushing aside her hair and grinning when her brows crease in the center. That's right, Dani, enjoy it now while you have it. I look at the space between them and snort. *If* you actually have it. I put the gun back in my waistband and walk back to the end of the bed, giving them a final look over. I walk to the door, my footsteps slow and deliberate, not wanting to disturb the awkward couple.

"Seb." My heart explodes, and I stand completely still, sweat gathering at the base of my spine.

I don't move for at least a minute, waiting to hear what else he has to say or how he'll react to my being in his house in the middle of the night. When there's no other sound, I turn and look at them over my shoulder, exhaling when I see they're both still sleeping. Even in sleep, Dixon looks confused. I slip out of his room. My heart is beating about a mile a minute as I hurry down the stairs and back outside.

He called me Seb.

The next morning at practice, it's quieter than usual. Even though Dixon is new to us, he quickly became part of the family. The guys are missing him today, and so am I. I head over to Coach's office, stopping short when I hear Dani speaking about Dixon.

"He's already left for Baltimore," she huffs. "I tried to convince him to let me drive him, but he's taking the Greyhound."

"That's good. He can spend some time with his family and recoup this week," Coach grunts.

"I think something bad is happening with his mom," Dani says like it's the hottest gossip bit. "I tried to get it out of him, but he wouldn't budge."

"Leave it be, Dani. His family life is his business, not yours, and stay out of his fucking bed. What did I tell you before?"

"It's not serious," she whines. "He's a nice guy."

"Yes, he is, and I'd like him to stay that way. Stop fucking my team members, Danielle."

I press my fist to my mouth and flatten myself to the wall

just as she thunders out of his office, her face a twisted mass of fury. She stalks down the hall without seeing me, and I head back into the locker room, completely satisfied with Dixon's lack of trust in her. He would've told her his family issues if they were dating.

I don't like that he's headed back to Baltimore, especially since his brother has a hit on his head. Maybe Dixon will be a fair trade if they can't find little North? I want to warn him to watch his back, but how can I do that without him knowing I've put feelers out? I could try to convince him that I did it because I care, but then he'll ask how I knew about his baby brother, and then I'll have to admit I was inside his house... Like a stalking psycho. Which I'm not, I just look after certain people, and I can't do that if I don't know everything about them.

Speaking of, now I have to get a few of my boys over to Baltimore, and I need to get them moving now.

Dixon

This bus seats are so cramped, but I like the fact that I'm alone. Dani offered to drive me, but I refused. I just don't want her around the shit that's going on with my family. She wouldn't understand, and it's nowhere near time to bring her home to Ma. Regardless, Dani is the furthest thing on my mind right now.

I had a dream last night.

Sebastian was in my room, and he was laying beside me in bed, his hand linked with mine. I was content, and I remember feeling complete, like nothing in life could bother me. Then I turned to look at him, and his face morphed into Dani's, an intense feeling of loss shattering my heart. I remember calling for him and begging him not to leave. It was weird, and reinforcing my need to get out of Buffalo. He's somehow become an integral part of my life, and my mind always gravitates back to thoughts of him no matter how hard I try to stop it, literally.

I called my mother this morning and told her about my injury. She was upset but calmed when I said I would be coming home for a few days. She wants to take care of me, and I think the worry she has over Danny is worse when she's alone. It's going to be hell trying to find him while I'm on crutches, but I'm hoping to find a few people to do the leg work for me. I have a few ideas of where he might be, but I can't figure out why he's not checking in, and I can't contact any of his gang friends for fear that's who he's hiding from. I can only hope he's trying to get out and laying low until they forget about him. I'm ready to bring him and Ma back with me. We could buy a new house and be a family again. I want nothing more.

I feel a pit in the base of my stomach, and I know it's my intuition telling me that something is wrong. Those old feelings of being inadequate for my family are resurfacing, and I can't stop worrying about screwing up all the things I worked so hard to achieve. Leaving my brother behind and chasing a dream of wealth and fame was my first wrong move. I should've forced them to follow me, we could've made it work. Maybe him just seeing what real work ethic looks like would've made him try to achieve it too.

I pull out my phone and begin texting a few of the guys I know from the old hood. I need to know what they've heard, then I need to convince them to look for him and to keep it quiet. I have a few season tickets up for bribes, and I'm not too proud to use them. After sending the texts, I rest my head on the seat and let my body relax. This will probably be the only time I will rest for a while.

CHAPTER TWENTY-FIVE

Sebastian

It's been nearly a week without Dixon, and we lost another game. The locker room is quiet as we sit here and listen to Coach berate us for not being focused. We really weren't, and this whole trip was a damn bust. The good news, though? We just played the Baltimore Ravens.

So instead of getting on that bus and going home with the team, I'll be staying behind to search down Dixon.

"Why aren't you coming back with us?" Jameson asks.

"Business," I shrug. He and Ortiz know what that means and don't question me further.

Coach doesn't question me, he just barks for me to be at practice in two days, and I swallow down the urge to flip him off. I get it … he's salty about us losing, but I will still slap him like a bitch if he pushes me.

I leave the stadium and hop in the cab that will take me to my hotel. It didn't take long to find the new home Dixon bought for his mom, so I will head over there tomorrow. I would've gone tonight, but I don't want to come off as obsessed because I'm not.

I get inside my room and throw my bag on the bed. I should

sleep, but I'm too amped, so I turn on the TV instead. Maybe I'll order porn and veg out after ordering room service. I open the menu on the screen for the porn titles and see *It's a Man's World*, a gay porn. I keep it highlighted for a while and then curse, turning it off. I need to get the fuck out of this hotel and get some fresh air.

I'm standing outside watching the cars drive by, a few of them cabs. Would seeing Dixon tonight be any different than waiting until tomorrow? I really don't think so, and honestly, we don't have a lot of time. Me attempting to sleep and it being half-assed will just make me feel worse anyway. Might as well get this over with.

I hail a cab and tell him the address. I know it's about a thirty-minute drive because I Googled it, wanting to be prepared. As I settle back in the seat, I wonder how he'll receive me. Will he be angry that I searched him out, or will he be grateful I'm coming to see how he's doing? It could go either way.

The streets of Baltimore look somewhat like Rochester's with ominous looking guys on the corners. To me, it feels like home. I remember being like them and running shit like they are. It was my life for so long. It still is in a way, that part of me will never die, so I will always be the Seb who runs Edgerton. No amount of money will change that, and I know that no matter how green the fucking grass looks, there's still dirt underneath.

His house is nice. It's a small bungalow, but it's on a quiet street, and the cars here are what I would describe as mid-class. I pay the taxi driver then get out of the car, noting that only one light is on inside that I can see. I can't help but wonder if all the doors are locked on this house, curious to know how pissed he'll be if I sneak inside. I decide against it and walk up the driveway. There's no garage and no car parked, so I can't be sure if he's even home. I stand on the small concrete front porch and hover my finger over the doorbell. If his mother is here, she may be sleeping, and I don't want her or Dixon pissed at me. So I gently rap my knuckles on the wooden surface and wait. After a few minutes, I do it again but a little harder.

"Coming," I hear his voice inside followed by a faint, "fuck."

There's a clicking noise, like something hitting the hardwood floor, and it stops on the other side of the door. I hear the lock turn and grin when I realize that while he's in Baltimore, he's a bit more cautious. The door opens, and I watch as Dixon hobbles out of the way on one crutch. The look of surprise on his chiseled face quickly changes into suspicion.

"What the hell are you doing here?" he asks and looks out to the street.

"I thought I'd check in on you. I'm alone."

"You came to Baltimore to check on me?" He has his brow raised.

"We had a game against the Ravens tonight." I raise my brow right back at him.

He scrubs his hand down his face and exhales. "Right."

"Are you going to keep me out here?"

"No, but wait." He shakes his head. "What are you doing *here*?"

I step up onto the ledge of his front door, just inches from his face, and watch as his eyes darken. I react to his nearness as well, my dick swelling in my jeans.

"Let me in," I rasp.

His eyes drop to my mouth, and I let them curl up at the corners. He hops back with a huff. "Come in."

I follow him inside. The warmth in this home is so vastly different than his house in Buffalo. There are pictures lining the walls, plants in all the corners, and it smells like home cooking. I've never lived in a home like this, so I envy him for what he's taking for granted. He should bring his mother to Buffalo with him.

"Sebastian," he groans. "What are you doing here?"

"I wanted to check on you, make sure you're okay."

"Why?" He looks at me with shock.

"Because you left without a word, and I didn't even have time to drop by to see you," I shrug.

His eyes squint with suspicion momentarily, but then he shakes it off. "I'm all right." Then his brows crash together. "How did you find me?"

"I have talents," I evade, and he continues to stare me down. "It's easy when you know what you're looking for."

I follow his hobble into the kitchen and nearly groan out loud when I see lasagna sitting on the counter. I didn't eat after the game. When my stomach rumbles loudly, Dixon shoots me a look. I shrug, and he rolls his eyes, opening a cabinet to grab two plates. He places one in front of me then nods his head at the pasta.

"Is your mom sleeping?" I ask as I plop a piece onto my plate.

"She's working," he answers quietly, his eyes never leaving my face. "Why?"

I ignore his question and moan over a mouthful of pasta, licking some sauce off my lip. It feels so fucking empowering to see the effect I have on him. He stares at me without blinking, and when I drop my head to get another bite, he adjusts himself in his pants.

"Miss me?" I ask around the next mouthful.

"No," he retorts and stabs at his food.

"Don't lie to me," I say quietly. "I hate liars."

"Whatever," he mumbles and eats another bite, leaning against the counter beside me.

"Thought so," I chuckle. "Dani was pretty pissed you wouldn't let her drive you here."

"She told you that?" he asks incredulously.

"Nah, I overheard her say it to Coach."

"Wow," he rolls his eyes.

"Looks like things are getting serious." The memory of them laying in bed together makes my stomach burn with jealousy.

He shrugs and takes another bite.

"How would she feel knowing about us?"

He puts his plate on the counter and looks at me. "What *us*, Sebastian? What the fuck are you even talking about?"

I push off the counter and stand in front of him, running a finger down his throat as he works hard to swallow. "This." My finger continues down over his chest and stomach, his intake of breath accelerating with my touch. My finger stops at the waistband of his pants, and I look back up into his eyes. "That."

His lips part, but before he can say a word, I'm invading his mouth with my tongue. His warmth, his scent, even the way he tastes … it's just so damn perfect, and when he fists my shirt in his hand to haul me in closer, I nearly come in my pants. He releases my shirt and works on my belt buckle, making me moan into his mouth. His frantic movements have me pulling away from his mouth so I can watch when he wraps his hand around my cock. My jeans fall to my feet, then he lowers my boxers to my thighs, groaning when my cock springs free.

"Grab it." I almost sound like I'm begging, but I can't bring myself to care.

He does as I tell him, and he squeezes me, chuckling when I jerk in his hand. "Miss *me*?" he taunts just as I drag his mouth back to mine. Yes, I fucking did.

He begins to pump my cock with sure strokes then spreads the drop of precum around my head. If he continues like this, I will come in his hand. I don't want that, I want to come *inside* of him. I pull his pants down to his knees and groan again when I see he has no underwear on, his cock bouncing off his thigh. I grab it in my hand and stroke him at the same leisurely pace he's stroking me, his moans being swallowed by my mouth. My other hand snakes around his hip and settles on his ass cheek. I give it a firm squeeze, letting my fingers graze his ass crack. He tenses at the touch.

He breaks our kiss and stares at me with his jaw clenched, but he doesn't stop me. I press in harder, and my forefinger dips into his tight hole just as his cock twitches in my hand. He likes it.

"I want to be inside you." I lick at his bottom lip. "Again."

I'm expecting him to draw away from me at those words, expecting anger in his features, but instead, he moans loudly and pushes back against my finger that begins to move in and out of him. I'm so damn hard, watching the bliss on his face and feeling the movements of him against my hand.

"Turn around, Dixon." There's a moment of hesitation, but then he turns around and plants his hands on the edge of the counter. "Jack yourself." I watch as his hand disappears down his front, and a guttural noise escapes his throat, making my cock jerk against his ass cheek.

I grab both ass cheeks in my hands and spread him open, his breaths coming out in harsh gasps. Just as my cock nestles in between them, his phone starts ringing from his pant's pocket. I groan but continue to glide my length along his ass crack.

"Ignore it." His voice is gruff as he bends for me, making his ass more accessible.

"I missed this pretty pussy," I groan as I continue to slide along his crack.

"Hurry up," he pushes against me again. I line myself up, and his phone starts ringing again, making him straighten up. "I should check it." His indecision means he's worried.

He bends as I step back and pulls up his pants, pulling his phone out of his pocket. "Shit," he mutters before he swipes it open. "Yeah?" I pull my pants up and buckle my belt just as a strangled, "No," escapes him. He falls against the counter, and I already know what's being said even before my phone pings with a message. "Where?" Dixon chokes out as I read Delano's text.

He's dead.

Nothing more than that, so I delete it, putting my phone away. Dixon's phone falls from his hand and crashes against the tile on the kitchen floor. I stand there watching him, my heart sinking and my stomach rolling. He takes a step forward—forgetting about his injury—and falls to the floor with a scream. I rush to help him up, but he pushes me off, tears streaming down his face and his chest bouncing with the force of his sobbing.

"What happened?" I sit beside him.

"My brother," he croaks. "I need to get to him."

I pull out my phone and call a cab, telling them to hurry.

Dixon

As the cab races us toward the hospital, I call my mother, getting her voicemail for the third time in a row. It can't be him. The police don't know for sure, and I'm on my way to identify the body. They found it down by the marina, inside a boat with a bullet hole between its eyes. It can't be my brother.

I have Sebastian with me, and he's quiet as he taps furiously into his phone. Maybe he's texting his wife. A large wave of guilt threatens to be the straw that breaks my fucking back, but I breathe through it. I can't deal with this shit right now. I need to get a hold of my mother, and then I need to pray that it's not my brother dead on a gurney.

"You don't have to be here for this," I tell Sebastian, who

quickly looks up from his phone. "We barely know each other."

"I don't see anyone else with you," he growls. "And tell me one more damn time that we barely know each other, I fucking dare you."

I chance a quick look at the cab driver and keep my mouth shut. Sebastian would have no qualms airing it all out because I'm being stubborn, and I can't have another thing on my plate right now.

"Besides," he continues, "you can't walk."

I scoff, knowing I have the crutch with me, yet I continue to keep my mouth shut because regardless of what I'm saying, I need someone with me. My mother still works the night shift at a clothing factory, and she's not allowed calls while she's on the floor. I don't know when her break is, so it looks like I'll have to call the factory to ask for her.

I'm staring at my phone, debating whether I should do it when Sebastian's voice breaks my thoughts. "Wait until you see the body."

"I have a bad feeling," I mutter.

"Do you know what happened? Why was he down there at the marina? If it was him," he asks me.

"My brother has never been the type of kid who wanted to change his future. Where we came from, you had two choices: be in a gang or make yourself great. I wanted to make my family great." I don't think I'm making any sense, but I hear him grunt in response.

"Gang life isn't all bad. It's a family, and for some, the only family they have. It's admirable that you wanted that and at a young age, but don't blame yourself for your brother's decisions."

"If I was there, maybe I could've prevented this," I argue with him.

"If you were there, then you both may have been shot in the head, and your mother would have no one."

"Football was for them," I murmur and drop my face in my hands.

"No." His hand wraps around my forearm. "Football was meant for you. Why do you think I hated you so much in the beginning? Here was this rookie showing up, and he had records that put us seasoned players to shame. Football is for you, don't misconstrue what you've achieved."

I know his words are true, I'm just having a hard time believing them, and I'm drowning in an ocean of guilt. Danny has been missing for two weeks, and the cops only recently filed the missing person's report because he was a known runaway with gang affiliates. I should've pushed harder and made people search for him, I have the means to do it now. I just always thought he'd be back home at some point, like he always is.

The car pulls up to the hospital, and Sebastian helps me out before slinging my arm over his shoulder. He carries my crutch in one hand then helps me walk into the hospital. After that, it's a blur of cops and nurses before going down to the basement. It's cold, and it smells like death. My body begins to shake with fear. Sebastian stops me in front of the morgue doors and grabs my chin.

"Stay strong."

I give him a quick nod and take my crutch, placing it under my arm. It feels like time is moving too slowly, all my movements weighted and my head heavy. I acknowledge the cop who opens the door, then I'm blasted with a rush of cool air. I turn to look once more at Sebastian, and he gives me a a quick meaningful look as he leans against the wall. He's not leaving me. That gives me the strength I need to walk inside. When the door bangs behind me, I take a deep breath.

The metal table in front of me has a body on it, covered by a sheet. Nothing is visible. I swallow hard when the cop nods to the ME to pull back the sheet. I see the hair first, it's grown out a lot, and then the forehead with the hole in the center. I can feel the lasagna I ate working its way up from my stomach, but I force it down. *Stay strong.*

I close my eyes and hear the rustling of the sheet as it moves down the body. When the sound stops, I open my eyes. My eyes fill with tears, and I can't seem to focus on the face. I take a few steps closer, and when I look down, my heart breaks. I can't see anything, and I can't hear anything save the scream ripping from my throat.

CHAPTER TWENTY-SIX

Sebastian

It's been two weeks since Dixon identified his brother, and he hasn't been back to Buffalo. I tried calling him and texting him, but he's not responding. I would've already made my way back there if Coach hadn't informed the team that he would be back next week, and he's bringing his mother. I know he purchased a new home, a larger home, and it's even closer to me. I can give him the time it takes for his ass to be back here, but then I'm forcing him to see me.

"Something weird happened last night," Jameson says as he sits beside me on the bench. I look at him with my brow raised as Ortiz sits on my other side. "Dani put her hand on my dick."

"What?"

"Is she still dating Dixon?" Ortiz asks.

"I don't know," I answer truthfully. "I haven't spoken to either of them."

"She was patting my chest and then her hand trailed down, landing on my—"

"Yeah, dick," I cut him off. "I heard you. What were you talking about?"

He moves in his seat, looking slightly uncomfortable, and I can already sense that I'm not going to like it.

"You," he clears his throat, "and Dixon."

"What about us?"

"She wanted to know why you stayed in Baltimore a few weeks ago," Ortiz speaks for him. "And she asked us if you talk to Dixon at all."

"Weird," I mutter, but my heart is pounding in my chest. "Why is she asking about Dixon?"

"Maybe he's not talking to her, which would be understandable with all that's happened," Jameson answers. "But why is she hitting me up?"

Why indeed.

"She's been flirting heavily with me too," Ortiz states, and that sends my blood on overdrive.

She's questioning and flirting with my two closest friends while asking for information about Dixon and me. What the fuck is she up to? I can't rely on these two to get me that information, I'll need to do it myself, and that means making the bitch believe I want to talk to her.

My phone rings, and I see Delano's name on the screen. I stand up and leave the locker room to take his call in the hallway.

"Tell me you have something," I say as soon as I pick up.

"We know the two guys who did it," he says. "They aren't being too quiet about it. They're using North's death as a warning to others who don't hold up their end of the bargain."

"Do you think you can get them?" I ask him quietly. "The two who killed Little North?"

"Yeah," he chuckles. "I can get them, but what do you want us to do with them?"

"Hold them until I get there." I scrub my hand down my chin. "We have a game tomorrow night, but I can be home Monday evening."

"Sounds good."

"Let me know the second you get them," I demand, and he grunts as he hangs up.

I can't give Dixon his brother back, but I can do something to rectify what happened. I can also use those fuckers as an example of what happens when you fuck with a North. And most of all, that way I can make sure Dixon and his mom stay safe.

Dani is striding down the corridor, probably on her way to her father's office, when I step out of the adjacent hallway and step in her path. She gasps as she stumbles to a stop, and her hand flies to her throat.

"Dani." I add longing into my voice as I give her a slow once-over.

"You scared me, Sebastian." She clears her throat and narrows her eyes. Not going to be easy at all. "What do you want?"

"What I know belongs to me." I bite into my lip, her eyes following the motion.

"I don't understand what you mean," she murmurs, sounding very suspicious.

I brush by her and continue walking out to the field, feeling her eyes on my back as I go. Baby steps. First, I need her to believe I'm once again interested in her, then I need her to trust me enough to talk to me. This wasn't always my plan but having her become a part of it will solidify everything, only now I've upped the timeline.

Dixon will be back in a week, and I have a lot to prepare before then. I'm pissed he hasn't replied to me, and I have a punishment in mind for when he's back in the city. After everything that's happened between us, I won't let him shut me out. I can be the person who helps him grieve. But first, he needs to be punished, and I love handing out punishments.

I run the same laps around the field that he used to. It makes me feel closer to him, and the ache that's been sitting in my chest dissipates. There's only one other person in this world who makes me feel this way and that's my daughter, Carla. She's always been my ray of sunshine in the storm that's my life, and she knows just how to wrap me around her little princess finger. When I get back to Rochester to deal with business, I can pop in to see her too, and my soul can be recharged until the next time I can visit.

With the game coming up tonight and Dixon on my mind, concentrating on anything else feels impossible. Dani is an added nuisance, but I'm dealing with her now before shit gets any worse. Females can be nasty, and a scorned one can be deadly.

That's why her suspicions are bothersome.

We buried Daniel last week in the same cemetery my father was laid to rest. I don't remember much after recognizing him on that gurney and waiting for my mother to get to the hospital. It would've been more agonizing if Sebastian wasn't there, but I didn't get the chance to tell him that, and during the hectic events after, he disappeared.

Both mine and my Ma's cellphones were confiscated for the investigation, and the cops tore through our home, looking for clues about Daniel's affiliations. Even when I explained to them that this was a new home, they still insisted upon the search, and since we wanted to find out who did this, we complied.

We were told he was killed execution style, and his body had been on that boat for at least a few days before the owner discovered it. I have heard what they have in terms of theories, but nothing is concrete. The cops said they've seen this type of killing before and in the same area. Apparently, it's done when someone has gone against the gang's demands. Was Daniel trying to get out?

My mother has been a wreck, and when I told her she was moving with me to Buffalo, she barely put up a fight. I know she feels like there's nothing else here for her, and that breaks my heart. I bought us a new home, and it's bigger than we ever could've dreamed about owning. I bought it in Daniel's memory, and I will still make sure there's a room just for him. Sebastian was right … I need to carry on with my career, and I need to do it for Danny.

My knee has healed enough that I can once again put my weight on it, but running still hurts, and the pain seems to be localized at the kneecap. The doctor said that's normal, and I should be ready to play again in a few more weeks. Coach has been incredibly supportive by checking in, not only about my knee but my brother too. I haven't spoken to Dani, and I really haven't had the urge to. I'll see her when I get back anyway. I don't know if she has been trying to get a hold of me or not. I'll know when the cops return our phones tomorrow.

It feels like time has been standing still yet rushing forward all at once. Sometimes I feel stuck in a moment only to pull out of it and realize hours have passed. Sometimes I'm taken back to a time when Danny and I were children and he didn't avoid me as much. I can lose hours in those memories. I've tried to pinpoint the moment things changed, when we reached the point of no return and when saving my little brother became impossible. I can't see it, which makes me feel even worse. I was away too often, and each time I came home, he was a little older. I didn't see the change from a delinquent teen into a disgruntled man, and that's what saddens me the most. No one paid close enough attention to Danny.

CHAPTER TWENTY-SEVEN

I follow Delano to the basement of his house. He pauses at the door, looking around before opening it. He stayed true to his word and had the two guys picked up, keeping them here until I could come. I follow him down the stairs, crinkling my nose at the smell of mold. These old houses in Rochester are full of it. This basement is especially bad because Delano sometimes leaves things to decay too long inside these walls.

He reaches up to turn on a pull string light, the single bulb washing the room in a dull orange hue. Two guys are sitting back-to-back on the floor with rope around their middles and bandanas stuffed in their mouths. They can't be any older than eighteen, yet they look hardened, like I did at that age. That's what happens when you call the streets your home before maturity.

I crouch down in front of the first one and pull the gag out of his mouth, his eyes spitting fire. "Do you know why you're here?"

"You'll die for this," he grits out.

"You're not in Baltimore anymore, you're in my city, understand?" When he stays silent, I take that as an assent. "Do you know why you're here?"

"No."

I stuff the bandana back in his mouth, and he does little to fight it, knowing I'm not to be fucked with. I get up and move to the guy at his back, pulling the material out of his mouth next.

"Same question."

"No," he answers, but I see something softer in his eyes. He may bend for me quicker than the other.

"Does Daniel North ring a bell to you?" The way his eyes round slightly and his jaw locks tell me it does indeed. "He was executed a few weeks ago."

He keeps his mouth shut, and I chuckle, liking that I get to take this to the next level.

"Take his boot off, and get me the torch," I tell Delano.

Delano grabs the kid's boot. He begins to scream as he struggles but proves to be no match for my boy. No, we've been through this many times before, so we've become a well-oiled machine. This is our niche, and we are just so fucking good at it. Once the kid's boot and sock are off, I stand towering over him, and we both watch as Delano grabs a plumber's torch. He hands it to me, and I make a point of pressing the ignitor, the sound loud in the soundproofed basement.

"Listen," the kid begins, trying to buy himself some time, "I can tell you who you really want. We just follow orders."

The guy tied at his back begins to squirm, screaming into his bandana and snapping his head back and forth.

"Hold his leg," I tell Delano, ignoring the kid. I already gave him a chance. I don't ever do second chances. "Did you eat today?" I ask Delano with a grin, and he answers me with one back, an excited gleam in his eye. We're so damn twisted.

"I love the smell of barbequed meat," he chuckles.

I crouch down and grab his foot around the center while

slowly moving the flame closer. "You're probably going to piss your pants," I say to the kid, and he begins to plead.

"Looks like this little gang in Baltimore recruited pussies only," Delano sneers.

I hold up the foot and bring the tip of the flame to his big toe, watching as the skin bubbles and blackens. His screams are loud and his body shakes, but I'm too far lost in the bliss of torture to give a shit. I move the flame down and start in on the next toe. The smell of ammonia hits my nostrils, and I laugh as the kid pisses himself. I knew he would.

I finally get to the last toe and pull back the torch. They are a lovely shade of black. I smirk at Delano when I see some fluids oozing out of the busted blisters. The kid passed out during the third toe, the scent of charred meat potent in the small room. I drop the foot, and it bounces off the concrete with a loud thud. His buddy tied at his back is panting loudly, sweat pouring down his face and his body shaking. I stand in front of him then crouch down, bringing us eye to eye.

"What was it you were telling people about killing Daniel North?" I ask him, and he mumbles around the bandana. "Oh, I remember. You were making an example out of him, right?"

His eyes squeeze shut like he knows there's no point, they're both never leaving this basement alive, and trying to fight that would be futile. I respect that. I respect it enough not to torture this one, but he still must die. I stand up and pull the gun out of the back of my waistband and point it at his forehead, in the exact same spot they shot Little North. I pull the trigger, and he slumps forward, jerking his partner into consciousness.

"Give me his phone," I tell Delano, jerking my chin at the guy I just shot. "I want to take a video."

Delano chuckles and searches the guy's jacket pocket, pulling out the newest iPhone. "These little gangsters have it good," I whistle, and Delano nods. I use the dead kid's thumb to open the screen then scroll through recent phone calls, *Baby mama 1* and *Baby mama 2* being the most used. But then I find *Boss* and fucking roll my eyes. The damn stupidity is astounding, but useful.

"Smile for your *boss*. I'm sending him a gift," I tell the kid as I record him moaning. "That hurts, huh?" I prod at his foot, and he screams again. "He pissed himself too," I say while keeping the video on the kid writhing on the ground. "Your other soldier," I get up and walk around, "got the same death he gave one of my little homies." I zoom in on the hole in his forehead. "I think you get the message, right?"

I stop the recording, send the video to their boss, then smash the phone under my boot.

"Find his, too," I tell Delano. "Dump them somewhere. You got that one?" I point to the kid still moaning in pain. Delano gives me a quick nod. I start for the stairs. "I'll see you in a couple weeks," I call out to him.

"You smell like you were at a cookout," Paola crinkles her nose, "but like the meat was bad."

I snort and lean in to kiss her cheek. "Nah, no cookout. I'm starving, though."

"I don't know how you have an appetite after roasting someone," she mutters before she heads into the kitchen. "Mami was here earlier and dropped off some paella."

My mouth salivates at the thought of her mother's cooking, and I follow her into the kitchen. I pull off my jacket, and a wave of seared kid hits me, the smell making my stomach clench in hunger. Yeah, I'm fucked-up.

"Carla's sleeping?" I ask her as she places a bowl in front of me.

"Si," she replies and sits across from me. "I told her you were coming to see her, so she's excited for when she wakes up."

"I'm excited to see the little mama too."

"You're different." She leans her head on her hand and watches me closely. "Are you seeing someone?"

"Nope."

"I've never seen you look like this before." She reaches for her pack of smokes on the table then pulls out a pre-rolled spliff. "You have this glow."

She lights the end, and the sight of the flame makes my stomach flop. The memory of a charred kid stealing my appetite. I push away the bowl of food and reach for the joint, my body craving the numbness it'll provide.

"I'm not glowing, Paola," I take a long pull on the spliff. "I'm sweating from torturing and killing two guys."

"You know it would be okay if you found someone. You've kept your oath to my brother, and I'm well taken care of."

"Enough," I snap, "there's no one else."

She sits back in her seat with a small smile on her mouth, and I look away, not wanting her to see any further into my soul. She's already seen too much.

"Papi!" A little squeal wakes me up, and the dip in the mattress warns me I'm about to be attacked.

"Hi, Mija," I chuckle as I feel her little body curl around mine, her breath hitting my cheek.

"Did you bring me a present?" her bright green eyes stare into mine.

"Nada," I shrug, "but we can go shopping."

She squeals again, the sound ringing against my eardrums, causing me to wince.

"Sorry Papi," she covers her mouth with her hand.

"It's okay, Mija." I ruffle her hair. "Let Papi get dressed, then we'll go."

Dixon

Being back here in the stadium is bittersweet. My goals have changed, and I don't feel like the same person who first stepped foot inside these walls. No matter how hard I try, I can't bring him back, so I know I must change my priorities. Yes, my mother is still important, but I've taken care of her, and Danny still means the world to me, but he's gone. I know I have to stop blaming myself for that, but it's going to take time.

Every decision made has a consequence. My mother's decision to have children with our father, my decision to pursue a career brought us to where we are today. It was both of our decisions to just hope Danny would come around that put him where he is today. I know once I face those realities, I will then begin to heal. Until then, I have a lot of work to put in.

"Dixon?"

I turn at the sound of Dani's hesitant voice and find her standing in front of her office.

"Hey," I give her a smile, and she runs into my arms.

"I tried calling and texting," her words are muffled as she buries her face into my chest. "I'm so sorry about your brother."

I stiffen at her words and try to relax. I need to start getting used to hearing that.

"Thank you." I rest my chin on top of her head.

"How's your knee?" She looks up at me.

"Stiff and a bit sore, but I need to start working with it."

"I'm so happy you're back," she whispers. "When can I see you?"

Her words make my stomach flip, and I try not to let the expression on my face change with it. "Soon. My mother and I are just settling into our new house."

Dismay is clear on her face, and I know I've disappointed this woman more than I've made her happy. That's a sign that I'm not ready for where she wants this to go, and I know I must tell her. Just not here inside the stadium. I'll take her out for dinner and break it to her over wine. Chicks love that shit.

"Your mother will be living with you?" I can hear the judgement.

"Yeah, considering I'm her only family left," I retort and step back.

"Sorry," she chews into her lip. "I didn't mean it like that."

She did, but I don't care. "It's all good. I'm going to head into the locker room and see the guys." I step around her and ignore her huff of frustration. She'll have to get over it.

I open the doors, and the guys' laughter fades as they turn to see who it is. Then slowly it picks back up as they rush forward, crushing me in the center of a large group hug and telling me they missed me. This is family.

"North, we missed you." Dex grabs my shoulder. "I'm sorry about your little brother."

I give him a nod, but I can't seem to get the words to come out. My throat is closing with emotion, and my heart is thumping wildly.

"Guys!" Sebastian shouts. "Give him some space."

The team parts in front of me, and then I see Sebastian. He has his arms crossed along his bare chest. He doesn't look pissed, but he doesn't look happy either, and I see he's schooled his features to be indifferent. Disappointment flares in my chest, and I can't help but compare myself to Dani. So this is how she feels. It's ridiculous, I can't expect him to walk over to me and then what? Kiss me? My heart thunders at the thought, and his mouth curls up on the right side, like he knows what I'm thinking.

I walk through the center of the sea of guys, my throat still working to remove the lump that has settled there. I start to walk by Sebastian, but he reaches out and grabs my shoulder, giving it a squeeze. I swallow and give him a small nod, avoiding his eyes. He was there when I lost it, when the mountain of pain crushed me at the sight of my brother, and he made sure I was okay. I don't think I can ever repay him.

"North," Zeal comes up to me as I open my locker, "how's the knee?"

I'm grateful for the change of subject. "Healing."

"That was a nasty hit you took," Ortiz chimes in. "Did you watch the playback?"

"Nah," I chuckle, "that would be psychological torture."

"My first concussion was my rookie year," Jameson offers, "and I watched that replay over and over again."

"That's because you have issues," Sebastian snorts, and the guys laugh.

"Coach said you'll be joining us in the next few weeks," Zeal says as he leans against the locker beside mine. "I can help you out with the rehab and weight training. Let's strengthen that knee up again."

"Thanks, man." I watch as he heads off to the field.

Today while the guys practice, I'll run the field and slowly bring up my endurance again. I follow behind Zeal and step out into the hallway, looking toward the large double doors and suddenly feeling nervous. How will it look out there now that my brother is gone? What will it feel like to dig my toes into the field and run along its surface? Will I feel guilty that I can do it while he rots into the ground?

"It still looks the same," Dani calls from her father's doorway. "Dad is out there waiting for you."

I hate that she seems to always be watching me, and when I want to have a quiet personal moment, she appears. I give her a tight smile and slowly make my way to the doors. I need to take her out soon to really lay down the boundaries. She has to feel it too, that lack of connection, and no amount of forcing it will make it work. Her constant disappointment should be enough of a reason for her to dump me, so I get the feeling she's clinging on for other reasons. Maybe she wants to marry a footballer so badly that nothing else matters.

Sad fucking life.

CHAPTER TWENTY-EIGHT

"Lucky guy," I say, holding in my smirk when Dani's eyes fly to mine. "He doesn't know what he has."

"He's been through a lot," she defends him and excuses his dismissal.

"He should lean on you more." I walk across the hall and stand in front of her. "I remember how good it felt."

Her eyes darken, and her tongue runs along her lip. So close. She still wants me, she's never stopped wanting me. It probably had a lot to do with the fact that I was married, being the forbidden fruit and all, but I also know Dani is looking to be a trophy wife. She's lucky because her father is in the position where she could easily find a husband that wants the same. That guy won't be Dixon North, I'll make sure of it.

I brush her hair back over her shoulder and internally pat myself on the back when she shudders. "I miss having you around."

"Don't fuck with me, Avando," she whispers. "You're married."

"Just for convenience," I shrug. "Is that what bothers you?"

"Of course, it does." She rolls her eyes.

"What if I said I would get a divorce?"

"Why?" Her eyes are wide.

"I just feel something," I motion my finger between us. "It's never fully left me, and now seeing you with North is so fucking hard."

I step back and watch the uncertainty on her face. It's not a flat-out rejection. I turn and walk toward the double doors and give her one more longing look over my shoulder. As I figured, she's still watching me. Finally, she ducks into her father's office. I nearly have her eating out of the palm of my hand.

After practice, North is limping, and he looks a bit sick. I jog up beside him and walk with him back to the locker room.

"Did you push yourself too hard?" I ask.

"Probably," he shrugs.

"Take it easy, you don't want permanent damage."

He scowls but nods, and I know exactly what he's feeling. He wants to be contributing to the team, and he hates watching them do what he could only a few weeks ago. Being an athlete with an injury is incapacitating. You feel useless and guilty that your team is picking up your slack.

"I heard a few of the guys talking about Toradol," he says as he drops his voice to a whisper. "Would it really help me get onto that field quicker?"

"Yes," I answer him honestly, "but it's only meant to be used for a short period of time. It eases the pain and reduces the swelling."

"But?"

"When you don't feel the pain, you lose the limit of your injury, and in most cases make it worse. It's only meant to be a short-term drug, but a lot of guys use it long term to cover up chronic injuries."

"If I want some of that, do I ask Coach?" he asks and glowers when I laugh.

"Nah, Coach won't give you that, he's straight and narrow. I've advised you about it but if you still want to take the chance, hit up Jameson."

"How's the leg?" Dani appears again.

"It's all right," Dixon shrugs, turning to stop to talk to her.

"You're limping."

"Just first day soreness," he answers her as I take a step inside the locker room. "Would you want to have dinner tonight?"

"Of course," she answers quickly, and I bite into my cheek. The whore.

So he's still wanting to date her, and she's still very eager to land herself a rich husband. That's what happens when you amount to nothing, and the only thing you can count on are your looks, which fade. Hope they don't mind me being a third wheel at their dinner tonight.

I followed him home and am now trailing behind him as he weaves through traffic. He's not going anywhere near Dani's house, and I laugh to myself when I realize he's arranged to meet her. That must be a bit of a slap in the face for Dani who likes to be spoiled and pampered. He pulls up to a steakhouse, and I continue, pulling down a side street. I park the Hummer and walk back to the restaurant, keeping my hoodie firmly over my face.

Dixon gets out of his car as soon as he sees Dani's car pull in, and I watch as he goes and opens her door for her. The jealousy I'm battling is something I have never experienced… I want to kill her. Fuck, if he doesn't stop this madness with her, I'll kill him too.

As soon as she stands up, he backs her into the car and presses his mouth to hers. My fists clench at the sight. The only saving grace is that he's kissing her with his eyes open, something he's never done with me. I know what this date is and what he's trying to convince himself of, but it won't work. She's not me.

They head into the restaurant, hand in hand, and I lean against a tree. I got nothing better to do tonight. I'll just wait here until they're done to see if they end up going home together later.

Dixon

Dani looks beautiful, so when I kiss her, I should fucking feel something. *Why don't I feel anything?* Sebastian's face floats into my mind, and I squash it quickly. I can't keep thinking about him like this.

We're taken to our table, and once we've both ordered, Dani leans forward on her elbows.

"Did you want to talk about what happened to your brother?"

The question is directly to the point, and I'm a little surprised by the anger that rushes through me. "Not really."

"You should talk about it, Dixon," she says as she sips her water.

"I have been." I shoot her down then look around the restaurant.

"What's it like having your mother living with you?" she crinkles her nose and chuckles.

"I've always lived with my mother," I tell her. "Except college and being out here."

"Oh." She sucks her bottom lip into her mouth. "I bet she'll want her own place eventually, though, huh? I mean, every parent must look forward to the day their kids leave the nest."

Is she dense? "Probably not since she just lost a kid."

"Right." She takes another drink of her water.

The silence becomes uncomfortable, and I exhale with relief when our food shows up. Dani is not your typical girl, she picked the most expensive dish on the menu, and she's eating every damn thing on that plate. Her most redeeming quality so far.

"Do you think you'll be able to play next week?" she asks.

"Maybe," I shrug. Which reminds me, I should talk to Jameson tomorrow.

"We need you."

Now, I don't know if it's the fact that she's already rubbed me the wrong way or if I'm just in a foul mood, but I am starting to get pissed.

"I'm no good to the team if I permanently injure my knee," I say through my teeth.

"Of course," she nods.

"Listen," I push my plate aside, completely ready to put a stop to us dating.

"Yes?" Her foot skims up my leg and presses into my cock. I'm surprised when it begins to swell.

What does that mean? Am I over Sebastian? Was it just a weird phase?

"Let's get out of here." The words are out of my mouth before I can even try to take them back. I need to know if I can follow through.

"Is your mother at home?" she asks.

"It's a big house."

I pay the bill for our half-eaten plates, then she follows me out of the restaurant. My cock pulses in anticipation, so I practically shove her into her car before jogging to mine. I don't want this moment to be spoiled, I will take any assurances that I'm not gay. I know I was supposed to end things tonight, but my reaction changes everything, and I need to put my mind to rest. The confusion has been too damn much.

When I pull out of the parking lot, she follows close behind me. She hasn't been to the new house yet, and to be honest, I hadn't planned on ever inviting her. I grab my dick through my pants and give it a good squeeze. I'm still hard and so ready to plunge inside of her.

Finally, we turn onto my street. Usually I drive it slowly, staring at the large, opulent homes. Not tonight. I need to get to mine and get Dani into my fucking bed.

I don't have to worry too much about Ma, she's been spending a lot of time in her room praying, and I made sure to put her on the other side of the house. No matter how much I want my mother with me, she's nosy and doesn't need to be in my business. I pull into my driveway and check the lights on the second floor. Ma's room faces the front, and right now all the windows are dark.

I park the car and step out just as Dani is rolling in. She gives me a sly look through her windshield, and my cock swells again. Maybe all I needed was time and space away from Sebastian, his presence always clouds my thinking. She steps out, and her bare legs gleam in the moonlight. I don't know how girls wear skirts when it gets this cold, but I'm going to have fun getting her out of it. She walks toward me, her hips swaying and those long legs eating up the Interlock driveway. If she keeps her mouth shut tonight, I will fuck her into tomorrow and then decide where I want this to go.

I pull her into my arms and slam my mouth onto hers, my tongue immediately slipping past her lips. I swallow up her moans and grab her ass. It's so plump. I grind my cock into her belly and yank my mouth off hers.

"Inside, now." I sound like a fucking caveman.

She giggles behind me, and I open the door, yanking her roughly in the direction of my bedroom.

"Nice house," she says with awe in her voice.

"Shh." It's harsh I know, but I don't want her voice to change what my body is reacting to.

I pull her up the stairs, and she stumbles a bit, whispering my name harshly. I don't stop as I push open my bedroom door and haul her inside, closing it quickly behind me. I press her into the door, my chest crushing hers and my hands sinking into her hair. She moans my name as I kiss her, my movements becoming frantic and my hands gripping the fabric of her shirt. I pull back and rip it off over her head, throwing it behind me, groaning when I see she's not wearing a bra.

I cup both breasts in my hands and lean down, taking a dusty rose nipple into my mouth. I nip it with my teeth, and she gasps, grabbing my head, her nails digging into my scalp. The feel of her long, pointed nails on my scalp has my mind pausing, not sure if this feels right. I shove the thought aside, latching onto her other nipple. Once I've ravished it, I grab her waist and hoist her in the air, bringing her to my bed. I lay her on her back and bite into my lip as her tits bounce with the motion of the mattress.

I grab the waistband of her skirt and pull it down, letting it skim over her legs. She's not wearing any panties either. Usually, that would send warning bells off in my head, like this one is too eager, and she was so sure this was where we would end up. I don't care right now, though. I want the same thing, and I don't even want to think beyond that. She yanks my shirt over my head and then literally purrs, running her fingers down my sculpted chest and stomach.

I work on my belt buckle and let my pants fall to the floor, my boxers tented with my erection. It feels so good to fucking see it. Her pussy glistens with arousal, and I spread it open with my fingers, preparing to dive right in.

"No," she whines and pulls on my chin. "I need you inside me."

My cock jerks at her words, and I yank down my boxers, preparing to sink inside her. I need a condom, groaning when I remember I never got the chance to buy any.

"Condom?" she leans up on her elbow. "My purse." She nods at the bag on the floor.

I race to her purse and toss it to her, watching as she pulls one out. She hands me the condom and I have it unwrapped in record time. Once I'm covered, I fall over her and slam inside. I cover her mouth with my hand when she screams my name. I don't need her noises spreading throughout the house. I really don't need to hear them either.

She's mumbling behind my hand, but I don't give a fuck as I lean up and start thrusting like a madman. She's screaming, and her eyes are rolling into the back of her head. Then I see Sebastian… the way his mouth turns up on one side and his eyes when they land on mine, heated and raw. I squeeze my eyes shut, trying to block out the image and concentrate on the warmth of Dani's wet pussy.

It doesn't work.

I begin to soften, and no amount of playing with her tits is helping. So I fake it. I throw my head back and moan loudly, her name mumbled in between. I look down into her face, and she stares up at me, her mouth slightly opened.

"I'm sorry." I slip out of her. "I know you didn't finish, you're just so fucking fine. Let's fix that."

She looks at me through hooded eyes as I kiss my way down her chest and over her stomach, my tongue dipping into her belly button. I don't really want to do this, the mood is gone for me, and my dick is flopping against my damn thigh, but I brought her in here. I spread her open, her juices running toward her ass, and bend forward.

I swipe my tongue through her folds then concentrate on that little, hardened nub. I used to enjoy eating pussy, the taste, even the way the juices would run into my mouth. Not anymore.

It takes me holding my breath as my tongue flicks against her clit and my fingers pump furiously into her to get through it. I pray she finishes before it becomes obvious I no longer want to be anywhere near her pussy. I'm an idiot for forcing myself into this, all because I'm so worried about the things I'm feeling and my obsession with blocking Sebastian from my mind.

Finally, I feel her tightening, and her pussy clamps down on my fingers. She lets out a moan, long and raspy, and I pull my head from between her legs. Breathing a sigh of relief. I get up and immediately head into the bathroom to dispose of the condom. I wash my face and gargle with mouthwash because the taste of pussy is something I no longer care for. When I come back out, Dani has my t-shirt on, and is lounging on my bed. Fuck, how the fuck do I tell her she isn't staying the night?

"Want to give me a tour of the new house?" She looks around with a wide smile.

"Tonight's not a good night," I answer her.

She stares into my face and gives me a small smile. "Sure, is it because of your mother living here?"

I grind my teeth and school my features. "Yeah, she would give you the third degree, and I'm not ready for that."

"I should go then?" she asks with her brow raised.

"If you don't mind?" I smile. "Just until I formally introduce you guys."

She rips off my shirt and begins dressing back into her clothes. "And when will that be, Dixon?"

"When I've gotten to know you better, Dani," I retort. "We've barely been dating, chill."

"Chill?" she shrills, and I cringe. "I'm leaving!" she huffs and pushes by me.

I follow her down the stairs where she yanks open my front door. "Do you have anything to say?"

"We'll talk later, Dani." *When I dump your ass.* She growls and stomps off back to her car, not giving me another glance.

I can't even bring myself to care.

10

CHAPTER TWENTY-NINE

It's been a week since I watched Dani stalking out of Dixon's house and looking murderous. She hasn't been back, and they've been avoiding each other at the stadium. I should let my plan go now since it clearly looks like they've broken up, but I know how Dani operates… She always wants what she can't have. She's been giving him longing looks the past two days, telling me her anger is dissipating, and she's going to try to make up with him.

Not going to happen.

We also have a game tomorrow night, and I know Dixon has asked Jameson for the Toradol. He won't be playing this game, but he told Coach he'd be back next week, even though I know he's not ready. He's still limping after long runs, and he can't practice for too long. If he wants to try Toradol, there's nothing I can do about that, he's a big boy. I've used it a few times, but I never had an injury like his. Sometimes getting sacked will make a shoulder swell or you hit your hip hard. In those instances, Toradol can numb the pain long enough to continue the game, but sprains and dislocations are different. That shit needs time to heal.

Coach tells us to cool down after practice then hit the weight room, specifically telling Dixon to strengthen his leg. Then he leaves, saying he has a meeting with the sponsors, which translates to happy hour at the local bar. I walk by his office, and Dani is sitting inside, reading a book by his desk.

"Hey," I say as I lean against the door.

"Hi." Her voice is husky as she watches the sweat drip down my chest.

"You're looking single lately," I say to her with a grin.

"I don't know," she shrugs and rolls her eyes.

"What if I want a taste?"

Her eyes darken, and she stands from the chair. "Of what, Sebastian?"

"Your sweet pussy." Straight up.

"Here?" She looks around.

"Why not? Haven't you always wanted to be fucked on top of your father's desk?"

She bites her bottom lip, and then her mouth spreads into a smile. "Okay. I need to freshen up first."

She slips by me and runs her hand along my chest. I pretend to shudder with want as she snickers and hurries off to probably wash her stank pussy. I see her purse chilling on top of Coach's desk and grab it, searching inside it for her phone. I already know that Dani doesn't have a password set up because she hates remembering anything, dumb ass hoe. I scroll through her contacts and find Dixon, pulling up the text box to write him a message. When I hear the click of her heels on the concrete, I stuff the phone back in her purse and lean against the desk.

She comes inside and closes the door, giving me a slow smirk.

"You remember how I like it, don't you, Dani?" I watch as she visibly swallows and nods.

I push off the desk and round to the other side, kicking Coach's chair out of the way. I motion for her to come stand in front of me, and she hurries over, knowing she needs to be compliant. I grab her shoulder and turn her roughly, pressing her down to bend over her father's desk. With my hand on the back of her head, keeping her face planted against the wood, I work her skirt up with the other. Dani never wears underwear unless she has to, and I'm thankful for it right now, knowing I don't have much time.

My shorts and boxers are next, pushed down around my thighs. I line myself up and slam into her, her cry of pain so fucking sweet. I pull out and thrust in again, grunting with the impact. She whimpers loudly and on my third thrust, the door opens.

"Dani?" Dixon says as he peers around the door.

I don't stop, and when she struggles to get up, I push her head even harder into the surface of the desk.

"Sebastian," Dixon breathes, watching me pound my cock into his girlfriend. "What the fuck are you doing?"

I raise my brow and ignore Dani's protests, the sound of our slapping flesh echoing inside the office. I don't bother to answer because that's rhetorical, right? I curl my fingers into her hair and lift her head, making her face Dixon.

"Tell him you want this."

"Dixon," she sobs his name.

I pull on her hair, feeling some strands give away under my harsh grip, and she whimpers. "Tell him."

"I wanted it," she whispers, and Dixon's eyes widen.

"Your girlfriend is a whore," I tell him as I slam her head back down.

"Whoa," his brows crash together. "You're hurting her."

"I know." I pick up my speed, my thrusts becoming harder,

her hip bones banging off the edge of the desk. She'll have bruising tomorrow. "This is the way I fuck, Dixon. Ain't that right?" I slam inside her and curl my body over hers. "I asked you a question."

"Yes," her voice shakes.

"Why am I here?" Dixon asks her, but she can't tell he's asking her, so I answer.

"I sent you that message."

His jaw clenches, and his hands tighten into fists. "For?"

"So you could see who she really wants."

"And what do you want, Seb?" He takes a step forward. *Seb.* "How about you pull out of her, or I'll show her exactly what it is you want."

I pull out of her, my cock wet with the evidence of how much she enjoyed it, regardless of her crying, then step back. She stands and pulls her skirt down, looking over her shoulder at me with accusation in her eyes. I raise my brow, my dick still out, and give her a wink.

"Get out," Dixon demands, and she grins at me. "You, Dani," he clarifies, and she gasps.

"Dixon, wait," she tries, but he raises his hand, shutting her up.

"This wasn't working anyway. Get out. I need to talk to Sebastian." Back to Sebastian.

Dani grabs her purse and shoves past Dixon, his eyes never leaving mine. When the door shuts behind her, he takes a few steps forward and stops on the other side of the desk.

"I'm here. Now what?" he asks.

"My dick is covered in her pussy juice," I taunt him, running a finger along its length before popping it in my mouth. "Mm."

"I know what her pussy tastes like," he snorts.

"Oh, yeah?" I tip my head to the side. "So I guess you wouldn't mind cleaning it off of me."

He looks thoughtful for a few moments but then comes around the desk and looks down at my cock. He licks his lips. "I could. Tell me that's what you want."

He wants me to hand him the control, making me admit this is what I want and taking the reins. My natural reaction is to refuse him and force him to do what I want, but Dixon won't let that happen again, and I really want his mouth around me. I swallow down my pride and give him a nod.

"Tell me." He leans forward, his mouth close to mine. "Use your fucking words."

I bare my teeth and growl. "I want you to suck my cock. Now." That's as good as it's going to get and he beams, knowing how hard that was for me.

He drops to his damn knees, and I groan, almost shooting cum all over his face. I've wanted this for so long, and now to finally have it, I don't know how to make it last. I want it to be permanently ingrained in my memory because I don't know what will happen afterward.

His hands land on my hips, and he leans forward, his tongue licking along my head. We both moan, and my cock jerks against his chin. I want to tell him to stop because once this is done, I'm afraid it'll be over between us, and I can't imagine that. Before I can even protest, he opens his mouth wide and swallows me down in one shot. My cock hits his throat, and he gags, the constriction forcing me to grit against the sensation to come. He pulls back, and I watch as a string of his salvia stretches from my head to his lip, making me almost lose my footing. I grip the desk and pant as he sucks on the tip, paying close attention to the ridged underside.

"How is my cleaning?" He grins up at me, and I shut my eyes. It's all too much, him on his knees and his eyes looking up through his thick lashes.

He once again sucks my length into his mouth, his hand working what his mouth isn't, and I can't control the sensations that swim up my cock.

"Dixon," I pant, "I'm going to come."

He moans around my cock, and I grab his head with both of my hands, shoving myself deeper into his throat. He moans, and it sets off fireworks behind my eyelids as I come, forcing him to take all of me. My cum shoots down his throat, and like a good boy, he swallows it without complaint.

I pull back and watch as he sucks in a lungful of air, my cock now glistening with his saliva. I instantly miss him, and I know it sounds insane, but I feel like he's already gone. I pull up my shorts as he stands up, wiping his mouth on the back of his hand. It's done and I feel deserted, my heart crashing in my chest. I haven't felt this way before, and it scares me.

He turns on his heel and heads for the door, opening it without a backward glance. He's gone, just like I figured he would be. I lean both hands on the desk in front of me. I have never felt such a feeling of loss, not even when my mother died, not when a few of my boys were killed. This is something entirely new, and the heartbreak is confusing.

And the heartbreak is so fucking painful.

Dixon

I can't believe that just happened.

I rush through the locker room, grabbing up my things and bypassing the shower. I was in the middle of my weight training when Dani texted me, and I can't finish it now, I need to leave. I just sucked Sebastian's dick. I just sucked a man's dick, and I enjoyed it. I'm still hard, fucking solid, and I know it's not going anywhere until I take care of it. This is nothing like when I had sex with Dani… My erection is going nowhere, and I am once again propelled into immense confusion.

I thought I had this sorted out, that Sebastian was a weird phase, and my lack of proper friendships was the problem. I don't think that's true, not after today. Not after swallowing his cum like it was my last meal. There's nothing about what I did that's confusing, it was gay, and it was unforgettable. I am gay for Sebastian Avando and no one else. He's ruined me for women, yet he's also ruined me for himself. He's married, and he has a child. I'm just a distraction, and that breaks my damn heart. I've never had a broken heart. I thought I was above that, that loving someone was something I had no time for.

I rush to my car and get in, starting it up. I rest my forehead on the wheel, mentally berating myself for letting shit get this tangled and knowing I'm at fault. He raped me, yet I got on my knees for him. What the fuck is wrong with me? When I look up to put the car in drive, I see him. He's standing at the stadium's entrance, still in his shorts, his bare chest moving rapidly. His breath is coming out in puffs of white in the cold December air. We lock eyes and stare at each other. Something huge transpired between us. There's no going back, and I don't know what that means for me.

I break the stare down and slam my car into drive, burning tires as I leave the parking lot. Thankfully, there's no traffic, so getting home takes minimal concentration. As I pull onto my driveway, large, fluffy snowflakes start hitting my windshield. It's the first snow of the season. As the flakes hit the window, they instantly melt, and the water runs down in tiny rivulets, transporting me into a memory.

"Dixon!" Danny yells as he runs into our one room apartment, "it's snowing!"

I jump up from our mattress on the floor and run to stand beside him at the window, watching as the large puffs fall slowly from the sky.

"Did you know that every snowflake is different?" I ask him, and he looks at me with confusion.

"They look the same to me."

"I know," I shake my head at him. "But close up, they have their very own designs. No two snowflakes are alike."

"That's impossible," he waves me off. "Everything has its pair, like soulmates."

"You don't know anything," I roll my eyes and step away from him.

"And you don't know everything," he retorts.

"Are you hungry?" I pull out a pack of ramen noodles, the last one.

"Can we go out and play instead?"

He's so small, and I know he's not eating enough, but I don't want him to be sad either.

"Okay, but then we come in, and you eat." I grab my jacket while he jumps up and down.

The snow falls harder and thicker, pulling the memory away from me, leaving me bereft. I miss my brother. I've been missing him since long before he was murdered. I blink heavily and exhale. I'm still fucked-up about Danny. I feel alone in my grief. Maybe Sebastian helped me forget for a short time. That must be why I did what I did in Coach's office. I need someone, and I'm tired of being alone. Sebastian proved to me that Dani's not that person, even though I already knew that. Maybe he was the next best thing.

I get out of the car and head inside, the smell of fried chicken hitting me. I groan out loud, dropping my bag in the mud room and heading into the kitchen. Ma is there in front of the eight-burner, industrial stove, and I feel hope that she'll be okay until she turns around. Her face has aged in the last few weeks, and her hair is greyer. Her presence is constantly shrouded in sadness, and her shoulders are slumped forward.

"Hello, Son." She tries to smile but fails. "I made your favorite."

It's not my favorite, it was Danny's, but I don't dare tell her that. I don't want to tip the delicate balance and shove her back into a depressive funk.

"Thanks, Ma."

"How was practice and your knee?" She looks at me worriedly.

"It's feeling great," I lie. It doesn't feel like it's getting any better, but I can't put her through any more stress.

"That's good," she nods and pulls me out a plate.

Silence falls heavily around us in the backdrop of this gourmet kitchen I always wanted to give to her. I begin to realize I never knew my family well. This is an extravagance my mother never really sought after, a gourmet kitchen and a large home. She was content living in a small apartment as long as we were all happy. I'm seeing that now, even though it may be a little too late. The second I could, I left to pursue my dream, and even though I was filled with good intentions, I lost my family along the way. Ma and I used to talk about Danny, where he was, what he did at school, and the shit he was getting himself into on the regular. Now we have nothing to chat about. She knows nothing about football, and I know nothing about the church.

After she serves me, she heads out of the kitchen without looking back, and my heart breaks some more. I don't know how much of it is left to break. I look down at my plate just as a sob works its way up my throat. How can I eat this? I like fried chicken, but Danny loved it, and the longer I stare down at it, the guiltier I feel. I'm so filled with guilt that it's threatening to consume me completely. I take the plate and put it in the oven, then head up to my room.

I open the door, and the first thing I remember is Dani laying on her back in my bed. I squeeze my eyes shut and try to shove it aside, but again, the guilt works its way in. I don't blame her for turning to Sebastian, especially if he was showing her attention because I didn't give that to her, and I feel so terrible. She's better off without me anyway. I don't have feelings for her, and I don't even know my sexuality anymore.

I don't know who I am anymore.

CHAPTER THIRTY

Sebastian

I've been sitting outside his house for the last hour.

This one has a gate, and it locks, so unfortunately, I can't let myself in. I can't get him off my mind, yet I can't bring myself to call him either. I don't think he wants to talk to me, and after what happened in Coach's office, I know he's going to go back to being elusive. I really didn't think it would go that far, but at the same time, I'm happy it did because he saw Dani for what she really is …: a gold-digging whore.

I grab my phone, fully prepared to call him when it rings in my hand. When I see Delano's name, I groan out loud and nearly throw the phone to the backseat. Instead, I swipe it open, bringing it to my ear.

"Yeah."

"We got trouble," he says, and I roll my eyes. When don't we?

"What now?"

"Those little gangbangers we took out," he huffs, "their leader is looking for them."

"Obviously." I squeeze my fingers into my eyes. "We sent that video, D."

"I know, but they are out for blood, and they're looking to get it."

"They can try," I chuckle. "Tell me you're not worried about some small-time Baltimore gang."

"I'm just filling you in so you know what's up," he explains.

"Thanks, but I wouldn't worry too much about it," I placate him and hang up the phone.

Those guys got off easy for what they did to Little North, and I don't give a fuck about some little crew running around the Baltimore streets like they're tough shit. I got other shit to worry about, one of them being the man who sucked the very soul out of me today. He fucking owns, me and he doesn't even realize it. Dixon North now owns what's left of my heart.

I know how this is going to go down… He'll try to avoid what happened and go back to pretending I don't exist. The joke's on him, though. I'm not going anywhere, and I'm about to make him face what the fuck is going on between us. I won't have an existential crisis about what's happening because I know I'm not gay. The only man I want is him. But it's more than that. I don't want him like I want a woman, and I'm not looking to fuck around every now and then. I plan on owning him too.

Maybe I need to make him face that before I give him too much time to force himself to forget. I swipe open my phone again and press his contact, listening to the rings. I would bet all my money right now that he's staring at my name on his screen and debating whether he should pick up or not. I'm kind of hoping he doesn't because I will unleash my crazy all over this street and laugh when he cries about it.

"What do you want?" he growls into the phone, and I pout. No crazy today.

"Is it too soon to say another blowjob?"

"I'm hanging up," he snaps, and I laugh.

"You don't want to do that. You live on a nice street."

"What the fuck are you doing on my street, Seb?" he yells, but I barely hear it. *Seb...*

"Open this gate, and let me in, or I will cause a fucking scene on your street, Dixon."

He's quiet for a bit, and I know he's debating if I'm bluffing or not. I'm not. He finally exhales, and I watch the gates open, a wide smile stretching across my face. I pull through the metal bars as they widen and drive up his driveway. It's a nice house, and I'm happy he finally got his mother to come be with him. I wonder if I'll meet her.

I park the Hummer and get out just as he's opening his front door and stepping on the porch.

"What do you want?" His arms are crossed over his chest.

"Nice house."

"I'm once again floored by your talent to find people." He rolls his eyes.

"Just you, North." I can see the effort it's taking for him to remain stoic. "Are you going to show me around?"

"Fuck no." His eyes widen. "My mother is here."

"Great, we can finally meet."

"What?" He straightens. "Are you stoned?"

"I wish," I shake my head. "I could fucking use it."

He stands there watching me, his arms still crossed over his chest and his body language closed off. He's trying hard to forget what happened today, but I won't let him. I step up onto the porch with him, and he takes a step back, his arms dropping to his sides.

"What are you doing?" he asks, looking from me up to the

corner of the porch.

I look up to the blinking red light and chuckle, stepping into him. He backs up, and when his back hits the door, I'm on top of him. My chest presses against his, and my hands land on either side of his head, our faces inches apart.

"Does your mom watch the camera feed?" I ask him with a grin.

"No," he shakes his head. "I don't think so—"

My mouth swallows his words as I kiss him. It's harsh, and it's violent as I force my tongue between his lips. He groans, then his hands land on my chest, pushing me away.

"Stop." His body is quaking.

"No." I grab his throat and lean in close. "I won't let you pretend this isn't happening. Now let me inside, or I will fuck you right here. The neighbors will find it interesting, I'm sure."

He slaps my hand off his throat and turns to open the door, looking at me over his shoulder. "You aren't meeting my mom."

"Maybe not today," I shrug and throw him a wink.

He leads us up the stairs and to the left, opening a door. I step in behind him, and I know right away it's his room. It has that same sterile, clean feeling his old house had. Like he doesn't live here. Dixon sits on his bed and watches me as I walk around his room, touching trophies and ribbons.

"All Star athlete, huh?" I murmur, and he scoffs behind me. "You didn't have these out in your other house." I realize all too late what I've admitted, hearing the rustle of his blankets as he stands quickly.

"What did you say?" His voice vibrates in anger.

Fuck. I can't take it back or cover it in any way, so it looks like I'm admitting I went through his house. "I was there once."

"I would've remembered that, Sebastian." Back to Sebastian.

"Not if you weren't there."

He grips my shoulder and forces me to face him, then his fist slams into my cheek. The surprise attack catches me off guard, so I don't get a chance to move when his fist sinks into my stomach. I bend over as the air whooshes from my chest, and his knee comes up, connecting with my forehead. I'm knocked to my ass, and my vision is blurry, rage exploding through me. All the pain is forgotten as I jump to my feet and grab the front of his shirt, throwing him down onto the bed. He tries to sit up, but I punch him in the nose, and he flies back, bouncing on top of his mattress.

My cock is pulsing and rock hard as I grab him and flip him over onto his stomach. He's still gripping his nose, blood dripping onto his blanket as I fall over his back, pressing my cock into his ass. He stills for all of two seconds before he's trying to buck me off. But that isn't fucking happening. I hold the back of his head down into his bed, much the same as I did with Dani earlier. I grab the waistband of his shorts, pulling them down.

"Seb, don't even think about doing this shit again," he growls and squirms underneath me. *Seb.*

I pull my shorts down in the next instant and press my cock into him. "Tell me no."

"No," he gasps as my cock slips between his ass cheeks.

"Now, say it like you mean it." I pull his ass apart and let my spit drip from my mouth, down to his crack.

I watch as it glistens around his puckered hole, and he moans as it continues down to his ball sac. He doesn't say no again, but even if he did, I wouldn't have listened. So I line myself up and begin to push into him. He resists me, clenching his ass. I crack my hand down onto the cheek, making him startle. While he's preoccupied with the slap, I slip in a few more inches and push past the tight ring of muscle. We both moan when he tips his ass up, giving me easier access.

"Now you want to fuck me sweetly?" he snaps when I bottom out inside of him, squeezing around my dick. "You forced me here, so fuck me."

I still inside of him, my cock pulsing and his ass gripping me. Forced him? He really thinks that way? *Fuck him,* he says? I grab both of his ass cheeks in my hands and haul him up, pulling out slowly. Preparing to do just that. He pants, dropping his head, and blood still drips from his nose. Doesn't look like I'm forcing a single thing. I thrust back into him hard, and he grunts with the force. I grind into him and pull back out, spitting down onto my cock. This will be the last time I fuck Dixon into submission. He's quickly becoming an addiction I can't afford.

"Stroke your cock," I demand. "Come with me."

His hand snakes between him and the bed, grabbing his cock. He lets loose a guttural sound, and my balls tighten, my orgasm looming. I start a punishing rhythm, knowing I'm not going to last long. Being inside of him, where I've wanted to be for months, is just too damn much. I hear him moan before strangled mumbles slip from his lips, shocking me when I realize he's coming.

It's like I've been given permission to finish, so I pump into his ass, chasing my release. Seconds later, I'm screaming his name as I shoot my cum into his ass. I continue to pump in and out of him a few times, savoring the feel of him and committing it all to memory. When I pull out completely, I spread him open and watch as my cum begins to leak out of his ass, dripping down to his balls.

"Fuck," I moan, "this is so fucking hot."

"Let me up." He's back to his grumpy ass self, so I move back, hauling back up my shorts. He gets up and rushes to his bathroom while I stand rooted to the spot, staring at the blood on his bed. It hits me all at once that I just fucked a man, and not just any man, the one I've been pursuing.

I wait for it, the feeling of contentment at accomplishing what

I wanted, knowing I can now move on to the next, but it never comes. Instead, my heart is beating wildly with panic, and my stomach rolls with fear. Why do I still want him?

When I hear his toilet flush, I turn for the door, throwing it open. I rush down his steps and out through the front door, jumping into my Hummer. I back out of the driveway until I come to the closed gate, my heart threatening to bust through my ribcage. When it slowly opens, I look up to see Dixon standing on his front porch, watching me as I speed away from his house.

Dixon

I open the gate, watching him panic inside his Hummer, feeling relieved that he's leaving without us having to talk about things. I don't want to talk about how tender I feel in places I shouldn't or that it's not as bad as I thought it would be. I don't want to talk about how satisfied I feel or that I can't imagine ever sleeping with anyone else.

I go back inside and close the door, my emotions running on high. I'm gay, right? I let him fuck me, and I let him do it even though he was my rapist first. I lean my back against the door and exhale, feeling my pulse in my backside. It's reminding me of what happened, but instead of feeling ashamed, I feel my cock swell. How did I get to this point? I shove off the door and wince as pain shoots from my knee up to my thigh. I need to hit up Jameson in the morning.

I struggle up the stairs, and when I get to my room, the blood on my sheets triggers something inside me. Something dark and sinister works its way throughout my body, and my ass hits the floor, sobs wrenching from my chest. There's something terribly wrong with me, fucking my rapist proves that. How did we both go from fighting to fucking out our frustrations? Why did I let Sebastian Avando fuck me? Why did I enjoy it so much that I came in record time?

As the tears fall and I struggle to breath through the sobs, I stare at the red drops on my bed. I touch my tender nose, and when I pull my fingers away, they are coated in a little blood. How did that happen? Then it hits me… Sebastian admitted to breaking into my house. My blood runs cold, and the sobs die down, my mind running with all the reasons he would've done that. I need to hear the reasons from him, and that means I have to come face-to-face with Avando to demand the answers. My stomach flips, but it's not with apprehension, it's anticipation. I have a reason to talk to him, and avoiding each other will be impossible.

We're playing the Steelers, but I have to watch from the bench. The Steelers are one of those iconic teams, yet I've missed my chance to play them tonight. We have a game against the Patriots next week, and I refuse to miss it. I will do what I must because I refuse to spend any more time on the bench nursing this knee. It just needs a bit of help in accelerating its healing. I sent Sebastian a text message, telling him I need to talk to him and to not even think about running out after… I know where he lives. I can certainly show up at his house and threaten to do the same shit he did at mine in order to be permitted inside.

It's been a weird twenty-four hours. I've been somersaulting between feeling angry and guilty for having sex with a married man. They looked happily married too. And then I think of his daughter, my stomach once again threatening to discharge my dinner. I'm not liking this person I'm becoming, and my heart squeezes when I think of how much I've changed.

I wish I could go back a year and take all my knowledge with me. I would've done almost everything differently. Now I must live with so many regrets, and I know they'll stay with me for a lifetime. I no longer have a little brother to be an example for, and that's the kicker of it all, because if he was here, I am not what I'd want him to be looking up to.

Jameson runs off the field, and I shake my head to bring me back to this moment, watching as my team gets destroyed by the Steelers. I wish I was out there running that ball into the end zone like my ass was on fire, but this fucking knee is just not healing fast enough.

"North," Jameson puffs as he tries to catch his breath. "Tell me you're coming back next week. We're getting pounded."

"I'll need your help," I say to him quietly, and he stares at me. "What we talked about before." I look around us.

"All right," he mumbles before he gulps down the Gatorade.

It's a miserable loss, and the atmosphere around the team feels heavy and depressive. Sebastian looks especially down, and I know it has a lot to with the fact that he was running laps around people out there, trying his hardest to get to the end zone. He doesn't look at me as he strips down and heads to the showers. He can't avoid me forever. I need to know what the fuck he was doing in my house. The guys come one by one out of the shower but no Sebastian, and when the last one says goodnight, he still hasn't come out.

Worry slices through me as I jump up from the bench and rush into the shower, finding him leaning against the wall, the water no longer steaming.

"What the fuck is wrong with you?" I snap at him, and he looks at me from the side of his eye.

"Are you stalking me now?"

"Funny you should ask that," I narrow my eyes at him. "I told you I wanted to talk to you."

"I'm tired." He shakes his head.

"I don't give a fuck," I retort.

His hand comes out and fists my sweater, dragging me into the shower with him. The cold water sprays over my face, and I feel it begin to soak into my tracksuit. I open my mouth to scream at him, but he hauls me into his wet body, his mouth instantly on mine. I moan, opening for him like his breath is the last I want in my lungs. I breathe him in, and when his tongue tangles with mine, I know there's no turning back. His cold, wet hand snakes down into my pants, and he finds me hard, fucking throbbing. He begins to stroke me, his tongue matching his movements in my mouth.

I try to clear the fog from my brain, the cold water helping. I pull back from his mouth, my hand going around his throat.

"Are you insane?" I yell at him, shoving him into the tiled wall.

"Remember the last time we were in a shower stall together?"

His words send my mind into a spiral because I remember the last time vividly. I remember being held against that wall by his friends while he forced himself inside of me, and I know I should be disgusted, but my cock is like steel. Sebastian chuckles as he grips it, knowing what I'm thinking about, apparently finding it humorous that I'm reacting this way. But what he doesn't know is along with arousal, I have a pulsing rage simmering just underneath. I squeeze his throat even harder.

He tries to draw in a breath, but I don't let him. Instead, I pump myself into his hand, and the sound of him struggling to breathe almost tosses me over the edge. I draw myself back out of his hand, and when his brows crash together in confusion, I chuckle darkly. I grab his shoulder and force him to turn, holding his face to the tile with my hand. The water hits his face, and he sputters while I pull down my pants, my cock jumping as I fist his ass cheek.

"How does it feel?" I ask him, putting my mouth to his ear while sliding my cock between his ass cheeks.

"Divine," he answers, then spits the water out of his mouth. Not for long.

I take my hand off his head and wait for him to fight me, but he doesn't. So with both hands, I spread him open and line myself up.

"What was it you said to me that day?" I taunt him in his ear. "Looks like a nice, wet pussy to me." Then I push inside of him, feeling the hard ring of muscle, and the moment it gives, I'm sinking into him.

He grunts through it. I know it's not pleasant at first, it burns. Serves him right for what he did to me. I lean back, the water hitting my chest. I watch as I pull out of him, groaning at the sight.

"Are you fucking me?" he taunts over his shoulder with a sarcastic snort. "Because I don't feel a fucking thing, North."

I snicker because he asked for it, so I'm not going to hold back any longer. I tighten my hold on his ass and slam back inside, my chest warming when he cries out. Bet he damn well feels it now. All the pent-up aggression I've had since the day I arrived combined with Sebastian's need to focus his hatred on me is slamming into his tight asshole. I don't care how much it hurts him, only that it feels amazing for me, so when I slam in for the final time, I grin as his face hits the tile. I come long and hard, my cock pulsing deep inside him. His breathing is rapid, just as mine is, and his eyes are wide open.

I pull out then smack his ass, watching as my cum slowly drips out. "Fuck, that really is hot."

He shoves me back and turns off the water, wiping a hand down his face. "Get the fuck out," he growls. When I don't move, he steps closer and screams, "get the fuck out!"

I forget the reason I was here in the first place, so I turn, rushing from the showers.

CHAPTER THIRTY-ONE

Sebastian

His street is dark, and the yellow hue of the streetlights make everything seem dull. I sit in the driver's seat and watch his house, the windows all dark. I let that shit happen again, cursing myself for the lack of self control. The second he stepped into that locker room before the game, I was a goner, and I knew in the back of my mind he and I were far from over. Why, though? Why can't I set Dixon North free?

The gates start to swing open, and I sit up straighter, watching to see who's leaving his house. I swear to God, if it's Dani, I will shoot her through her windshield then go inside and shoot him too. It's not Dani—luckily for them both—but it's not Dixon either. I assume it's his mother since she looks the right age, and I know there's no one else living in that house. As she drives away, I wait, watching the gates as they stay open. After ten minutes of watching, the gates don't close, and I curse his mother for not being careful.

I pull onto his driveway and ride up to the house, everything still dark inside. I grab my gun out of the glove box and get out of the Hummer, tucking my piece in my waistband. I walk up to his door slowly and look at the blinking, red light in the corner. I knock on the door and wait. It's late, so I don't ring the doorbell. These large homes have some ridiculous chiming doorbells, and I don't want to disturb anyone inside. I don't know for sure if that was his mother, so she could still be here.

When no one comes to the door, I try knocking again a bit louder and look up to the camera, raising my brow. Is he watching me? I'm standing here at his damn door, hours after he fucked me in the same stall I first forced him to take my dick, and I can't help but wonder if he's laughing while I stand here. I refuse to be a needy bitch and wait for him, so I reach for the door handle. I'm shocked that it's open, the door swinging open wide.

Did he not learn anything when I said I was inside of his house?

I shut the door with a loud resounding thud and wait, but nothing happens. There's no noise, and the house is eerily still … too quiet. I jog up the steps then run to the room I know is his, kicking open the door loudly. Fuck whoever is disturbed. None of this feels right, and if his mental state is anything like mine, then he may be in trouble.

"North!" I yell into his bedroom, but I don't hear any response.

I see the curtains billowing around his sliding door and run for that, tripping over the ledge. I end up out on a balcony that faces the backyard, sucking in a lungful of fresh, cold air. Just as I look to the sky, snowflakes begin to fall, and I hear a sarcastic snort from my right.

"I should've known you would break in again." I turn to see Dixon sitting in the corner with a whiskey bottle in his hand.

"Are you fucking stupid?" I yell at him. "Didn't you hear me call your name?"

"I did." He takes a swig from the bottle. "I was just hoping you'd go away. But you never do, do you?"

"Nah," I stare down at him, "and I can't break into a home that's left completely open."

"It doesn't matter." He takes another swig.

"Was that your mom who left?" I ask him as I swipe the bottle out of his hand, taking a gulp.

"She left?" he chuckles, and the sound sends chills down my spine. "She called me Danny."

His words hit me like a freight train, and I feel his pain as if it was my own. The heavy feel of it is palpable in the air as I sit down next to him, gulping from the bottle before handing it back.

"She's sad," I tell him. "Seeing you probably constantly reminds her about him."

"I didn't get mad at her." He sounds so small. I watch as he takes another sip. "I broke down."

That crushes me a bit more, and I feel for him. His only family left in the world just left him, and he's struggling with survivor's guilt. I see it and I know it well. I live with it daily. Having the life I do has never been easy, and even though I have money now, it doesn't change where I came from. I had friends murdered similarly to Little North, and I still ask myself every day why I'm here and they're not.

"You can go now," he sneers. "And you need to stop breaking into my shit."

"This time I rode right up." I stand, anger pulsing in my chest and shooting straight to my cock. This is our own brand of foreplay.

"Then you can ride right back out." I know I should take it easy on him, that his heart is broken and his soul is bruised, but I think he's goading me on purpose. He wants me to help him forget for a while.

I can do that.

I grab him by his shirt and haul him up out of his chair. He puts up a struggle, but it's no use. He tries to swing the bottle at my head, but I block his arm, and the bottle crashes onto the concrete, smashing into pieces. He bares his teeth and tries to headbutt me, but I grab him around his throat, forcing him into his bedroom.

"What else do you need, Dixon?" I whisper against his mouth, and he tries to bite me. "Do you need me to fuck you?"

He growls and tries to twist out of my hold, but I tighten my grip, his eyes widening at the lack of air. I can see the exact moment when the anger in his eyes burns bright with lust, and I know he wants more than just a fight. I let go of his throat, and he surprises me with a quick left, connecting with my cheek. My blood boils with rage as I reach for my piece at my back and press it to his forehead.

There's no reaction, he just stands there, staring me down. "Do it." His voice is low and defeated. "Kill me!" he screams and grabs the barrel, pressing it in harder. "Fucking do it!"

I pull back a few inches and hit him with my left fist, making him fall on the bed, away from the gun. "Why do you want to die?" I ask him, but he stays motionless on the bed. "Tell me." I kick his leg, worried he's passed out.

"Because I hate it here." So damn defeated. He has given up.

I crawl over him, my gun still in my right hand as I press myself into his ass. "I can't kill you, Dixon North," I whisper in his ear.

"Why not?" he mumbles and presses his ass against me.

"Because I don't want to be here without you, even though I hate it too," I hear his breath catch at my admission.

"Use the fucking gun on me, Seb." A sob catches in his chest. *Seb.*

"Use the gun, huh?" I push myself up and pull down his track pants. He doesn't fight me, and when the cool metal of the gun barrel slips between his ass cheeks, he barely flinches. "Like this?"

When he doesn't pull away, my heart begins to speed up. I like when he's submissive like this. I continue thrusting the barrel between his ass cheeks, warming the metal before I press it into his ass. I watch as his hole widens and swallows up the tip of the gun, his back moving rapidly with his breaths.

"Do you like how I'm using my gun?" I ask him as I push it in farther. He moans at the intrusion and widens his legs.

I take that as a yes and begin to fuck him hard with the gun, my hand hitting his flesh with my thrusts. His moans become louder, and my cock is straining against my pants, desperate to take the gun's place. I pull out the barrel and toss it onto the bed, quickly yanking down my pants. I spit onto my hand and rub it along my length then line myself up.

"We need to get lube," I tell him as I thrust into him.

"No, we don't," he grunts with the intrusion. "This isn't a regular thing."

I grit my teeth at his words and punish his asshole instead, slamming into him forcefully. "Don't talk shit." I grunt, and my eyes roll back into my head when he clenches around me. "It's already a regular thing."

"You're fucking married," he counters, but his words lose their fire when he moans.

I am married, there's nothing I can say to defend my actions, and I won't disrespect him by trying. If I tell him I'm married in name only or that I have never fucked my wife, it'll sound like lies. But I don't want to explain my situation, I'd rather he just think the worst of me. It's not like my marital status is changing at any point, and I won't lie.

"Come for me," I command as I continue to thrust into him. "Come."

When he begins to jack himself off onto the bed, I clamp my eyes shut to try to hold off, but it's no use. I watch as stars burst behind my eyelids, and my mouth drops in a silent scream, my cum shooting inside Dixon. His groan follows right after, and I keep myself seated inside of him as he comes undone.

His body is shaking with his release, and my cock is still

pulsing inside of him. I pull out then slowly stand up , hiking up my pants. I grab my gun and tuck it away again, biting my lip when I watch Dixon stand up. He pulls up his pants then turns to face me, his eyes a mixture of confusion and despair. I don't think as I grab him around the neck and drag him to me, wrapping my arms around him.

He sobs into my neck as I hold him tight. I don't know what to say to help him, but I do know how to give him comfort.

Dixon

"This is potent, North," Jameson warns as he hands me five syringes filled with a clear liquid. "You need to inject it into your knee about fifteen minutes before you want relief."

I nod and look up, finding Sebastian leaning against the lockers across from us. He looks pissed, but he'll have to get over it.

"Let me know if you want more." Jameson squeezes my shoulder.

"Thanks, man." I watch him head out to the field.

Sebastian's eyes follow him until he disappears, then he looks at me with anger.

"What?" I ask him.

"I don't want him touching you," he growls, and I look at him with shock.

"You're seriously fucked-up." I shake my head.

"When you want more of that," he points to the syringes in my hands, "you ask me." Then he pushes off the lockers and heads out to the field. He's being ridiculous with the jealousy bit considering the fuck is still married. We have our game against the Patriots in a few days, so I want to get onto that field to practice today.

I take the top off the syringe then slowly insert it into the outer side of my kneecap, making sure to get underneath. When I depress the plunger, the cold liquid spreads inside, and I can feel it seeping through my knee. After ten minutes, the throbbing has already lessened to a dull ache. I stand up and put all of my weight on it. It hurts, but only a fraction of what it was before. I can work with this. I put the other syringes away in my bag, lock my locker, then jog out to the field. I feel rejuvenated… My knee has never felt better.

When I tap Coach on the shoulder, he looks at me closely. "What's up, North?"

"I'm ready to go in."

"You sure?" He looks down to my knee. "Are you feeling up to it?"

"Never better," I smirk, and he nods.

"Zeal, North is in," he calls out, and Zeal hoots with excitement.

Four hours later and my knee feels like it's been put through a grinder. The pain has intensified, and my thigh is now swollen as well. I long for the sauna, but I know the heat won't be good for the swelling. I throw on my clothes and skip the shower. I'd rather take it at home where no one can see the damage. I try not to limp as I leave the locker room. As I step out into the hallway, I come face-to-face with Dani.

She opens her mouth to talk but I hold up my hand. "Not now."

I try to move around her, but she grabs my arm, her eyes boring into mine. "I am so sorry."

"Forgiven." I shrug her off and continue my way out of the stadium.

"That's it?" she calls out, and I turn to look at her. "Everything is fine?"

"You and I were over long before that," I shrug and turn my back on her again. "Good luck, Dani."

I don't bother to wait to hear her reaction because my knee feels like it's three times it's actual size. All in all, it was worth it. I couldn't sit on that bench another practice, I need to be in for the game this weekend. There was no other option. After this game, I'll take some time off to let it heal.

I hop into the car and hiss when the pain radiates into my groin. It just needs ice and some rest. When I get home, I see Ma's car in the driveway, and my heart sinks into my stomach. It's been four days since she left, and I have no idea where she went. I was worried she'd never come back, and seeing her car means we'll have to talk about what happened.

I get out, wincing when the pain becomes worse, then limp to my front door. It opens before I can get up the steps, and Ma rushes forward to grab my arm.

"What have you done, Son?" She sounds worried, and I hate that I'm causing her more pain.

"Just a rough practice. The doctor said it would act up as it healed," I lie. "When did you get back?" I ask as we step inside and close the door.

"I shouldn't have left, Dixon, but I'm so far away from Danny, and I just needed to see him."

"You've been gone for days. Where did you stay?" I ask her as I make my way to the kitchen to grab my ice pack.

"With one of the ladies from work," she answers, looking nervous.

I really want to ask her why she left without saying goodbye, and I wish I could tell her how her calling me Danny made me feel like she wished I was the son who died.

"Okay, Ma." I nod and walk by her to go to my room. "I'm glad you're back."

"Me too," she whispers behind me, but I don't look back.

CHAPTER THIRTY-TWO

The liquid spreads throughout my knee, and the cooling effect is instantaneous. Seb keeps watching me with his eyes narrowed and his arms crossed, like the hypocrite he is. I know he does drugs, I've seen it, and I know he still suffers from his last concussion. He's self medicating to get by as well, so he shouldn't judge me.

"I need more," I tell him without looking up, flexing my leg and sighing when the pain subsides.

"You're always going to need more," he retorts, and I stand, getting in his face.

"Don't even stand there and judge me." I poke my finger into his chest.

He grabs it and sucks it into his mouth, his tongue swirling around the tip. I'm hard in a split second, and I can think of nothing else but having his mouth on my cock.

"You can't use this forever," he says when he pops my finger out of his mouth, "or your knee will only get worse."

"I need it for this season, that's it," I reply, my voice husky with need.

"Too long," he rasps as his other hand cups my swollen cock, clutching it through my shorts.

I fall forward into him, and my forehead hits his, the pleasure too much. He releases my finger and cups my cheek, pulling me in so he can suck on my bottom lip. He presses his cock between us, and I groan into his mouth, wanting him inside me. He chuckles against my lips when I begin to whimper. The need coursing through me is almost too much when his hand moves from my cock to my ass. He gives it a squeeze, bringing me in closer and pressing our cocks together.

He slips a hand beneath my shorts then runs his fingers down my crack, stopping at my asshole. He pushes a finger inside and begins to fuck me with it, watching my face closely.

"Fuck, Seb," I pant.

"Dixon?" Dani's voice calling into the locker room has us flying apart, and I nearly pass out from the fear surging through me.

Sebastian rolls his eyes and falls back against the lockers, crossing his arms again. "Looks like your girl wants in on our action now," he grins.

"Shut up," I snarl at him then head toward her voice. She's standing at the locker room entrance, her face a bit pale and her eyes wide. "What's up? Is everything okay?"

"I'm late," she whispers, and I swear I hear a snort behind me.

"For?"

"My period," she huffs, and what she's trying to say dawns on me.

"And you're telling me ... because?"

"Because I was only with you," she grits through her teeth.

"Not from what I saw," I rebut before adding, "plus, I wore protection." And the second time, I didn't even come. But I don't tell her that.

"You need to face this, and when you're ready, we'll talk." She storms off toward her father's office and slams the door.

"That bitch is crazy," I turn at Seb's voice.

"It's probably yours," I snarl, and he laughs.

"It could be anyone's, and you know I didn't come in *her* that day."

No, he didn't. I swallowed everything he had that day. The memory makes my hard cock jump in my shorts, and I wonder if Dani noticed I was sporting an erection while talking to her. I follow Seb out to the field where I try to drive Dani from my mind. If she is actually pregnant, I know the kid isn't mine.

Practice is good, and I feel amped for the game tomorrow, excited about playing against one of the teams I've looked up to for so long. The feeling only lasts until I get home where the pain crashes in on me worse than ever. Walking is impossible, so I hop to my front door, praying my mother doesn't see me like this. She'll freak and call Coach. How would I explain to him that I'm fine during practices, yet I come home like this?

Thankfully, I hear her in the kitchen cooking, and when she calls out to me, I tell her I'm going for a soak. I make it upstairs, but just barely, and I have tears coursing down my face because the pain is too fucking much. I fall on my bed and decide not to move for the rest of the night. I take out my phone and message Seb, telling him to have more for me tomorrow because one more won't cut it.

Sebastian

I find Dixon in his car the next morning, breathing rapidly with sweat pouring off his face. When I come up to the driver's side, I see the used syringe and groan into my fist. I knew this would happen, using Toradol to mask pain only makes it worse. He uses me as an example for self-medicating, but my head is different from his knee.

I tap on the window, and he doesn't even look to see who it is as he lowers it. "I'm good," he pants, and I growl at him.

"No, you're not." I toss in a bag with five more syringes. "That's all you'll get. After the game tonight, you're going to the hospital."

"No," he sits up and winces. "Don't, Seb, I can deal with this."

"I'll be taking you there myself." I tap on the hood of his car, then I stride back to the stadium. I can't see him like that. It reminds me too much of my addict mother, and it gives me the feeling that I'm about to be abandoned again.

I swallow it down because Dixon isn't mine. If he wants to leave, he can. Doesn't mean I won't find him, though. And he knows I would, I'm damn good at it. With that thought, I forget my mommy issues and head back inside. It's fucking frigid outside, Christmas right around the corner. In a few days, I will be watching my little girl open Barbies, dollhouses, and nail things. I can't wait.

We're playing in the snow, my favorite time to play football, and we're up by a touchdown. Dixon has been on fire, and on his third syringe of the day. I wasn't joking… I will be taking him to the ER later.

It's the last quarter, and Dixon is looking a bit green, his knee at least twice the size it should be. I pray he makes it to the end, but I can see him declining quickly. Zeal calls out the play, and Dixon takes off. I'm not sure if anybody else notices, but I see the slight limp in his run. He's not nearly as fast either. He skips to the side to avoid a tackle, and I watch as he slips and lands on that leg, knowing what comes next.

The scream that tears through his throat is filled with pain. I watch as the game is paused, medics running to the field. It's the worst possible thing that could've happened, but at least I can be assured he's on the way to the hospital, just like I wanted.

The rest of the game is spent with me worrying about Dixon, and we end up losing by a few points. It's the Patriots, and honestly, we're happy we weren't pounded into the dirt. A few points loss is not bad. I get to the locker room, and Dixon is gone, just like I knew he would be. That knee was looking way worse than the first time he injured it, and I'm kind of pissed Coach didn't care to check it out. I get that Dixon is his own man, but coaches are there to guide and make sure we're doing well. He throws piss tests, but that's about it.

I change quickly then leave the stadium, getting in my Hummer to drive to the hospital. When I get inside, the nurses tell me he's in x-ray, but I can wait in his room for him since he'll be admitted for at least the night. All good things. I go to the room they tell me, and when I walk inside, I see his mother sitting on one of the beds. She sees me, so it's too late to back out.

"Hi there." She gives me a once-over and a smile. "Are you a friend of Dixon's?"

"Yes, ma'am." I step forward and hold out my hand. "Sebastian. I'm a teammate."

"You must be more than that to come by." She smiles, and my heart begins to pound. Maybe I should've just called instead. "He's in x-ray and will be back soon."

"Sounds good." I nod. "Would you like a coffee?" I need to

get out of this room. The way she's looking at me is like she knows everything I've done to her son. Both willing and non. I hope I'm just being paranoid.

"No, thank you." She just keeps smiling, and it's creeping me out.

I turn quickly and leave the room, rushing down to a set of elevators. I press the buttons rapidly, cursing when the damn things take forever. And then I feel heat on the side of my face. I turn to look back the way I came and find Dixon's mom leaning against the door frame of the room, just watching me with that creepy smile.

The elevator dings open, and I go to rush in, only to bump into a stretcher.

"Shit, sorry," I say as I back away.

"Seb?" Dixon's voice hits me, and my relief is immediate. "What are you doing here?" He sounds groggy and out of it.

"I wanted to make sure you were okay before I went home for the holidays." I follow the stretcher as the nurses push it toward his room.

"Looks like a severe strain," he huffs and rolls his eyes. "I'll be out tomorrow."

"That's good." They push him into the room, and his mom looks from him to me, giving me that creeped out feeling again. "Anyway, I should go. I've got a long drive ahead of me."

"All right, man." Dixon holds out his hand, and I grasp it. "Thanks for coming by."

"Happy holidays," I say to him and his mother.

"Merry Christmas," his mother replies, her eyes on mine like a hawk's.

I walk out of that hospital and back to the Hummer, my mind flicking through everything between Dixon and me. Could she have overheard us that first time? I get inside the Hummer and drive back to my house. I have a long drive in the morning, and I don't want to spend what time I could be sleeping by worrying about secrets coming to the surface.

Rochester has a nasty rep, not that it hasn't been earned.

The good folk stay away, but I can never wait to get back here. My wife and child live in Tribeca, and that's as close as they'll ever get to Rochester. Paola grew up in Rochester with me, and we both agreed that Carla would not be subjected to it. I don't think she needs to be tough like we were growing up. She needs to be tough in other ways, especially because she'll have money, and she'll be my only child.

Delano's small house is lit up with Christmas lights, and the scraggly bushes in the front have Christmas ornaments on them. Growing up, we never had much to give each other for Christmas, but we always decorated and had a good time. I unload the bags I have in the back—I bought him and his mom some food, and there's clothing as well. There was a time when they gave me everything they could, so I never miss an opportunity to give back.

Delano also has three boys. I leave the back open because it's filled with gifts for them to open Christmas morning. I open the front door and the screams of kids assault my ears. Thank God I only have the one.

"Ho, ho, ho!" I yell through the house followed by a chorus of 'Uncle Seb' sounds around me. "Get out to that vehicle, and bring in all your gifts," I tell them before they run outside screaming.

"Thanks, man." Delano comes out of the kitchen, and I haul him in for a hug. "We need to talk." His voice lets me know that it's about business. He leads me into his office. It's small and cramped, but this is where a lot of our decisions go down.

"What's up?"

"A few suspicious things have happened over the last few weeks," he begins, tossing me a baggy to cut up. "Two of our grow ops were raided. We caught one of the guys and forced some info out of him." Tortured, he means, and I can't help the envy I feel. I wish I'd been there for that.

"And?"

"Looks like that little Baltimore gang is starting a war."

"No way." I look up at him. "How?"

"We killed his son."

"So?" I shrug. "That's life."

"Truth," he nods and leans forward. "But he's out for blood, and he's out for you."

"Me?" I raise a brow. "How do you know that? And how does he know me?"

"He also ran into some of our women and left a few messages carved into their dead bodies," he takes a breath and shakes his head. "It said, 'Bring me Avando and this will stop.' "

"Really." I sniff a line then look up at Delano. "He recognized my voice in the video."

"I guess so," he shrugs. "There's really no other way."

"How are we contacting him?" I ask.

"He said to come to the Marina where we found Little North."

"He'll have to wait until after Christmas," I snort. "It's the holidays, after all."

We laugh and finish the lines, taking me back to when we were younger. Times were hard, and we had death creeping around us constantly, but we never let it control our lives. We grew up with the mentality that we're on borrowed time, and death was something we never feared. Nothing has changed.

CHAPTER THIRTY-THREE

Looks like Paola had someone come by and decorate our house in those fancy dangly Christmas lights. I bet Carla freaked out when she saw them on, she's done that every year. I walk in the house and yell out to my family, excited to finally hold them close.

"Papi," Paola chastises as she comes into the foyer. "Must you yell?" She leans up and kisses me softly on the lips. "Welcome home."

"Thank you." I smile down at her. "Where's Carla?"

"She's at Mami's for a few days. they probably wanted to give us some alone time." Paola's parents believe we are married in the traditional sense, and I would never reveal otherwise to them. I want to see my daughter, but it can wait a day. "I ordered food, and there's wine." She tries to distract me, knowing I miss my little girl.

Paola's parents do know that Carla is not mine and they are extremely grateful that I stepped up and claimed her as my own. Paola has never spoken about who the real father is, but I can say the guy must have bright green eyes.

I follow Paola to the kitchen where she pulls apart the food bags, taking out the portions. Then she's pouring some wine into glasses. I swallow mine in two gulps.

"I need a shower before I eat." I kiss her cheek. "I'll be down in a bit."

She nods and begins to hum a Christmas carol as I leave the kitchen, smiling to myself. This time of year makes me feel warm and thankful for everything I have, including the people around me. I think of this year and everything I've gained, Dixon being the main thing. I know we started off on the wrong foot, and things got real messy really damn fast, but I'm liking where we're headed. I like what we have. I'm not ready to figure out what it all means, but I am happy to have him.

I get to my bedroom—I have my own room in the house— where I strip down before heading for the shower. Carla asked us once why Mami and Papi don't share a room, and I told her it was because her mother snored. It was funny at the time, but it made us realize that as she grows older, she'll have more questions, and she'll demand proper answers. I guess we'll cross that bridge when we get to it.

I step under the hot spray and let it soak into my muscles, groaning when I finally feel the events of the night l leave me, it's good to be home. This whole thing with Dixon's knee and now the Baltimore gang is adding to my stress, I just want to let it all wash down the drain so I can enjoy my family without thinking of what might happen later. I hear a muffled bang and roll my eyes, Paola probably popped open another bottle. She'll be passed out in an hour tops.

I get out and dry myself off, dressing in a tracksuit. My gun is laying on my bed with my wallet and keys, so I open my bedside table to put them away. That's when I hear a low mumbling, and I freeze on the spot. Someone else is downstairs with Paola. Usually, I would stay out of the way, knowing it was one of her guys and giving them some privacy. But something tells me it's not. She didn't tell me she was expecting anyone.

I grab my piece and stick it into my waistband, creeping out into the hallway.

"Where is he? I see his Hummer outside," a voice I don't recognize demands.

"Fuck you," Paola snaps back, before I hear a hand connecting with skin. She cries out as I slowly make my way down the stairs, remembering where to avoid the creaks.

"Check upstairs," he tells someone, then I hear a set of boots coming closer. I slip into the closet and watch as a guy in a ski mask walks by, heading for the stairs. Everything is covered on his body, but I did see light eyes and the white skin around them. Rage consumes me as I step out and grab the back of his shirt, slamming my gun into his temple. I gently lower him to the floor then creep toward the kitchen.

There are two entrances to the kitchen, so I go to the other one, that way this guy won't see me coming.

"You have a piece of shit husband, you know that?" the guy sneers. "He fucking kills kids."

Paola doesn't say anything, and I wait to hear if he has other men with him. When I hear nothing, I shake my head, surprised that this fuck came with just one guy and thinks they'll leave here with their lives. Not a damn chance. Thank God my daughter isn't here because I would be in a rage so uncontrollable.

I step into the kitchen and find Paola on her knees with a gun to her head. My girl doesn't even flinch, though, she's been through worse. I am so proud of her strength. I raise my gun and cock it, the noise loud in the silence of the large kitchen.

"Step away from my wife," I growl, and the guy looks at me over his shoulder. He also has a mask on, but I can see his eyes are a dark brown, the skin around them also white. Nothing about them seems familiar, so I don't know what I'm dealing with.

"Where's my partner?" he asks, and I laugh.

"Dead." I want him to believe that he's alone. I'll kill this one, but the other one will be used for information. The guy's eyes flash with anger, and his body shakes. "Aw, was that your boyfriend?"

He presses the gun harder into Paola's head, and she hisses

with the action, making me flatten my lips. "I'll kill her."

"I'll kill you," I shrug.

"You'll go to jail," he counters, pulling another laugh from me.

"Nah, I wouldn't."

"Yeah, you would. We're undercover cops." he refutes, and my stomach bottoms out.

"Why the fuck are you in my house?"

"Investigating Baltimore drug distribution and it led us to a few murders," he tsks. "You see, those kids you killed a few weeks ago? I was their boss, and they were gathering information for me."

"No cop would be in my home with a gun to my wife's head!" I snap.

"No, probably not," he shrugs and cocks the gun. "I have a drug distribution I need to stay covered, and your meddling is bringing some heat."

An undercover cop who's a double agent working for the fucking gang he was supposed to be infiltrating... I can't even fault that since I own a few cops of my own. But these guys never play fair. They can use both sides, and right now, I don't have many options.

"So what do you want?" I keep my gun trained on him.

"First it was to warn you to fuck off, but now that you killed my partner..." It's like time slows, and I watch helplessly as his finger squeezes the trigger, sending a bullet into Paola's head. Blood sprays all over the fridge, and I scream as I spray my own bullets, hitting the piece of shit in the neck. Blood spurts from his wound, and he falls to the floor as I run for Paola.

I pick her up and look down into her open, lifeless eyes, a sob breaking free from my chest. "No, no, no," I chant as I rock her back and forth. I hear the front door open, and my head snaps toward the noise, fuck. I forgot about the fucker I knocked out.

I jump to my feet and slip on the blood pooling on the floor, running for the front door. It's wide open and too dark to see anything. I look behind me and find the floor empty, meaning the piece of shit got away.

I slam the door and scream. What the fuck do I do?

EPILOGUE

"Dixon!" His voice reverberates out of my phone's speaker. "Everything I did was to protect you!"

"Seb, where are you?" My voice shakes as worry clutches at my chest. "What is that noise?"

I can faintly hear sirens like an ambulance or cop cars.

"I can't go to jail," he whispers, his voice drowning out.

"Seb!" I yell. "Do I hear cops?"

"I just needed to make sure you were kept out of shit, that you were safe." His voice cracks, and I roll off my couch, grabbing my crutch. It's Christmas eve, and I was sinking into depression before I heard his voice.

"Seb." I hobble down the hall and into my TV room, skidding along my Persian rug. "I need you to tell me what's happening."

I almost trip over an Italian leather ottoman as I grab the remote from my glass end table. Sebastian's panting over the speaker phone along with his random cursing has my stress ramped to an extreme high. I turn on the TV and flick to a local Buffalo news station, cursing when I hear the breaking news.

There's a high-speed chase on the I-90…

"Fuck, Seb!" I scream. "Why are you running from the cops?"

"They know, Dixon!" he screams back. "They know what I did!"

"Pull over before you kill yourself!" My breathing is coming out in short gasps, and I can feel my skin coating in sweat. This is fear unlike any I've ever experienced.

"I can't go to jail." He sounds eerily calm, and I know this is his game only voice. No feeling, just a completely tactical mindset.

"No," I stutter, "no, Sebastian. Please pull over." I reach up and dig my fingers into my hair.

"Take care of yourself, North."

The line goes dead, and I drop my phone, hearing as it clatters against the marble tile. The news is saying a Buffalo footballer is on the run from police, and they will update everyone when they learn more. I feel moisture stealing its way down my cheek, knowing it's just a matter of time until they get Sebastian's name.

How the hell did we get here, and where do we go now?

ACKNOWLEDGEMENTS

To my readers who decide to open the pages of my imagination and go on each and every dark, crazy ride with me, I love you. Thank you for taking this leap with me.

To my Alpha/sensitivity reader, Crystal Partin, thank you for all of your help in making this book feel so damn authentic. You are amazing!

To my Betas, Jocelyn, Gemma, Kristen and Amber! Look how long we've been doing this together now! Thank you for all your help, I love you guys so much!

To my ARC readers, thank you for recommending my books and supporting me. It really means so much! I love you guys!

ALSO BY C.A. RENE

The Whitsborough Chronicles

Through the Pain

Into Darkness

Finding the Light

To Redemption

The Whitsborough Progenies

Ivy's Venom

Carmelo's Malice

Saxon's Distortion

Gabriel's Deception

Desecrated Duet

Desecrated Flesh

Desecrated Essence

The Reaped Series

The Reaper Incarnate

Hunting the Reaper

Claiming the Reaper

Hail Mary Duet

Blue 42

Red Zone

C.A. RENE

Sacrificial Lambs

Sing Me a Song

Song of Tenebrae

A Verse for Caelum

To the Grave

Mimic

For all book updates and social platforms, check out my website

ABOUT THE AUTHOR

C.A. Rene lives in Toronto, Canada with her family, where most of the year varies from chilly to frigid. Most days you'll find her wrapped in her many blankets in bed while reading or writing her next dark, twisted story.

Her stories boast of inclusivity and refusal to be conformed in any small box. Writing across genres is a hobby and drinking wine is a must… Or coffee … with a splash of Baileys.

www.ingramcontent.com/pod-product-compliance
Lightning Source LLC
Chambersburg PA
CBHW060516220726

48290CB00015B/1569